RISKY REVENGE

White Eagle's heart was filled with grief and outrage over the death of his mother and grandfather. To steal away quietly unnoticed? Or to strike a blow for his people? He fingered the blade of his knife, his mind in a panic of confusion while he stared down at the snoring warrior. The man lay helpless before him, but what if he struck and he didn't kill the Sioux? Suddenly the warrior's eyes popped open, and White Eagle took a step backward, staring horrified at the Sioux.

"What is it?" the warrior asked, still half drunk and groggy with sleep. He reached for the edge of his blanket to pull it over his shoulders.

There was no time to think. Acting on instinct alone, White Eagle quickly knelt down and grabbed the blanket as if to help cover the sleepy man. Then he whispered, "Die, Sioux dog. . . ."

Son of the Hawk

Charles G. West

A SIGNET BOOK

SIGNET
Published by New American Library, a division of
Penguin Putnam Inc., 375 Hudson Street,
New York, New York 10014, U.S.A.
Penguin Books Ltd, 80 Strand,
London WC2R ORL, England
Penguin Books Australia Ltd, Ringwood,
Victoria, Australia
Penguin Books Canada Ltd, 10 Alcorn Avenue,
Toronto, Ontario, Canada M4V 3B2
Penguin Books (N.Z.) Ltd, 182–190 Wairau Road,
Auckland 10, New Zealand

Penguin Books Ltd, Registered Offices:
Harmondsworth, Middlesex, England

First published by Signet, an imprint of New American Library,
a division of Penguin Putnam Inc.

First Printing, November 2001
10 9 8 7 6 5 4 3 2 1

For Ronda

CHAPTER 1

Booth Dalton sat watching the string of twelve heavily loaded mules as they filed through the narrow part of a rocky canyon some three hundred feet below. He squinted against the afternoon sun in an effort to study the four riders, each leading three of the mules. He shifted his position in the saddle slightly, contemplating the possibilities that might develop for an enterprising man like himself. He didn't concern himself when the lead rider disappeared from his view, blocked out by the trees on the ledge. Booth knew where the canyon led. He felt no sense of urgency—there was plenty of time to decide how best to approach this unforeseen stroke of luck.

Just what in hell are four white men doing smack-dab in the middle of Injun country? And where the hell are they goin'? This wasn't just Indian territory, this was the sacred hunting grounds of the Sioux nation. Booth knew he was taking a sizable risk himself just being in this part of the hills, but he had traded with the Sioux, and he figured that if they did catch him in the Black Hills, they might go easy on him. But this mule train moving through the pass below him might as well be carrying a big sign saying, *Come and get us!*

"The last of 'em's goin' outta sight. What're we gonna do?"

Booth turned to look at Charlie White Bull as the

chunky half-breed walked back from the rim of the ledge where he had been watching the progress of the mule train. Booth smiled to himself as he considered his witless associate. Charlie claimed he had been kicked in the head by a horse when he was a young'un, and that was the cause of his thoughts sometimes being a little behind schedule. Booth figured it more likely that Charlie had been kicked by that horse on a regular monthly basis, judging by the elementary level of the man's reasoning. Most men would find it uncomfortable to have Charlie hanging around, but Booth found the simpleminded half-breed useful for any number of troublesome chores—such as slitting some miner's throat.

"Why, what do you think we oughta do?" Booth finally replied, knowing what Charlie's answer would be.

His face absent of all expression, Charlie answered just as Booth expected. "Go down there and kill 'em and take them goods."

Smiling patiently, Booth chided his partner. "There's four of 'em, and they all got rifles cradled across their saddles. You wanna just ride down there blazin' away?" Charlie shrugged. "That might not be too smart," Booth finished.

"Maybe you know what to do," Charlie finally said, his phlegmatic facade never changing.

"Maybe I do. Maybe I *always* know what to do— right, Charlie?" He didn't expect an answer. "I always know how to git what we need without riskin' our asses. Now mount up. We'll just take a little ride across the ridge and wait for 'em on the other side. I'd druther they made camp so we don't have to go chasin' after them mules when the shootin' starts." He pulled his horse's head around and pointed him toward the ridge. Talking more to himself than his stoic partner, he said, "I'm mighty curious to git a look-see in them packs. And I damn shore wanna git to 'em before the damn Injuns find 'em."

Booth continued to marvel at this unexpected good fortune that had wandered deep into Indian territory on this late summer afternoon. He was pretty sure the four were prospectors looking for gold, but they were a long way from the gold strikes west of the Absarokas. Booth had long held a suspicion that there might be gold in the Black Hills, so it shouldn't have been a huge surprise that some bold miners might be brave enough—or dumb enough—to prospect in the Indians' sacred grounds.

Booth might have searched for the precious metal himself, but he and Charlie weren't suited to the work involved in washing it out of the streams. Confiscating it, along with anything else he could get his hands on, from those who had labored for it was more Booth's style. The two of them had done quite well by themselves by bushwhacking greenhorn miners. There was some gain from the dust their victims occasionally found, but the real profit was in selling the equipment and supplies to the other, more established miners. Booth considered himself an entrepreneur in the hunting and retailing field. He and Charlie would hunt for some tenderfoot with his back turned, kill him, and sell his goods at an inflated price. It had worked to perfection in the Montana territory until the miners around Turkey Creek became wise to the source of Booth's inventory. He and Charlie had just managed to strike for Indian territory a step ahead of a vigilante committee.

Booth smiled again when he thought about how soon he was back in business—this time selling guns and ammunition to the warring Sioux. Old Iron Pony was anxious to get his hands on as many rifles as

Booth could bring him, along with the powder, flints, and balls. But Booth was well aware of the fact that the Lakota chief wouldn't tolerate the two in his country for one minute after the rifles they supplied stopped coming. Of course even the plunder Booth and Charlie provided might not be enough to save their hair if Iron Pony found out that Charlie was half Flathead. Booth had told the chief that his stoic partner was the product of the union between a white man and a Santee Dakota woman. He almost convinced Iron Pony that Charlie White Bull was his cousin, a thought that always amused Booth.

The four men led their mules through the narrow mouth of the canyon only to find a flat stretch of shale and gravel leading up to another line of pine-covered hills. The leader, Tom Farrior, raised his hand to halt those behind him. "I swear, Ned, I sure thought there'd be water on this side."

Ned Turner pulled up beside Tom, concern etched in his face as he stood up in the stirrups and gazed all around him. "I did, too. We need to find a stream soon. It's been a good while since these animals had a drink." He paused to look around again before adding, "I could damn shore use one myself."

While they considered the formidable line of hills dead ahead, the other two members of their party caught up to them. "What's the trouble?" Anson Miller wanted to know. The afternoon sun was already beginning to settle over the mountains, and if they didn't find a place to camp soon, he feared they'd be stumbling around in the dark.

Tom turned in his saddle to face both Anson and Jack Stratton. "There ain't no water here. I thought there would be. It just seemed like a likely place, looking from those hills on the other side of the canyon."

"Damn," Jack Stratton murmured. The other three felt the same about prospects for making a dry camp.

Ned Turner, not being one to give up easily, pointed toward a long line of trees that led down from a mountain about five miles distant. "That looks like a stream coming down that mountain. I say we get a move on and—"

Before he could finish, Anson growled a warning. "We got company."

The heads of the other three turned as one to follow the direction he pointed out. From a narrow ravine that led down from the eastern ridge that formed one side of the canyon they had just passed through, riders came into view. All four men instinctively grabbed their rifles.

"Keep your eye on 'em," Tom Farrior warned as he quickly scanned the treeless slope to the west, looking for a likely defensive position.

"There ain't but two of 'em," Jack said. "They look like white men—leastways one of 'em does. The other one looks more like an Injun." All four frantically searched the slopes on either side of them, fearful of having been surrounded by a swarm of hostiles.

When no more riders appeared anywhere around them, Tom cautioned his partners to be ready, anyway. "We'll just see who they are and what they want. Keep your rifles ready." It was mighty surprising to meet a white man in this part of the territory, and Tom was especially leery of one riding with an Indian.

Booth Dalton affixed his most engaging smile in place and waved his arm back and forth as he and Charlie made for the four men now sitting motionless, watching their approach. He was well aware of his best asset in his chosen line of work, an amiable facade that betrayed no hint of ill intent. It had been said by one of the miners in Turkey Creek that Booth had the face of a Methodist minister and the guile of Satan himself. The same miner originated the rumor—false though it may have been—that Booth was a man who might backshoot you, but he would give you the Lord's blessing to send you along. In simple fact, Booth had no religion—no notion of God, Man Above, the Great Spirit, or any other symbol of a world beyond this one. It seemed simple logic to him that, if there was a God, He wouldn't have made men like himself and Charlie. The only truth he accepted from the Bible was, "From dust thou art, to dust returneth," and he reckoned that he had returnethed more than a few to their origin.

"Hallo, friends," Booth called out once he was within earshot.

Tom and his partners made no response to the greeting but continued to watch the two closely as they approached. He glanced briefly to each side again, watchful for any sign of treachery, but the barren little valley appeared to be deserted save for the six of them. The two strangers were an odd pair. The white man did not wear the trappings of a mountain man, dressed as he was in black trousers, broadcloth shirt, and a broad-brimmed, flat-crowned hat. His companion, a solid-looking block of a man, riding a gray pony with an Indian saddle, was definitely an Indian, or a half-breed. The beaming, openly friendly face of the white man contrasted with the sullen countenance of his companion—a face devoid of expression, discouraging even the seed of a smile.

"Boy, am I glad to see some white faces," Booth exclaimed as he and Charlie pulled up before them. When there were no more greetings from the four miners other than a couple of nods, Booth pretended to take no notice of their suspicious stares. "I'm Booth Dalton," Booth went on, "special aide on Indian affairs to the Secretary of the Interior." Making a sweeping gesture toward Charlie, he said, "This here is my guide. We're on our way to Fort Laramie."

Booth paused, beaming brightly, as he evaluated the effect of his story upon the four cautious miners. It evidently had the effect he wanted, for Tom glanced at Ned Turner briefly, and both men relaxed a bit. "Tom Farrior," Tom responded courteously, still a bit leery of any white man in this wild country. His three companions nodded politely but said nothing. "What brings you alone in these parts? Don't you know this is Injun country?"

Booth laughed good-naturedly. "Indeed I do, sir, and might I add that you do well to question anyone you meet in these hills. This is dangerous country, and my guide and me wouldn't be west of the Cheyenne River if my packhorse hadn't broke his hobbles and run off the other night. Most of our supplies and a packet of important dispatches for the post commander at Fort Laramie was on that horse, so we've been trackin' him ever since." He paused again to judge the effectiveness of his story. Pleased to see more of the stiffness dissolve from the faces of the four, he silently congratulated himself—he kinda liked the idea of being an aide to the secretary.

"Well, Mr. Dalton," Anson Miller offered, "we ain't seen sign of no packhorse. Leastways, it sure didn't come through that canyon behind us." Jack Stratton nodded his head, agreeing.

Booth grimaced and shook his head as if perplexed. "I guess we're just gonna have to give it up for lost, and hard luck at that. We'll just have to make do with the supplies we've got in our saddlepacks, won't we, Charlie?" The half-breed did not respond. Booth turned back to Tom. "You fellers look like you're fixin' to do some prospectin'. I've heard there's some color in some of the streams in these hills, but I feel it my duty to warn you that you're in some country that the Injuns are mighty particular about. So you boys best be real careful. Keep a sharp eye all the time, and it wouldn't be a bad idea to keep a guard over your animals at night."

"I reckon that's good advice, all right," Tom said. "We know we're in dangerous country. We aim to be mighty careful." Booth certainly seemed to have an honest face, and Tom had no doubts that the man was who he said he was. "What we're looking to do right now is find a place to camp. You run across any water back the way you came?"

Booth smiled warmly. "Matter of fact, we did. There's a suitable spot to make camp about two miles on the other side of that ridge. It's gittin' late—me and Charlie was fixing to find us a place to camp, too. We could camp together, if it's all right with you gentlemen." When there was no immediate response to his proposal, he continued. "I'd be happy to offer my protection in case we have any Sioux visitors. Charlie here is the younger brother of old Iron Pony himself, so the Sioux won't hardly bother nobody ridin' with him."

This seemed to encourage a favorable reception from the four miners, and the atmosphere suddenly became free of tension, jovial in fact, as Booth cordially shook hands with each man. As far as Tom was concerned, it was a stroke of luck to run into Mr. Booth. It might not be a bad idea to ask for some token from his guide, something that would identify the four of them as friends to the Sioux in case they were unsuccessful in avoiding a war party after they parted company with Booth.

True to his word, Booth led the small mule train to an ideal camping spot in a grove of trees beside a clear stream that fairly sparkled with the last faint rays of the setting sun. Tom marveled that Booth had been able to stumble upon it because it had been necessary to cross a ridge and ride down an almost hidden ravine to reach the stream. He supposed that Booth's somber guide had found it. There was a little more excitement among the four prospectors when they looked back up the mountain toward the source of the rushing stream. Without discussion, the four of them decided it to be a likely spot to start their search for gold.

When advised that his camping companions had decided to set up a permanent camp on the spot, Booth seemed genuinely pleased. "Well, now, I'm mighty happy that I could show it to you. Maybe, when you strike it big here, you'll remember ol' Charlie and me."

It was a lighthearted camp that night. Tom and his friends found Booth Dalton to be a most entertaining guest, full of stories about the frontier—some of them possibly true—tales of the California territory, and mining towns in between there and here. Iron Pony's younger brother remained apart, whether from cold detachment from white men or some other reason— Tom couldn't say. But Mr. Dalton was a close friend to them all before it was time to unroll their blankets. Still, Tom did not feel it wise to discard all caution. When it was finally time to bank the coals for the night, Tom took Ned aside. "I don't think we've got anything to worry about from Mr. Dalton, but it might be a good idea for one of us to have one eye open all night." Ned agreed, and they quietly worked out a guard schedule with Jack and Anson, so that only three of them would be asleep at any time during the night.

Meanwhile, Charlie White Bull was showing signs of impatience to see what manner of plunder the prospectors' pack train contained, so Booth found it

necessary to remind his associate once again that he
would be the one to decide the proper time to strike—
and Booth was in no particular hurry now since Charlie had not turned up any sign of Sioux in the area. He
reasoned that the job would be a whole lot easier if the
four men came to accept him as a friend. If it took a
couple of days to reach that point, he was content to
bide his time and enjoy the company of four pleasant
companions. After cautioning his half-breed partner to
be patient, and not to try anything during the night,
Booth retired to his bedroll, content in the knowledge
that there would be a sentinel on guard all night to
protect and watch over him. Of the half-dozen men in
the camp, only Booth and Charlie enjoyed a full
night's uninterrupted sleep—snoring peacefully while
the four prospectors took turns watching them.

When morning came, Tom awoke to find Booth already up and preparing to set a kettle on the fire to boil
coffee. Glancing around him, he saw that his three
partners were still huddled under their blankets—including Jack Stratton, who took the last watch during
the night. After watching Booth for a few moments,
Tom said, "We've got a coffeepot that might be a little
easier to work with than that kettle."

If Booth was startled by the sudden voice behind
him, he didn't show it. "Good morning," he offered
cheerfully in response. "That might work a little better
at that. I had me a good coffeepot, but a Blackfoot warrior put a hole in it when we was attacked last spring
on the Missouri." He waited while Tom got the coffeepot and handed it to him. "I'm aiming to get me another one—just like this one," he said, smiling. There
was a smidgen of truth in his story. He *had* discarded
his coffeepot after it received a bullet hole. But the rifle
ball that did the job had come from the flintlock of a
miner Booth had left for dead—and he did have plans

to replace the pot with the very one he was now holding.

Just then, Tom noticed that Charlie White Bull's horse was missing. "Where's your guide?" he asked, glancing toward the horses and mules tethered in the trees.

Booth's smile broadened. "I sent Charlie out a little earlier to see if he couldn't git us some fresh meat. I noticed that you boys weren't packin' anything but salt pork last night—and I know I ain't had nothing but jerked buffafo for a while. Figured we *all* might enjoy a little fresh meat."

"Why, that sure sounds good to me," Tom replied, a second or two before another thought occurred. He quickly glanced in Jack's direction and was met with an expression of puzzled bewilderment on his young partner's face, as Jack threw back his blanket. *How the hell did he get outta here without you knowing it?* Tom wondered. The knowledge that the guide had been able to untie his horse and ride out without anyone taking notice bothered Tom more than a little. After thinking about it a second, he also realized that Booth had said he had sent Charlie to hunt. That meant that the two of them were awake and talking while Tom and his partners slept unaware. He shot Jack an accusing look.

Tom remained a bit uncomfortable knowing that the half-breed was missing. Mr. Dalton seemed jovial enough, however, serving coffee to the four prospectors as if he were the host. Tom's concerns were lessened somewhat when, after half an hour, a single shot was heard about a mile off in the distance.

"Well, boys," Booth announced, "that'll more'n likely be breakfast." He looked around the fire, grinning at each man in turn. "Charlie don't hardly miss.

I'm thinkin' we'd best rig us up a spit to roast the meat on."

Just as predicted, the half-breed returned with a fresh kill draped across his saddle. They spent the day in camp, calling it a holiday, while they stuffed their guts with strips of roasted meat from Charlie's white-tailed deer. Tom was beginning to believe his suspicions of their new friends were completely unfounded. It would be hard to imagine a more congenial companion than Mr. Dalton. After a while one even became accustomed to the stoic presence of Iron Pony's younger brother. Tom was glad that the two had decided to stay with them a couple of days—he would be sorry to see them start back on their way to Fort Laramie.

After the second night, Tom and his partners became wholly convinced that Mr. Dalton and his guide were no more than honest men involved in honest work. Ned was certain that Lady Luck herself had caused the two to cross their path because Booth spent a generous amount of his time educating the four novices on the proper methods of placer mining. Having nothing to qualify them as gold prospectors, other than desire and the money to equip themselves, the four men had counted on compensating for their lack of knowledge with hard work. To Tom's delight, they found Booth Dalton to be a veritable gold mine of information on the subject of mining. When Tom wondered why Booth didn't try his own hand at prospecting, he was advised that Booth felt that serving the government in his capacity with the Department of the Interior was much more gratifying. Tom wondered what Annie would think now if she could know of their good fortune.

It had been troubling to Tom that his young wife was not more supportive of this venture to strike it rich. Although she had argued that it was risky to invest what money they had on what she considered a pipe dream, Tom was convinced that her real concern was being separated from her husband after only three months of marriage. She had journeyed as far as Fort Laramie with him, and had remained there with Ned's wife Grace. Tom missed his wife, but he was convinced that prospecting was the only opportunity he had to amass enough to set Annie and himself up with a farm of their own. And now he was even more certain that he had made the proper decision, what with Mr. Dalton's glowing reports of likely signs of gold throughout the Black Hills country. *Why, we might be back at Laramie well before the two months I promised*, he thought as he spread his bedroll and checked it for uninvited critters. Mr. Dalton had promised to draw them a map in the morning, showing over a dozen promising streams for prospecting.

Of the four partners who started out from Fort Laramie, Anson Miller was the loudest snorer. He could probably outsnore the other three combined. Ned Turner had expressed concern that Anson's snoring might be heard by a passing Sioux war party and be the cause of all their deaths. Worse yet, Anson was always the first one asleep, usually deep in his slumber almost as soon as he pulled his blanket over his shoulders. Anson maintained that he only snored when he rolled over on his back. So it had become a ritual with the other three to place a large stone or stick of wood behind Anson's back as he lay on his side, figuring it would prevent him from rolling over.

All four of the partners had eaten heartily, and after a long evening of conversation about prospecting and planning for the beginning of their search for gold, everyone turned in later than usual. Consequently, no one bothered to place a rock behind Anson. The fire was no more than a bed of dying embers when Anson rolled over on his back. Within seconds, his mouth dropped open and the first nasal bass tones rumbled up his windpipe. He had issued no more than two or three notes before a beefy hand was clamped tightly across his open mouth, causing him to snort briefly before Charlie White Bull's razor-sharp skinning knife laid his throat open from ear to ear.

Held firmly by the half-breed's powerful hands, Anson Miller's life drained from his body, his arms and legs thrashing helplessly while his last breath bubbled from his severed windpipe. Charlie glanced over at Jack Stratton's bedroll where Booth was performing the same execution. With two members of the prospecting party disposed of, Charlie went to the other side of the fire to slit Ned Turner's throat.

When Charlie reached down to clamp his hand over Ned's mouth, Ned awoke and yelled, causing Charlie to struggle with him before subduing his flailing victim with a knife thrust deep in his belly. Awakened by the struggle, Tom opened his eyes to discover Booth standing directly over him. Alarmed, Tom asked, "What's wrong?"

"Why, nothin'," Booth replied, smiling, "nothin' at all."

While Tom fought to rid himself of his blanket, Booth pulled his pistol from his belt and put a ball in Tom's forehead, killing him instantly. He stepped back as Tom's body slumped back to the ground.

"Waste of lead," was Charlie's stoic comment, as he cleaned his knife blade on Ned's shirt.

"Quicker," Booth replied simply. He would not have wasted a bullet if Tom had not awakened before he could slit his throat. Since he did, Booth saw no reason to struggle with his victim, risking a wound himself. Pausing to reload his pistol, he said, "Now wasn't that a sight better than chargin' into four men with guns like you wanted to do the first day?"

Charlie grinned, transforming the somber face into a comical brainless facade. "I reckon."

"Let's git some sleep," Booth said, "we can take inventory of our goods in the morning."

Charlie was not ready to retire yet. "I wanna take the scalps now—so I can dry 'em in the morning."

Booth shook his head, exasperated. "What the hell do you want 'em for, anyway? You can't trade 'em." He watched for a minute while Charlie sliced the skin around Anson Miller's pate. "I swear, Charlie, I ain't never gonna make a civilized man outta you." Booth pulled his boots off, rolled up in his blanket, and was soon on his way toward the peaceful sleep of a man satisfied after a good night's work. Other men might have been a bit uneasy going to sleep while a brainless half-breed was loose with a bloody knife. Booth wasn't worried in the least. Charlie was like a child in most ways, and he would be lost without Booth to tell him in which direction to start every morning.

Most of the following morning was spent stripping the bodies of all useful items and pulling the packs apart. Booth was a little disappointed to find no more than a couple of kegs of black powder and a likewise small supply of flints and lead. There was a large quantity of dried beans and salt pork, as well as several tins of smoked oysters, one of Booth's favorites. Of course there were mining tools and other supplies, but the item that delighted Booth most was a silver pocketwatch that Annie Farrior had given Tom as a wedding present. He rewound it and held it up to his ear, a wide grin on his face when he heard the steady ticking of the timepiece. THOMAS L. FARRIOR, LOVE FROM ANNIE, was the inscription on the inside cover of the watch. It brought a wide grin to Booth's face. Charlie, until then busy pulling Anson Miller's shirt from his body, paused to watch Booth wind the timepiece—regretting the fact that he had not found it first.

Reading his partner's expression, Booth said, "Hell, Charlie, you can't tell time, anyway." Feeling real pleased with himself, he looked down at the body of young Tom Farrior. "This here really shines—I swear it does—and I reckon I can at least give you that map I promised you." He pulled his knife from his belt, and after cutting the shirt open, drew the point across Tom's bare belly, opening a long slash. "This here's the creek you're laying beside." Carving a couple of X's across the first slash, he said, "And here's where the gold's at—and now you got your map." He stood there giggling at the joke.

Curious, Charlie walked over, stood next to Booth, and stared down at the almost bloodless lines drawn on the corpse, the blood that had not drained during the night having settled in the body. Puzzled by Booth's obvious enjoyment over the slashes, he turned to stare in his partner's face.

"That's his map," Booth tried to explain, still laughing.

Still confused, Charlie shook his head and said, "Not much map." He returned to his plundering of the packs.

Booth decided to stay where they were that night, and start out for Montana territory the next morning. He knew there were a couple of mining camps out there that his reputation had not reached. They could sell most of the tools there, and all of the food supplies.

That decided, they dragged the bodies away from camp since they were already attracting a horde of flies. Booth intended to get an early start the next day. It wasn't healthy to stay too long in the Black Hills.

CHAPTER 2

Blue Water sat before her father's tipi, pounding the kernels of wild grain into a meal that she would make into cakes. The entire camp was preparing to set out on a long journey in a few days to a place Blue Water had never seen. After returning from a meeting with the other elders of the village, her father, Broken Arm, had told her that she must make preparations to pack up the tipi. Chief Washakie had told the council members that a great conference had been called for at Fort Laramie, between the North Platte and the Laramie rivers. The purpose was to propose a peace treaty between the whites and the warring tribes along the Medicine Road that the whites called the Oregon Trail.

She looked up from her work when a group of boys ran between the lodges, laughing and shouting in a game of war. Blue Water smiled at the tall sturdy youngster leading the pack, running with the grace and strength of an antelope. Broken Arm had given her son the name of White Eagle because the boy's skin was lighter in color than that of the other boys. It was no secret that White Eagle's real father was a white trapper.

Blue Water had been a young girl when she had fallen in love with a sandy-haired young man at the rendezvous on the Green River eleven summers ago.

She would have gone with him wherever he wanted to go, and at the time, she felt in her heart that he returned her love. But it was not to be. Broken Arm would not permit the union, and when he realized something had happened between Blue Water and the white man, he broke camp in the middle of the night and took his daughter with him, leaving the rendezvous and the young white trapper behind.

She paused to think about that time. Her young heart was broken, even then carrying the seed that would bring her a son, but she knew it was best to leave. She only regretted that she had left without saying goodbye. Stealing away in the middle of the night may have been unnecessary, but her father thought he was acting in her interest. Perhaps he was right, for the trappers no longer came to the summer rendezvous after that year. Since then troubled times followed between the white man and the Indian, although her people, the Shoshoni, remained at peace with the white men. Looking back, she could see that her place was here with her people, with the mountains to protect them from the ever increasing numbers of wagon trains following the Medicine Road. The aching in her heart for the young trapper eventually subsided, and when Eagle Claw talked to her father about making her his wife, she was not reluctant to agree to the proposal. White Eagle needed a father, and who among the warriors of her village would have been a better father to her son than Eagle Claw?

As she had hoped, Eagle Claw had proved to be a good father, teaching the boy the many skills he would need to become a warrior. Little White Eagle was an attentive pupil, and Eagle Claw soon found that his adopted son showed promise to be a leader among his peers. A frown settled upon her comely features when she thought of Eagle Claw. White Eagle was only ten summers old when Eagle Claw was killed in the war with the Gros Ventres. Blue Water had not yet taken another husband, although a year had passed since Eagle Claw's death. There had been opportunities, for she was a handsome woman. Perhaps she would marry again, but for the time being, she preferred to live in her father's tipi. White Eagle missed the man he called father, but there were many uncles, as well as Broken Arm, to oversee his training.

"Trace," she murmured as her thoughts drifted back to that moonless night on the Green River. Trace was the name the white men had called the young trapper.

"What?" Broken Arm asked, as he came around the side of the tipi, thinking she had spoken to him.

Startled by the sudden appearance of her father, Blue Water hesitated before replying, not wanting to let her father know her thoughts. "Nothing, Father, I was just singing to myself." Even though many years had passed since the rendezvous on the Green River, Broken Arm was still troubled whenever he suspected his daughter had thoughts of the young trapper.

"I have just been talking with the elders and we have decided to start for Fort Laramie tomorrow, so you must finish your preparations today," Broken Arm stated.

Blue Water nodded and continued grinding the kernels of wild grain. After a thoughtful moment, she paused again and asked, "Why does Washakie want to go to the council with the white chiefs? Fort Laramie is a long way from our country. Why should we worry about the soldiers?"

Accustomed to his daughter's habit of questioning the decisions of the elders, Broken Arm patiently answered her. "Washakie is right. It is important that the soldier-chiefs know that the powerful Shoshonis should be informed of any treaties made with the white men. Bridger, the great friend of the Shoshoni, has told Washakie that the soldiers called this meeting with our enemies, the Sioux, the Cheyenne, Arapaho, Crow, Arikara, Assiniboine, Gros Ventres, and Mandan. Although the Shoshonis have been friendly with the white man for many years, we were not asked to attend this meeting which may greatly effect the future of all Indians. We must be there to protect our traditional hunting ground. The Great White Father in Washington must know that the Shoshoni people will not permit the Sioux and the Cheyenne to trespass on our lands."

Blue Water nodded without further reply, indicating that she understood. Washakie was a wise chief, so she was sure that this was a necessary journey. Inside she still wished that her people would stay away from the soldier forts. She felt reluctant to leave the land of the Shoshoni. Here they were strong, protected by the lofty ridges of the Bitterroots to the west, and the massive Bighorns to the east. The soldiers had no business here. Let them build their roads through the Arapaho country to the south. *It is not for a woman to decide*, the words of the elders rang through her head. She sighed to herself and went back to preparing her meal.

Early the next morning, the village prepared itself for the long journey to Fort Laramie. Blue Water helped her aunts take down the tipi, folding the buffalo-hide covering and tying it to a packhorse. Fashioning a travois with two of the lodge poles, she loaded the entire contents of the tipi and strapped them down. After she had prepared food for her father and White Eagle, she packed her cooking utensils in a parfleche and strapped it to the loaded travois. The village was on the move before the sun had climbed to the tops of the pines on the eastern ridge. Blue Water rode on a bay pony, leading the packhorse with the travois. Her son rode beside his grandfather on a spotted gray pony that Eagle Claw had given to him. The sight of the boy's confident posture as he rocked gracefully in rhythm with his pony's gait, brought a warm smile to Blue Water's face.

Buck Ransom walked his pony across the wide parade ground, past the post headquarters, heading toward the post trader's store. Laramie had changed quite a bit since the old days when the inner courtyard of the old fort used to be busy with Indians and trappers. The old fort by the Laramie River had been abandoned since the army took it over a couple of years ago. Now it looked more like a town than a military fort. He'd heard that it was officially designated Fort William, but nobody called it that. The trappers were mostly gone now, but the Indians still came there to trade at the post trader's store. He had passed a camp of Sioux about a mile from the fort, next to a Cheyenne camp. In the next few days, there would be many more bands arriving for the big medicine treaty the government had called for—Arapahos, Crows, Assiniboines, Rees, Hidatsu, Mandans. These were some of the tribes the government had invited. To add a little more spice to this already volatile stew, he had heard from Bridger that Washakie—though uninvited—intended to bring his Snakes to the party. Buck was curious to see what was going to happen when all those Indians were camped so close to each other. Some of the tribes invited to the conference were blood enemies, and he figured it was going to take a miracle to keep some of them from going after each other. Pretty soon, there were going to be thousands of Indians around the fort, and as far as Buck had seen, there were probably no more than three hundred or so soldiers to keep the peace. They had set up a camp near the fort and called it Camp Macklin. It was going to be interesting, and Buck decided it was a spectacle he didn't want to miss.

"Buck Ransom," Lamar Thomas called out when he saw the grizzled old mountain man walk in the door. "I thought you was dead."

"I ain't took no inventory lately," Buck replied, "but last time I looked, I was still here." Lamar always greeted Buck with the same statement, no matter how long it had been since Buck was last in Laramie. Sometimes Buck wondered if the sutler's clerk was disappointed to find him still among the living. "I could use a little something to cut the dust in my throat," Buck said.

"Bottle or glass?" Lamar asked, reaching under the counter.

Buck thought it over for a moment before replying. "You better just pour me a drink. I wanna do a few things before I dive into a whole quart of that poison." He watched while Lamar filled a shotglass and then handed it to him. Then, after wiping his mouth with the back of his hand, he tossed it back, closing his eyes tightly as he endured the burning in his throat. "Damn! It's been a while," he rasped hoarsely when he opened his eyes again. "Better give me another one." After chasing the first with a second dose of the fiery liquid, he waited for a moment until his voicebox was operative again. "You seen Trace McCall?"

Lamar shook his head. "Not since spring. He come through not long after the last good snow."

Buck didn't bother to ask if Trace had said where he was heading when he left Fort Laramie. Trace probably hadn't known himself. At least Buck now knew that Trace had made it through another winter with his hair intact. Nowadays, that was quite an accomplishment for a man who spent his time living in the midst of so many warring Indian tribes.

Ordinarily Buck didn't spend much time worrying about the welfare of Trace McCall, the man the Blackfoot Indians called the Mountain Hawk. In all his years trapping in the Rocky Mountains, Buck had never seen a man become as natural a part of the mountains as Trace had—he was more Indian than most Indians—as good with a bow as he was with his Hawken rifle. He could damn sure take care of himself, but Buck had been a wee bit concerned for his old partner lately because it had been longer than usual since Trace had come to Promise Valley to visit.

Trace had no family. The closest thing he had to kin were the friends he had in Promise Valley where Buck had a cabin in a small settlement of emigrants from back East. Until this spring, Trace had never failed to show up in the valley to visit with Buck and look in on Jamie Thrash and her father. But this year he didn't come, and Buck had wondered if the Blackfeet had finally tracked down their Mountain Hawk. He was relieved to hear that Trace had shown up at Fort Laramie.

Glancing up from his empty whiskey glass, Buck met Lamar's steady gaze and realized his mind had wandered. "Looks like you got a few extra folks around," he offered for the sake of conversation.

"I reckon," Lamar quickly agreed, "but not as many as we'll likely have in a few more days."

"I don't mean Injuns," Buck said. "I seen more white folks than usual, too."

Lamar shrugged. "Well, we got the commissioner here for the big meetin', Colonel Mitchell's his name, and his folks. One of your old friends is here—Tom Fitzpatrick—he's done got hisself named government agent for all the Injuns on the upper Platte."

"I heard," Buck commented dryly.

"Some of them fellers you see walking around in brand-new buckskins is newspaper reporters from back East, come to write about the big treaty. There's two ladies staying with the missus and me. Their husbands got the gold fever and traipsed off into the Black Hills."

This stimulated Buck's interest. "The Black Hills, you say? How big a party was they?"

"Just four of 'em."

"Four? My God, why didn't you just shoot 'em here and save 'em the trouble of riding all that way? Didn't nobody tell 'em that they ain't supposed to be in that country?"

Lamar shrugged. "Sure they did—I did, myself. But you know you can't tell a prospector anything. They left outta here the first of May—said they was planning on being back here in two months. It's been four months and they ain't back yet. I reckon they've gone under or they struck it so rich they can't leave it." He took Buck's glass from the counter and swished it around a few times in a bucket of water behind the counter before replacing it on the shelf. "I hope they show up soon. Their womenfolk are just about beside theirselves worrying."

Foolishness, Buck thought, *I'll bet them Sioux have somethin' to say about that at this here treaty meetin'.* If he had to guess, he'd say that there were probably four corpses full of arrows laying beside some stream up in the Black Hills, and those women might as well get used to the idea of being widows.

Private Noah Bostic, company clerk, stuck his head inside the office door of Captain R. H. Chilton, his commanding officer. "Captain Chilton, sir, there's two ladies out here that wanna talk to you."

"What about?" Chilton asked, obviously annoyed at having been interrupted during what was becoming a busy time for him. He wasn't at all comfortable with the ever-increasing hordes of savages that were gathering for the peace talks, and he didn't welcome any additional distractions.

"I don't rightly know, sir. But they made out like it was mighty important," Noah replied.

"Damn," Chilton exhaled quietly and then sighed impatiently. "All right. I'll be right out." It seemed to the captain that every civilian thought the army was created just to listen to their trivial complaints.

Captain Chilton was surprised to find two young and not at all unattractive women awaiting him when he walked out to greet them. He unconsciously buttoned the top two buttons of his blue garrison jacket and pulled his shoulders back. "Ladies," he acknowledged, "Captain Chilton at your service."

Annie Farrior stepped forward. Grace Turner, somewhat less outspoken than her friend, and extremely intimidated by this obvious symbol of military authority, preferred to let Annie act as spokesman. So she took a step backward and moved in behind Annie.

"Thank you for seeing us, Captain," Annie started. She went on to explain that the purpose of their visit was to seek the army's help in finding their missing husbands and their two partners.

Captain Chilton did a masterful job of disguising his annoyance at hearing that four civilians had wandered off into the Black Hills. He had many more serious problems on his mind than four gold-seeking idiots who were apparently anxious to lose their scalps. Nevertheless, he endeavored to demonstrate some concern for the benefit of the distressed young ladies. "How long have your husbands been missing?" he asked.

"Well, sir," Annie replied, "Tom promised to be gone no longer than two months, and it's been four months now."

Chilton stroked his chin thoughtfully. "Four months . . . well, if they were riding up into that territory looking for gold, four months isn't a very long time to do much searching. Perhaps it's just taking a little longer than they had anticipated."

"If my husband said he'd return in two months," Annie insisted, "he would either be here now, or would have sent word to me somehow. I fear something terrible has happened." She glanced at Grace Turner, a look of distress in her eyes. "Mr. Lamar Thomas suggested that we talk to Mr. Fitzpatrick. We went to see him and he sent us to you." Annie searched Chilton's face for some sign of compassion, then added, "Mr. Fitzpatrick said the army was being sent out here to protect us."

Chilton twitched uncomfortably. He wished he could accomodate the two women, but his mission at present was of far more importance. And he was already concerned for his effectiveness with less than three hundred men, dragoons, infantry, and mounted infantry combined. "Unfortunately, madam, I am unable to assist you at present. Perhaps you are aware of the purpose of this great gathering of Indians for peace talks. It is my assignment and responsibility to protect the commissioner and his people, and I'm critically outnumbered as it is. So you can understand why I can't spare a man at this time." Seeing the disappointment in her eyes, he hastened to add, "I am genuinely sorry for your predicament, and I truly wish I could help."

The despair apparent in the faces of both women, as Annie turned to console her friend, was enough to cause a feeling of guilt in Captain Chilton. When the women continued to gaze into his face, helpless and not knowing who to turn to at this point, he offered the only bit of hope he could. "As I said, I am unable to spare a search party at the present, but after the treaty talks—if your husbands are still missing—I will see if a patrol can be formed to look for them. Mind you, I cannot promise to do it, because I have been instructed that the area around the Black Hills is to be avoided by the military due to the importance the Indians assign to it. I'll try, that's all I can promise. Now, if you'll excuse me, ladies . . ." He turned and went back inside.

An interested witness to the conversation between the captain and the two women was one Robert Dimeron of *The Chicago Herald*. A reporter for over nine years, it was his natural inclination to keep his ears open for the unusual story that might please his editor. For that reason, he had been hanging around outside Captain Chilton's office all morning, talking to as many of the officers as he could corner. Captain Chilton had granted him a few minutes earlier but provided him with no more information about the treaty talks than Dimeron already knew. Curious about the arrival of the two women, he had parked himself on a stool outside the office door where he could hear the conversation that ensued.

Two women whose husbands were missing deep in Indian country—*Now that might be a story there*, he thought. He remained seated until the captain ended the interview and returned to his office. Then he quickly got to his feet and approached the women. Offering his card, he introduced himself. "Pardon me ladies, but I couldn't help overhearing your conversation with Captain Chilton." He doffed his hat. "I'm Robert Dimeron, reporter for *The Chicago Herald*, and I'm grieved to hear about your husbands."

Annie Farrior looked at his calling card, puzzled by

his interest in Grace and herself. Looking up at him, she smiled politely and handed the card back to him. "Thank you," she said, and taking Grace by the elbow, started to leave.

Dimeron turned with her and fell in beside them as they walked. "I know it must be terribly hard for you and your friend, Mrs. . . ." He paused, waiting for her to fill in the blank.

"Farrior," Annie said and nodded toward Grace. "This is Mrs. Turner."

"Farrior," he repeated, tipping his hat. "I would like to offer my help, and the services of *The Chicago Herald*, in soliciting a search party to find your husbands."

Annie and Grace continued walking. "How can you help us?" Annie asked.

"Well, to be honest, I'm not sure I can, but I'm thinking that if I tell Captain Leach that I'm doing a story for *The Herald* about you ladies trying to get help in finding your missing husbands, it just might influence him to become involved—maybe send a patrol out to the Black Hills after the treaty talks."

"Captain Chilton said he would try to do that if he could," Annie replied.

"I know," Dimeron quickly answered, "I heard him. But I think there's a good chance Chilton might not be staying here, and my guess is he'll be escorting the peace commission back to Washington as soon as the talks are finished. I'm sure the captain would like to help you, but he most likely will have no choice in the matter." Seeing the distress in their faces that this piece of news caused, Dimeron hastened to reassure them. "Captain Leach, on the other hand, just arrived here and he'll be on permanent assignment at Fort Laramie for the sole purpose of protecting the folks traveling the Oregon Trail. He'll still be here when the peace commission moves on, and he's the one I'll have to persuade."

Annie's hopes were rekindled. "Do you think he might?"

"I think he might feel that he has no choice, especially when he sees how your story will appear to all our readers. Why even right here at Fort Laramie, he'll feel some pressure to respond to your distress call, what with so many prominent folks here for the talks—Colonel Mitchell, Mr. Fitzpatrick, Jim Bridger, why even Father Jean DeSmet is coming all the way from Flathead country. A lot of people will be watching Leach to see how he responds to the needs of the people."

Dimeron was satisfied to see that his proposal was eagerly embraced by both women, and he was soon filling his notepad with information about the four men who had embarked on the likely ill-fated trek. It wasn't a bad idea at that, he admitted to himself, even if his motive was not altogether to come to the aid of two damsels in distress. He would jump at the chance to actually see some of this wild frontier where the savage redman roamed. What a story it would make to venture into the heart of Sioux hunting grounds. And he would make sure Annie Farrior and Grace Turner insisted that he, and only he, must accompany the patrol. This would be his price for bringing their cause before the public eye.

Colonel D. D. Mitchell was more than slightly annoyed. His task as commissioner was to bring these tribes to the council table to smoke and speak of peace. And now, before the actual peace talks had even begun, Captain Henry Leach brought this distressing news. "This is not a good time for this, Captain. Why weren't these four civilians stopped?"

"Sir," Leach was quick to point out, "this was not my doing. I only arrived in Laramie this week, and I only learned of the prospectors today. Captain Chilton informed me that two wives of the men came to him for help in finding their husbands." Noticing the colonel's deep frown, he added, "I'm afraid I reacted to the news much as you have, sir, although Captain Chilton appeared not to be overly concerned."

Mitchell thought for a moment. "It may amount to nothing," he mused, rubbing his chin as he turned the matter over in his mind. "But, dammit, I've got to convince these Indians that we mean to keep settlers and gold miners out of the territories we set aside for them. Four men you say?" Leach nodded. Mitchell continued. "I think it might be wise to tell the Sioux chiefs about the four men—if they don't already know—and tell them we'll send soldiers to find them and punish them. Maybe that'll placate them." He got to his feet, indicating the meeting was ended. "And captain, get a troop out right away and find those idiots."

"Yes sir," Leach replied. "What about the reporter that started this mess? He insists that the two wives want him to accompany the patrol."

The colonel had other things on his mind already. He was ready to dispense with this problem. "Hell, I don't care. Let him go if he wants to. It'll be one less reporter around here."

"Yes sir. He also recommended that we ask Jim Bridger to act as guide for the detail."

"The hell you say? By God, he's got a helluva lot of nerve, doesn't he? Well, you can tell Mr. Reporter that Bridger has more important things to do than chase into the wilds looking for lunatic husbands."

Annie Farrior sat alone by the tiny stream that trickled down to the river where Lamar Thomas had built his cabin. The skirt she was supposed to be mending lay untouched across her lap, the threaded needle still held idle between her thumb and forefinger. Some thirty yards away, she could hear the sounds of supper being prepared, so she told herself that she mustn't tarry. The light was rapidly fading from the evening sky, anyway. Off in the distance, she could hear the almost-constant sounds generated by the Indian camps gathered for the treaty talks as voices, some shouting, some singing, were carried on the wind. Occasionally the tinny peal of a bugle split the late-afternoon air with a series of staccato notes that held some message for the soldiers. It would be dark soon, and the nightly dancing and drum beating of the various Indian camps would begin—sometimes continuing on through the night.

Even though it was not really autumn yet, still there was a slight chill to the constant breeze, causing Annie to shiver. She couldn't help but wonder if the shiver might be caused in part by the thought of being surrounded by thousands of savages. The newspaper reporter, Robert Dimeron, had assured her that there was no real threat of danger—it was a peace conference. However, Lamar Thomas had said that anything could happen when this many Indians were gathered together—especially with the long history of bad blood between some of the tribes. To make matters even more volatile, old Chief Washakie had promised to bring in a couple of hundred of his Snake warriors, all armed with rifles and prepared to back down to no one. They were sworn enemies of the Sioux and Cheyenne, and Lamar hoped that Tom Fitzpatrick would be able to keep the peace between them.

Annie's thoughts were brought back to the cabin when she heard her name called from the doorway. "I'll be there in a minute, Grace," Annie replied. She slowly folded the skirt and put her needle and thread away. *A few more moments*, she thought, gazing out toward the shallow river. She didn't care if the skirt was mended tonight or next week. She had only used it as an excuse to be alone for a little while, saying the light would be better outside. She truly was fond of Grace, but she needed some time to herself lately. It seemed that with every week that passed, with no word from their husbands, Grace became more and more dependent upon her, fretting constantly over the cramped conditions and the uncertainty of their future. Rose and Lamar Thomas had been extremely generous in taking them in. Tom and Ned had paid Lamar a small sum to help with the food, but Annie knew that that amount had long ago been depleted. Now, with winter not far away, Annie found it difficult to keep dire thoughts from her mind—even contemplating the possibility that her husband might not return to her.

This directed her thoughts to the newspaper reporter. Mr. Dimeron had been somewhat effective in garnering some response from the military regarding her situation—although negative in reality, for Captain Leach was infuriated that her husband and his three partners were not stopped from venturing into the Black Hills in the first place. Still, the net result was a planned patrol, headed by a young lieutenant named Austen. Rather than wait for the completion of the treaty talks, Leach was adamant that the patrol should be sent out at once, and when Colonel Mitchell was informed of the mission, he insisted that the Sioux and Cheyenne chiefs be informed as well. He thought it crucial at this stage that the Indians know these gold-seeking forays were not encouraged by the government.

Mr. Dimeron had hoped to persuade Jim Bridger

himself to guide the search party, but Mr. Bridger was needed as an interpreter for the peace talks. Bridger had, however, recommended a man who happened to be in Fort Laramie at this time. The man's name was Buck Ransom, an old mountain man and former comrade of Bridger's, who according to Bridger knew the territory as well as he did.

Unlike Grace Turner, Annie did not spend much of her time brooding over their situation. She missed Tom, and she prayed for his safety every night before going to sleep. However, if something happened to her husband, and he didn't come back, she knew she would deal with it. It wasn't that she didn't love Tom—she did—but it v as a love that was still being cultivated on her part. In truth, she had accepted Tom's marriage proposal in large part because of her desire to escape the dominance of her parents and a chaotic home life with four younger brothers in one tiny house. Tom was a good man, but she admitted to herself that she was hardly swept off her feet. Instead, she had resolved to learn to love him, and given more time than the few months they had spent together, perhaps she would have by now. Even so, Annie did not take her marriage vows lightly, so Tom never knew that his wife was not as passionate for him as he was for her.

Maybe a more sensible mind should have prevailed when the four friends had first contemplated the notion of coming west to search for the gold that was rumored to be lining all the streams in the mountains. California was the initial destination, but Anson Miller had persuaded the others that too many prospectors were descending upon the new claims there—it would be wiser to search in an area where they would not be competing with hundreds of other prospectors. And Anson had been told by an old trapper for whom he had bought a drink that the reason the Indians were so adamant about keeping the whites out of the Black Hills was because there was gold laying around everywhere in the streams there. It seemed flimsy information to plan an entire life upon, but Annie was as anxious to leave Illinois as Tom was, so she did not try to dissuade him. She had supposed that, if there was no gold, then they could continue on to the Oregon territory.

"Annie."

"Coming, Grace," Annie called back. Getting to her feet, she looked toward the glow of campfire that now lit the darkening sky. The chanting and dancing would soon begin.

CHAPTER 3

Young White Eagle kicked his heels hard, urging his spotted gray pony to gallop as the boy sought to chase after the large group of Snake braves now riding out before the column of women and children. Fort Laramie was on the other side of the rise, and Chief Washakie was even now assembling a force of close to two hundred warriors upon the brow. The wily old chief wanted to show the other tribes gathered there the strength of his warriors, all armed with rifles that Jim Bridger had supplied. Though grossly outnumbered by their traditional enemies, the Sioux and the Cheyenne, Washakie feared no one. His Snake warriors were among the fiercest fighters of all the western tribes. He had come in peace, to smoke with his old enemies at the council fire. But he would demonstrate his potential for war just in case someone might think of settling old scores.

White Eagle urged his pony on. Up ahead, he could see the Snake warriors filing out across the rise to present a solid line where they would sit while their chief rode out alone to meet the white men who stood ready to greet him. When no more than twenty yards from the line of warriors, White Eagle was intercepted by a stern-faced brave who scolded him and sent him back to the women and other children. White Eagle knew better than to protest. Disappointed to be treated as a child, he nevertheless turned his pony around and reluctantly started back at a slow walk. He had so wanted to stand with the warriors as they gazed silently in solemn dignity upon the assembly below them. His mother had warned him that he would be ordered back, but he had to find out for himself.

As the spotted gray walked leisurely back to the women and children, White Eagle continued to gaze back at the warriors, wishing he were old enough to take his place beside them. Then something east of the rise—maybe half a mile distant—caught his eye and he pulled his pony up to take a longer look. It looked to be a column of soldiers, riding two abreast. White Eagle's sharp eyes counted thirty-five blue uniforms and three others, one an Indian, the other probably a white scout. Only slightly curious, the boy watched the column until it rode out of sight behind a hill in the distance. Then he nudged his pony and continued on.

Buck Ransom wondered whatever possessed him to give in to Robert Dimeron's pleas to guide a patrol into the Black Hills. He had tried to explain to the newspaper reporter that he was getting too long in the tooth to do this line of work anymore. Dimeron was insistent that Buck was the only one who could guide them, only because Jim Bridger recommended him. In the end, it was Dimeron's promise of a handsome sum from his newspaper in addition to the pay he would receive from the army that made up his mind. It was just too much for Buck to pass up.

Look at him, Buck thought, *thinks he's out on some kind of Sunday picnic.* Dimeron *was* quite cheerful as he bobbed unevenly along, fighting the natural rhythm of his horse. *As out of place as a pig in the parlor.* The thought made Buck snort with contempt. In spite of the money, he might not have agreed to go if he had been told there was going to be a woman riding with them. He didn't find that out until the patrol was assembled and ready to ride.

Buck had openly questioned the advisability of a woman accompanying a detachment of soldiers in the field. The officer in charge told him that he agreed with Buck on the matter, but he wasn't given any choice. One of the party they were setting out to find was the lady's husband, and she had convinced Captain Leach that she would not hinder the patrol. The newspaper reporter had assured the captain that he would look after her, taking full responsibility. It amounted to little less than insanity to Buck, and he told the young lady that, but nothing could dissuade her. Buck tried to convince anyone who would listen that the mistake they were making was in thinking that all the Indians were gathered there at Fort Laramie for the council talks. "It might seem that way," Buck had told them, "but there's a whole lot more Injuns that ain't ever signed a treaty, and ain't ever plannin' to." He soon saw that he was wasting his breath and nobody believed him, so he gave up arguing. If she wanted to traipse her sweet young fanny into those hills, then why should he give a damn?

Buck's reverie was interrupted when Lieutenant Luke Austen suddenly joined him. "Well, Mr. Ransom," Luke said, "looks like we're gonna miss all the excitement back there."

"I reckon," Buck replied, "but we'll be mighty lucky if we don't run into more excitement than we can handle."

"You're doing the guiding. How do you want to handle it?"

Buck had not yet had time to evaluate the young lieutenant, but his first impression was that Luke Austen might have the potential to survive the frontier. At least he was smart enough to know that Buck knew the country and had a hell of a lot more experience in Indian territory than he did. "I reckon it's best if I stay out ahead about a half a mile or so, so's I can git a chance to see what's what before you boys ride into an ambush or somethin'."

Luke nodded. "You think there's much possibility we might run into trouble with the peace talks going on?"

"Lieutenant, there's a heap of Injuns out there that don't care spit for them peace talks, and I don't know if I blame 'em. The Oregon and California trails have cut a wide road right through their huntin' grounds." He gestured to the side. "All this used to be good grazing land. Now look at it, beat out by all them wagons and oxen till there ain't enough grass to feed an antelope. And now prospectors," he went on after taking a quick look back to make sure Annie Farrior was not in earshot, "like them four fools we're lookin' for." He pulled his shoulders back and puffed a little. "Oh, there's a chance we'll run into trouble, all right."

Luke Austen watched the old scout ride out ahead of the column, his horse kicking up miniature clouds of dust from the dry prairie. Luke wondered if the old man still had the stamina to lead a mounted patrol into the mountains. *I guess I'll find out*, he thought and turned back to check on the two civilians.

Luke had protested only slightly less than Buck had when told that a woman was to accompany the troop. A reporter was bad enough, but a woman put an extra hardship upon the men. Typically, a troop of soldiers in the field were a pretty rough bunch to be around, and Luke didn't appreciate the added responsibility of insuring a lady's privacy, not to mention the men's manners. He had halfway expected her to show up in a frilly dress and a bonnet, but was relieved when she

arrived wearing army-issue trousers and had her hair
rolled up under a wide campaign hat. It was obvious
that she had endeavored to make herself as unfemi-
nine as possible, and Luke appreciated that. He had
made quite a speech to his men before she arrived, letting them know he expected nothing short of sterling
behavior on their part. His speech was followed by
one by Sergeant Grady Post which, though not as
lengthy as that of the lieutenant's, served to deliver the
message in a language the soldiers understood. Grady
was a sizable man with fifteen years of soldiering, and
he promised to bury his size-twelve boot in the ass of
any man who demonstrated the slightest disrespect toward the lady.

"You folks doing all right?" Luke asked as he
wheeled his horse and fell in step with Annie Farrior's
horse.

"We're doing fine," Robert Dimeron answered immediately, still cheerful after half a day of bouncing up
and down in the saddle.

Luke couldn't help but notice the contrast in the riding
styles between the woman and Dimeron. "You look
like you've done some riding before, Mrs. Farrior."

"Well, no, not really," Annie replied. "I rode my father's mules once or twice when I was a girl."

"Oh?" Luke responded. "Well, you could have
fooled me." He studied the young woman's face for a
moment until she lowered her gaze and he realized
that he must have been staring. Looking quickly away,
he said, "I hope it isn't too uncomfortable for you," although he could see that it wasn't. *A right handsome
woman, even in a man's getup*, he thought, *and she's got
enough sense to go with the horse's natural motion.*

"Are we in hostile territory yet?" Dimeron asked.

"We've been in it ever since we got outta sight of the
fort," Luke replied, causing Dimeron to quickly glance

all around him as if expecting to find an Indian behind every scrub or bush.

Seeing nothing but the big open prairie, the reporter relaxed and concluded, "They must all be at Fort Laramie for the treaty talks."

Luke's lips parted slightly in a thin smile. "Just because you don't see 'em, doesn't mean they're not there." Then he touched the brim of his hat respectfully to Annie and rode off to the head of the column.

Dimeron looked from right to left once more before saying, "I think the lieutenant is being a bit overdramatic, don't you?"

"I don't know," Annie answered. "He doesn't strike me as the dramatic kind." She decided at that moment that she liked the young officer. He had an easy way about him that spoke of a quiet confidence. She was glad that he had been assigned to this search party, although she guessed that he didn't necessarily appreciate being stuck with a woman on his patrol.

They made camp the first night in a little grove of dusty cottonwoods that jealously competed for the attention of a shallow stream. Buck promised better water the following night when they would strike the south fork of the Cheyenne River. Although the day had been hot and dry, when the sun slipped beneath the line of low ridges to the west, the evening air took on a definite chill. Annie was thankful Captain Leach had suggested that she should include a garrison jacket along with the other garments borrowed from the quartermaster.

As was the summertime custom, the men packed no half-tents, preferring to sleep in the open, even though the nights were already chilly. Sergeant Post detailed two men to set up a tent for Annie, however, as well as one for Robert Dimeron. Dimeron, seeing that he was the only man sleeping in a tent, insisted upon sleeping in the open like the troopers, so after that first camp, Post only concerned himself with the lady's comfort. Several small fires were started and the soldiers gathered around them to cook their evening meal of salt pork and hardtack, to be washed down with bitter coffee. Annie shared the same fare as the men, and while it was not particularly appetizing, she did not complain, soaking the hard crackers in her coffee to make them easier to chew. She understood that there was no time to hunt for fresh meat, since the lieutenant's orders were to make haste whenever possible.

Luke did not confide in the lady that his specific orders were to mount a patrol for fifteen days. Regardless of the success or failure of his mission, he was to return to Fort Laramie within that span of time. Luke speculated that Captain Leach, while irritated that the four prospectors might have jeopardized the peace talks, was not really concerned with their safety. The captain was concerned, however, about sending out a troop of cavalry from an already skeleton force. In deference to the young woman's anxiety for her missing husband, Luke determined to push the troop on the trip outbound in order to have as much time as possible to search for the prospectors.

Luke Austen harbored no illusions as to why he was chosen to lead this seemingly foolish patrol into a country so wild that four men might hide there for a year without being found. It was no secret that Luke was Henry Leach's least favorite officer. Luke didn't waste a great deal of time speculating upon the reason. Basically, he supposed that it was because he was a graduate of the military academy, and his father was a general who had served in the war of 1812. Leach, not having the benefit of an academy background, had earned his captain's bars through the ranks. Aside from that, Luke knew his popularity with the men was another sore point with Leach.

For those reasons, Luke wasn't surprised that he had caught this assignment. Seated with his back against a tree trunk, sipping his coffee, he glanced around him at his command. The irony of it brought a smile to his face. Of the men selected to ride with him, over half were deadbeat soldiers, troublemakers, drunks, and slackers. Most of the rest were foreigners who barely understood English. He looked across the stream to where his scouts were lounging. Buck Ransom obviously knew his business, and had probably been as good a scout as Bridger had testified. But Buck was old, maybe too old for this line of work now. The other scout, a sullen Sioux named Bull Hump, was rumored to have participated in a raid against a party of emigrants during the early summer. Bull Hump denied it, and there was no witness to prove it, but Luke wouldn't put it past him. Captain Leach assured him that he could trust the Sioux scout.

What a crew, he mused, *a troop of misfits, a broken-down mountain man, a turncoat Sioux*—he turned his gaze to the two sitting before the tent—*and a woman and a damn reporter*. He had to hand it to Leach, the captain had fixed him up with a real command.

"Maybe you can tell me why you're smiling, sir, so I can enjoy it, too."

Lost in thought, Luke had not heard Sergeant Grady Post behind him until he spoke. He glanced up as Post kicked a cottonwood limb aside and sat down beside him. "Why, I was just mulling over this patrol, Sergeant."

Grady Post did not have to be told what prompted the ironic grin on the lieutenant's face. The one solid element in an otherwise shaky detachment, Grady knew the score full well. "It's a ragged bunch, all right.

I expect the guardhouse will be a lonely place until we get back."

Buck Ransom rode out about a mile ahead of the column as the morning sun spilled over the dry prairie. Glancing out toward the east, he watched for a moment as the Sioux scout disappeared beyond a rise. Buck hadn't made up his mind about Bull Hump. The Indian seemed a bit standoffish. Buck wasn't sure if he would trust him or not. *We'll wait a bit on that one*, he thought.

Turning in the saddle to look back at the double line of soldiers trailing him, Buck wondered if he shouldn't have turned this job down. More and more lately, he was feeling the rigors of long hours in the saddle. His kidneys hurt and his joints were stiff, and for the first time in his life, he had begun to miss the warm comfort of his cabin in Promise Valley. Buck detested the thought of old age, but it had gotten to the point where he was unable to deny it. *I shoulda took me a squaw a long time ago.* "Shahh," he spat, and nudged his horse hard. Thoughts of aging depressed him.

Some eight hours later, Buck sat in the saddle and gazed ahead toward the mountains before him while his horse drank from the waters of the south fork of the Cheyenne River. He would wait there for the lieutenant to catch up. Off to his right, Bull Hump was cutting across a low ridge on a course to intercept the column. The Sioux scout showed a tendency to range a little far ahead, sometimes Buck didn't see him for hours. *I hope to hell he's keepin' his eyes peeled*. Buck turned his attention back to the hills ahead. *If the Injuns find out we're in these parts, they ain't gonna like it too much*. It was not the first time the thought had entered his head that day.

While he waited for the others to catch up, he

worked away at an upper tooth that had been aching
for the past two days. With his fingers, he wiggled it
back and forth, trying to loosen it to the point where he
might rid himself of it. He knew he should have let the
doctor in Laramie pull it, but it had not been so painful
while he was there. Half of his teeth were gone already, and he kind of hated losing this one—it was on
the side he chewed his plug of tobacco. *This keeps up, I
ain't gonna be able to eat nothin' but corn mush.*

"Where in hell would a man start lookin' for four
greenhorn prospectors?" he wondered aloud. Then he
took hold of the offending tooth again and launched a
vigorous wiggling assault upon it. The tooth refused
to yield. "Damn!" Buck gasped in exasperation, giving
up for the moment. Back to his previous thought, he
tried to remember the various game trails he had followed through these mountains many years ago. It
had been a while since he had risked his neck in these
sacred grounds. *That damn Injun oughta know where to
look; he's a Sioux, and the Sioux seem to think the Black
Hills belong to them. Hell, them four fellers could be anywhere, and most likely their bones is already bleaching in the
sun.*

When the column caught up to Buck, Luke decided
to follow the river upstream for a few miles before selecting a campsite. After Sergeant Post assigned pickets for the night, he saw to the placement of Annie
Farrior's tent to insure the lady the maximum amount
of privacy. While she watched two troopers assemble
her tent, Annie gazed longingly at the inviting river,
wanting desperately to be able to clean some of the
trail dust from her body. But she hesitated to suggest
something that might be a little too awkward, given
the company she traveled in. Lieutenant Austen, prov-
ing himself to be the gentleman that his commission as

an officer stated, read the lady's thoughts and suggested that she might desire a bath.

"Oh, I most certainly would," Annie replied, "but I'm afraid I wouldn't be very comfortable taking one under the circumstances."

"Well, I think we can manage to protect your privacy long enough for you to clean up a bit," Luke said, then turned to look for his sergeant. "Sergeant Post," he called.

When Grady Post responded, Luke told him to set up a camp schedule with the men. Any man who wanted to bathe in the river would be required to go downstream one hundred yards. The lady would go upstream one hundred yards or so. To further insure the lady's privacy, she would be provided an escort. When Post turned to pass on the lieutenant's orders, Luke turned to Annie again. "I will escort you myself, Mrs. Farrior. You have my word that no one will bother you."

Annie was still hesitant, but she so wanted to rid herself of the day's grime. "It would be nice, but perhaps I should wait until after dark."

"As you wish, ma'am, but it'll be a little chilly after dark." Seeing her indecision, he smiled and said, "You don't have to worry, Mrs. Farrior, I'll make sure nobody sees you—including myself."

She immediately blushed. "I'm sure you would be the perfect gentleman," she hastened to assure him. "I think I *would* like that bath." She fished around in her saddlepack for a towel. "And, Lieutenant, please call me Annie."

"Yes, ma'am . . . Annie."

Luke walked with Annie, following the river upstream until reaching a bend that afforded her respectable privacy from the soldiers' camp. Luke suggested a spot for her bath where he could stand watch on the bank above. "I'll stand right up here with my back turned." He smiled and added, "You can take my pistol if you want. Then if I turn to look, you can shoot me."

Annie blushed again. "I'm sure that won't be necessary." She strode off down the bank to the water's edge. Luke took a position at a high point on the bank some twenty or so yards downstream. With his back toward her, he stood watching in the direction of the camp. As quickly as she could manage, Annie removed her army trousers and waded out from the bank, splashing the chilly water over her arms and legs, and scrubbing her face with her hands. Although she was shivering all over when she waded back to shore, the refreshing effect of her bath seemed to take the weariness from her body that riding horseback all day had caused. While she stood there, drying her legs and arms, she found herself gazing at the young lieutenant, standing straight and tall, his broad back to her. She wondered if he was married—he had made no mention of a wife. She hoped that he wasn't. Suddenly realizing the direction her thoughts were leading her, she silently scolded herself, and reminded herself why she was out in the middle of hostile country with a cavalry patrol. *Forgive me, Tom,* she thought, feeling ashamed for her speculations regarding the young officer.

"You can turn around now," Annie said, and walked back up the bank where he awaited her.

Back in camp, Buck and Grady Post were discussing the different possible directions to start a search for the four prospectors. When Luke and Annie returned from the river, Luke invited Annie to join the discussion, hoping she might remember something her husband might have said that would give them a clue. She sat down with them by the fire but could offer very little information to help. The problem, as she pointed out, was that none of the four knew anything about the Black Hills. The only lead they had was a creek the old trapper had told Ned Turner about. After Ned bought the old man a second drink, the trapper told him that a good place to start looking was a place the Indians called Bitter Water.

"Well, I reckon I know where that is," Buck commented, his face twisted in a frown caused by his toothache. "But I'd be the most surprised one of us if there's any gold in that little crick."

Bull Hump joined the little group around the fire, having just returned from scouting the area north of their camp. When Grady looked at him, his eyes questioning, Bull Hump reported, "No Injuns anywhere." Like Buck, the Sioux scout was familiar with Bitter Water. He was adamant in seconding Buck's opinion that there was no gold there. "I know best place to look for yellow dirt," he said, "much yellow dirt in valley, one day's ride."

Luke looked at Buck, who simply shrugged his shoulders. Maybe the Indian knew what he was talking about, maybe he didn't, but starting the search in one place was as good as another. So Luke decided to let Bull Hump lead them to this valley he spoke of. The lieutenant was less than enthusiastic about the possible success of such a random search—as was Buck Ransom—but he didn't know any better plan. Annie's husband and his three partners might just have stumbled upon this valley Bull Hump was so sure about.

Annie studied the old scout's face while the discussion was going on. Finally she asked, "Are you feeling all right, Mr. Ransom?"

Buck was surprised by her question. "Well, I reckon I've felt a heap better, ma'am. I've got a tooth that's painin' me some. I've been tryin' to pull it all day, but I reckon it ain't done tormentin' me yet."

Annie got to her feet. "Here, let me take a look at it. I've pulled a couple of teeth for my pa."

Buck situated himself in a position to try to get some light from the fire. It wasn't enough so Annie produced a candle from her bag, along with some thread, which she always carried, and she was ready to examine her patient. Buck, grimacing, demonstrated the degree of looseness in the offending tooth with one hand while holding the candle up to his face with the other. Annie tested the resistance of the tooth, but like Buck, she found she could not get enough grip to apply a forceful enough pull. Annie suggested tying a band of thread around the molar to provide a grip that wouldn't slip. Buck agreed, so she carefully wound strand after strand of thread around the tooth until she had a sizable wrap.

With a grip that offered more friction so her fingers wouldn't slip, Annie tried to extract the tooth. She was not strong enough to do it. By this time, several of the men had gathered, fascinated by the project to separate Buck from his tooth. Soon there were many volunteers who wanted to take a stab at pulling the tooth. Buck held up under the assault admirably while one after another pulled and strained, pulling his head this way and that until he finally called, "Enough!"

An interested spectator to the exercise was the Sioux scout, Bull Hump. A solidly built man with short stubby fingers, he waited until Buck had called a recess in the contest before he stepped forward and stated, "I can pull."

Buck was not anxious to continue the torture. In fact, he was at the point where he had just about decided to live with the constant toothache. But Bull Hump's stoic announcement was delivered more as a fact, and not simply a wish to try his luck. So Buck agreed to submit to one more assault. But Bull Hump had conditions that Buck had to agree to first.

"I pull tooth, tooth mine," the stoic Sioux stated.

"You want the tooth?" Buck asked, amazed. "What in tarnation for?" When Bull Hump made no reply, his face as void of expression as a stone, Buck shrugged and said, "All right, you can have the blame tooth. I sure as hell warn't planning to keep it."

That settled, Bull Hump planted his feet solidly before the old scout and prepared to perform the extraction. Buck opened his mouth wide and squeezed his eyes closed. Bull Hump clamped his stubby fingers around the threaded tooth, and with his other hand on Buck's forehead for leverage, administered a slow but powerful pull. Buck could not contain a long yelp of pain as the roots of the tooth steadily gave way to the overpowering force, finally parting from Buck's gum.

Buck backed away, staggering as he scrambled to his feet, spitting blood and shaking his head violently. "Goddamn! 'Scuse me, ma'am—I ain't ever gonna do that again! If I have another tooth go bad, I'd druther shoot the blame thing out than go through that again."

Bull Hump, his expression the same blank facade as before, turned the tooth from side to side, examining his token. Satisfied, he placed it in the pocket of his buckskin shirt and returned to his own cookfire, pausing briefly to gaze at Robert Dimeron, who was writing furiously in an attempt to record the entire operation.

When Bull Hump had moved out of earshot, Grady Post chuckled silently, shaking his head. "That is one spooky Injun." He turned back to Buck, who was probing his empty socket with his finger, and periodically spitting blood. "He's got your tooth now, maybe he's planning on getting your scalp next."

Buck took his finger from his mouth long enough to answer the sergeant's tease. "I reckon this old, thin, gray straw on top of my head don't appeal to him that much. I think he's been admirin' that fine head of black hair on that reporter feller. Did you see how he give it a look just now?"

"I did notice that," Grady returned, grinning broadly.

Robert Dimeron looked up from his notebook, a forced smile upon his face. "I'm sure I don't have to worry about that with a whole troop of soldiers to protect me," he said, perfectly aware of their attempt to tease him. Still, it made him uncomfortable—the Sioux was a sinister-looking man who appeared to have little use for a pleasant expression.

By the time Buck turned in for the night, the throbbing in his gum had stopped. Spreading his blanket close to his horse, he sat down and propped his rifle against a bush, where he could get to it in a hurry. Satisfied that all was well in the camp, he glanced across the clearing and was met by a steady gaze from the Sioux scout. When their eyes met, Bull Hump broke it off, and lay down, turning his back to Buck. Buck gave it no more than a moment's thought before going to sleep himself. *Damn Injun—probably thinks he oughta be the number one scout.*

Annie pulled her army blanket up around her shoulders. Already the snores of the soldiers outside her tent provided an assortment of low rasping notes, like a chorus of oversized katydids. She wondered if Tom was nearby in the mountains that loomed before them, perhaps listening to the snoring of his three companions. Then her mind drifted to the image of Luke Austen, standing guard over her bath. The picture was still in her mind when she fell asleep.

CHAPTER 4

The scouts were out early the next morning—Buck to the east, along the river—Bull Hump to the west. By the time the troop was ready to move out, both scouts had returned to camp to report no sign of any Indian activity anywhere. When Lieutenant Austen gave the order, "To horse!" Buck indicated the line of march, pointing toward a line of low hills to the northwest. Since Buck didn't know what valley Bull Hump had in mind where all this gold was supposed to be just laying around waiting to be picked up, it was decided that Buck would lead the troop as far as Bitter Water. It was Bull Hump's suggestion. Explaining that he had been to the valley only once himself, Bull Hump preferred to be free to scout on ahead of the troops to make sure he could find the landmarks that would take him to the right valley.

"That sounds all right to me," Luke said, upon hearing the scout's proposal. "What do you think, Mr. Ransom?"

"Hell, it don't make no difference to me," Buck replied. "I can sure take you to Bitter Water. If he don't git lost, we'll meet him there." The hint of sarcasm was not lost on Luke, but in case it was, Buck added, "I can't wait to see that valley with the gold laying all over the ground. We can all go back rich men."

Bull Hump sat on his horse, waiting. If Buck's comments bothered him, it didn't show on his expression-less face. When Luke nodded to him, he immediately wheeled his pony and galloped away. They watched him for a few moments, then Luke put the column in motion with a wave of his hand. Buck backed his horse a few yards and watched the troops start out before moving out in front.

"Good morning, Mr. Ransom," Annie Farrior called out as Buck rode by. "How's the toothache this morning?"

"It don't hurt a'tall, ma'am. I'm much obliged." He tipped his hat, then nodded to Robert Dimeron, who was riding beside Annie.

It took most of the day to reach Bitter Water due to the roughness of the terrain and the ridges that had to be crossed. When they reached the little creek in the middle of the afternoon, Luke saw at once why Buck had doubted the existence of any gold in the dark, slowly moving water. Unlike most of the mountain streams, Bitter Water flowed from an opening in the side of a hill, making its way leisurely down through a belt of pine trees. The bed of the stream was almost black, no doubt caused by the minerals that washed out of the hill. The resulting odor of the water was probably the origin of the stream's name.

When the column pulled up, Buck was sitting there waiting for them. After Luke gave the order to dismount, Buck motioned him over to where he stood. "Damned if them fellers weren't here," he said, pointing to the remains of a campfire. "I didn't really expect them to even find this place."

"How do you know it was them, and not an Indian hunting party?" Luke questioned.

"Tracks," Buck said, his attitude suggesting that the answer to Luke's question was fairly obvious. He swung his arm around from side to side. "Look around you. Them's shod horses and mules, about a dozen or more of 'em, I expect."

Luke nodded, realizing he should have noticed that himself. It was a good sign, however, for it meant that they were at least on the trail of the four white men. Then a thought crossed his mind, and looking around him, he asked, "Where's Bull Hump?"

Buck shook his head. "Ain't seen him all day, not since he rode out this morning."

Luke pushed his hat back and scratched his head thoughtfully. "Well, we've still got some daylight left, but I expect we'd better wait here for him. You think he can find that valley he was talking about?"

Buck shrugged. "I don't know—maybe." Buck had his doubts. It had been a while since Buck had ridden this part of the country, but old age had not dimmed his memory of places he had been. And he had no idea what valley Bull Hump might be thinking of. Buck had explored every valley and canyon in the Black Hills, from the Cheyenne River to the Belle Fourche, and he had never seen a valley with gold all over the ground like the one Bull Hump had described.

"I suppose we could camp here for the night," Luke said.

"Well, it ain't the best place to camp," Buck said. "That water ain't fit to drink—the horses won't even drink it—but if I recollect correctly, there's a better place no more than three or four miles beyond that ridge to the east. There's better water and a little grass for the horses."

"What about Bull Hump? We're supposed to wait for him here."

Buck snorted. "Hell, he can damn shore follow our trail. If he can't, he ain't much of an Injun." He turned his head and launched a brown stream of tobacco juice that spattered on a rock a few feet away. "'Course you're the boss, whatever you say."

Luke laughed and turned to Grady Post, who had joined them. "Sergeant, get 'em mounted up. We're going to a better camp."

As Luke suspected, Buck's memory was reliable. They arrived at a grassy knoll below the pines on the eastern side of the ridge, where a clear stream made its way down the mountainside. There was still at least an hour of daylight left with no sign of Bull Hump as yet. The troop went about setting up camp. Sergeant Post put out pickets while Luke checked to see that Annie was comfortable. Buck decided to scout the area around them to make sure they didn't have any neighbors.

Luke paused to look at his scout as Buck crossed the stream and disappeared into the pines. Then he turned his attention back to Annie Farrior. "I don't know if you overheard back there, but Buck is pretty sure the campfire at Bitter Water was that of your husband and his friends." Annie's eyes brightened—evidently she had not heard.

Dimeron, busy at that point with his bedroll, had paused to listen, and hearing the lieutenant's statement, walked over to join them. "You think we might be close to finding them?" he asked.

Luke only glanced briefly in the reporter's direction before directing his answer toward Annie. "According to Buck, that fire is pretty old, weeks maybe. If it had been recent, I would have told you right away. But I thought you'd like to know we've at least crossed their trail."

It was almost dark when a picket called out, "Rider coming!" It turned out to be Buck, returning from his scout. He reported to Luke that he had found no sign of anyone else in the area. Glancing around the camp, he noticed that Bull Hump had not shown up yet. Although Luke was mildly concerned, Buck was not. He didn't have that much faith in the Indian's ability to begin with. "Hell, Lieutenant, if he can't find a whole troop of soldiers in these hills, he ain't much good to us no how."

It was early the following morning when the Sioux scout came riding in, stolid and unperturbed. He rode straight over to Luke and slid off his pony. "I find valley," he said simply, "white men been there."

Buck, walking stiffly as a result of his usual morning back pain, made his way over to Luke and the Sioux. Questioning Bull Hump in his own tongue, he asked, "How long ago?"

"Not long," Bull Hump answered, "maybe one or two days, no longer."

"Any sign of a war party?" Buck asked.

Bull Hump shook his head vigorously. "No war parties. No sign of anyone else."

Buck translated for Luke. "He thinks they were there only a day or two ago."

"We'd best get moving, then," Luke decided, and instructed Grady Post to hurry the men to finish their breakfast and get ready to move out. "And, Sergeant, tell Mrs. Farrior what the scout said—she'll want to know that."

Buck continued to question Bull Hump. "Where is this here valley?"

"Three or four hours' ride, that way." He pointed toward the northwest. "I'll show you."

Buck scratched his head, thinking hard in an effort to recall what valley Bull Hump might possibly be referring to. The somber Sioux scout was not very adept at transmitting information. But Buck figured it couldn't be many miles from where they stood, if it was no more than three or four hours away, because it would be slow travel in the direction he pointed out. It would require following a series of valleys and canyons to make their way through the high hills.

Within half an hour, the troopers were in the saddle and moving out behind the stoic Sioux scout. Buck rode beside Luke Austen and Sergeant Post, a few paces behind the Indian. Annie and Robert Dimeron were next in line before the column of troopers. There had been no rain for weeks, promising another dusty ride, so Annie and Dimeron rode near the head of the column to avoid most of the dust. Leaving the grassy knoll, they followed a dry canyon through a low line of mountains. After approximately two hours' ride, Bull Hump turned back east, following a narrow cross canyon that appeared to make a blind turn some two hundred yards ahead.

Buck stood up in his stirrups, peering intently toward the point where the canyon turned. "I ain't too sure about this," he mumbled, wondering if the Indian had made a mistake in his directions. He nudged his horse and moved up beside Bull Hump. "You sure this is the canyon you found? It don't look like it leads anywhere."

If Bull Hump was insulted by Buck's lack of confidence in his sense of direction, it did not register on his face. He only gazed intently at Buck for a few moments as if considering the old scout's question. In fact, Bull Hump's answer surprised Buck. "Maybe you are right. It was dark when I found it yesterday. Before we go any farther, maybe it is best if I ride on ahead and make sure this is the way."

"Well . . ." Buck hesitated, "all right." He pulled his horse to a halt and turned back to tell Luke what the Sioux scout had said, shaking his head in wonder. *That might be the first Injun I ever met that couldn't find his way outta his own tipi.*

Luke halted the column before proceeding any farther up the narrow canyon, and they sat and watched the Sioux scout until he disappeared around the bend. "I guess a lot of these canyons and draws look alike, even to an Indian," Luke offered in defense of his scout. He knew what Buck was thinking, though, and he himself was beginning to wonder about Bull Hump's ability.

Buck inwardly scoffed at the lieutenant's remark. None of these canyons looked alike to him. To Buck, the greater part of his life spent in the mountains, every canyon, draw, coulee, gulch, and gully had its own distinguishing characteristics. They might be small and undefined by the casual eye, but a real mountain man could tell one from another right enough. He was about to share that opinion with Luke when Bull Hump reappeared at the turn of the canyon, and signaled for them to come on.

"Looks like he knew where he was going after all," Luke commented as he signaled his troopers into motion.

"Shit," Buck mumbled too low to be heard as he gave his horse a tap with his heels.

Bull Hump waited at the bend of the canyon, watching stolidly until the soldiers were within fifty yards. Then he wheeled his pony and disappeared again around the turn. Buck went on ahead at a fast trot to catch up with the Indian. The canyon's walls closed in even more before the bend, and when he made the turn, there was no sign of Bull Hump anywhere. Buck was confused for only a moment before he realized what was happening, then immediately alarmed when he glanced ahead and found himself in a box canyon, the end of it no more that four or five hundred yards away.

At once, he wheeled his horse and raced back to

warn the lieutenant. It was too late. As his horse skidded around the bend, its hooves spraying a shower of dirt and gravel as it sought solid footing, Buck's eyes were met with a terrifying sight. For from out of nowhere, hundreds of Sioux warriors suddenly emerged from the rocks and gullies, and filled the narrow canyon behind the troopers.

Luke was not even aware of the trap closing behind him until he saw Buck come flying around the bend in the canyon, his eyes wide as saucers, his arms flailing in a frantic effort to warn the column. The Sioux, also seeing Buck, held their silence no longer. The canyon suddenly exploded with rifle fire and ear-splitting war whoops, as the rearmost troopers were cut down from their mounts as if a giant scythe had taken a bloody swipe across the rear of the column. So great was the surprise, that there was no immediate return fire from the soldiers. The narrow corridor filled up with a screaming half-naked horde of warriors, firing rifles and arrows in almost constant volleys. Eight army saddles were emptied before Luke could respond.

Buck was yelling and waving his arms frantically for the lieutenant to come on as fast as he could. Since there was no cover on the canyon floor, there was no option but to run, hoping to find a place to take up defensive positions at the box end of the canyon. At breakneck speed, the soldiers ran for their lives amid a chaos of war whoops and bullets snapping around them, punctuated by the frequent screams of their comrades as the deadly Sioux bullets found their marks.

Annie, her heart pounding with terror, bent low on her horse's neck, the echoes of the ambush reverberating around her ears as she urged her horse for more speed. Now she found herself being jostled and bounced back and forth as the terrified troopers com-

peted for the limited space at the narrow bend. Chaos
reigned and it was plainly every man for himself, even
though Luke Austen tried to maintain some form of
discipline in the retreat. Her horse stumbled and almost went down when Robert Dimeron's mount
wedged in ahead of hers, trying to escape the wave of
bullets and arrows. She got only a glimpse of the reporter as his horse charged ahead. He had dropped the
reins and had both arms clamped around the frightened animal's neck, his eyes wide in panic.

"Annie!" Luke yelled and forced his horse between
those of two wildly retreating troopers. "Stay in front
of me!" He pulled back hard on the reins, straining to
slow his horse long enough to allow Annie's mount to
forge ahead. Then he followed close behind in an effort
to shield her from the hostile fire behind them. She
made no effort to control her horse. It would have been
to no avail, anyway, for there was no way she could
have kept the animal from galloping after the mob of
horses sprinting toward the end of the canyon.

With no cover from the devastating shower of arrows and rifle balls, Luke's troop was cut to pieces as
the Sioux warriors' fire claimed one trooper after another. Buck, fifty yards ahead of the frantic retreat, circled his horse and tried to direct the soldiers toward
the trees that girded the steep sides of the canyon—the
only available cover in which to make a stand. Grady
Post, seeing what Buck was trying to do, wheeled
around when he caught up to Buck and tried to help
the scout guide the desperate rush to safety.

"Get 'em into that gully there!" Buck shouted,
pointing to a low rock-strewn defile at the base of the
steep wall of the canyon. The sparse growth of trees
near the floor of the canyon was not sufficient to give
them adequate protection, so without waiting to be or-

dered, the troopers starting digging shallow rifle pits in the rim of the gully.

Even as they labored to carve out defensive positions in the hard, rocky soil, their numbers were still being methodically reduced as first one man, then another, screamed in agony as Sioux rifle shots ripped through their bodies. Lieutenant Luke Austen's distress was written across his face in bold concern as he tried to hurry his men in their digging. As he witnessed the devastating destruction of his command, one man at a time, he struggled to maintain some semblance of order. In those first few minutes of the ambush, it was a hopeless endeavor because his troop of misfits, drunks, and foreigners abandoned all thoughts of military discipline, concerned only with thoughts of self-preservation. The dead and wounded lay like strewn firewood before the rim of the gully, and some of the survivors could be seen pulling the bodies of some of their fallen comrades up closer to the edge of the defile to provide protection against the continual hail of missiles.

Annie, at Luke's direction, laid behind him as flat as she could in the bottom of the gully. Her hands clamped tightly over her ears, she tried in vain to shut out the terrible noise of the massacre. The horrifying bedlam of guns, agonizing cries, shouted commands, horses screaming, mixed with the blood-chilling war whoops of the savages, left her shaking with fear. She didn't even remove her hands from her ears when Buck suddenly grabbed her arms and roughly dragged her out of the path of a terrified horse that almost trampled her. The confused animal had scrambled over into the gully with the embattled soldiers, trying to escape the deadly hail of bullets.

Finally Luke and Sergeant Post were able to organize return fire, and the attack was beaten back some distance as the Sioux warriors now sought cover. After a few more minutes, the continuous firing subsided, replaced now with individual sniping from the steep sides of the canyon. Luke looked around him at the bodies before the gully, and those slumped over their rifles on the rim. He could only count four troopers in addition to Buck, Grady Post, Annie, the reporter, and himself—nine survivors from a troop of thirty-four. There was no time to dwell on it. The task now was to find a way to save those who were left.

Buck crawled over beside Luke. "We can keep 'em off us for a while here, but when they decide to climb up the sides of this canyon, we're gonna be sittin' ducks down here in this hole."

Luke looked at the old scout, the young lieutenant's eyes burning with anxiety. "You're right about that, but I don't know what else we can do but sit tight and keep our heads down. Have you got any suggestions? Because if you do, I'm damn sure open to them."

Buck shook his head slowly. "We're in a fix, and that's a fact." He looked behind them at the sheer rock wall that rose for some fifteen or twenty feet before breaking away to a tree-covered ledge, above which the mountain sloped steeply up to a high ridge. "Well, that's the only way out, and that don't look too promisin'. 'Course, Injuns is unpredictable sometimes. They might just figure they've had enough fun with us and go on about their business before they lose any more of their warriors. Maybe the best thing to do is to just wait 'em out a while—see what's on their minds." He didn't voice it, but he hoped the Sioux would figure they were satisfied with the plunder they had already gained. He didn't have to call Luke's attention to the gruesome activity taking place near the bend of the canyon where the braves were stripping the bodies and taking scalps.

"Those savage bastards," Luke murmured under his breath, and Buck knew the lieutenant had seen the same thing he did. Back to the question for the moment, he said, "I guess we don't have a lot of choice. We'll wait them out for a while before we try to scale that cliff behind us. We can make it plenty costly for them to try to overrun us here."

So they lay low behind their breastworks of rocky soil and human bodies, watching the desecration of the bodies of their former comrades, helpless to avenge the outrage. Not knowing how long they would have to hold out, Luke ordered the men to hold their fire, shooting only if the hostiles ventured within range. Sergeant Post slid along the length of the gully on his belly, collecting as many cartridge slings and canteens as he could from the bodies.

Annie, able now to sit with her back against the rock wall behind her, had regained some of her composure. She asked Grady Post for one of the rifles he had collected, determined to contribute what help she could. She took a second rifle and thrust it toward the still-shivering reporter, encouraging Dimeron to make himself useful. Dimeron was in no state of mind to be of much use. For the first time realizing that the end of his life might very well be within the next few hours, his zest for firsthand knowledge of Indian territory ran down his pantsleg to form a dark stain in the sand. He had abandoned his notebook during the wild dash for the cover of the gully and now sat staring at the rifle Annie pressed upon him with terrified eyes.

"Git down!" Buck yelled, his warning followed a few seconds later by a hailstorm of arrows that thudded into the ground and clattered against the rock wall behind them.

"Artillery," Luke commented, then called out, "Anybody hit?"

No one was, but they soon found that it was only the first of a series of attacks as wave after wave of arrows rained down upon them. Everyone there knew that it was impossible for all of them to escape the deadly rain. A trooper near the far end of the gully was the first to be hit. He cried out in agony as an arrow pierced his chest. The soldier next to him tried to comfort the injured man, but there was little he could do. In spite of Luke's order to maintain a vigilance in case the hostiles decided to charge the gully, he, Grady, and Buck were the only men willing to expose their heads enough to keep watch. The remaining three troopers chose to cringe beneath the brow of the defile. Buck and Luke were too occupied to notice the huddled conference between the three, and were taken by surprise when they made a sudden desperate attempt to escape.

Without announcing their intentions, one of the soldiers, a big raw-boned fellow named Logan, who had spent a good portion of his enlistment in the guard house, suddenly jumped to his feet and ran to the stone wall. Right on his heels, the second man followed him and scrambled up on his shoulders—the third man moved quickly behind the two.

It had happened so fast that Luke was unable to prevent it. Their plan was obvious. The two smaller men figured to be able to reach the ledge by standing on Logan's shoulders. Once both of them were up, they could pull Logan up and make their escape up the steep slope above.

"Logan!" Grady Post roared, but it was too late to prevent the escape—the second man was already scrambling up on the ledge and reaching down to grasp Logan's hands.

"Logan! No!" Luke shouted when he saw what was happening. "You men, get back down here—now!"

Logan, his feet kicking at the sheer rock wall frantically while the other two strained to lift him, finally managed to struggle onto the ledge. Once on sound footing, he looked back at the lieutenant. "You can sit around and wait for them bastards to kill you. Not me. I aim to be long gone when that next bunch of arrows hit."

"Logan, that's crazy," Luke pleaded. "Our only chance is to wait it out. Get down here! I order you to get back down here."

"You can go to hell, Lieutenant. We're savin' our ass while there's still time."

Grady Post turned his rifle on the big man on the ledge above as if to shoot the insubordinate soldier. Buck gently, but firmly, pushed the barrel of Post's rifle down, saying, "Don't waste your ammunition, we're gonna need it. They're done for, anyway."

Robert Dimeron, until that moment cowering in the bottom of the gully, scampered to his feet and ran to the stone wall. "Wait! Take me with you!" Moments later, two rifle shots were fired from the side slopes at almost the same time and two slugs thudded into Dimeron's back. One yelp of pain and he was dead, slumped at the foot of the wall. Annie stifled a scream as the two black holes in Dimeron's white shirt rapidly became larger red stains as the reporter's blood spread across his back.

The three on the ledge needed no further incentive, and turned at once to scramble up toward the trees. A half-dozen shots rang out from the sides of the canyon, and Logan and one of his friends tumbled back down the steep slope, landing at the foot of the stone cliff, both dead. The third trooper, hit in the heel and spun around, nevertheless regained his balance and, using his hands and feet, clawed his way into the trees before a lucky shot split his head like a melon.

Buck looked around him, considering the four of them left to hold off what he estimated to be close to two hundred Sioux warriors. "Well, we sure coulda used them three guns," he said. "But they wouldn't have made a whole lot of difference at that, I reckon."

With no options before them, they sat back and waited. Their fate was in the hands of the Indians now, because there was no way the four of them could hold the hostiles off if the Sioux decided to rush them. Buck felt that the reason there was now a lull in the attack was because the Sioux were having a powwow to decide whether it was worth the losses they were sure to have. As it now stood, they had won a great victory with very little loss of life. They had horses and plunder—why risk even one more warrior's life?

Buck was partially right in his speculation. After talking the matter over, the main body of warriors decided to withdraw, but a small party of twelve decided to stay behind, not willing to let any of the white men escape. They planned to climb the ridge and work around behind the trapped soldiers.

"Uh-oh," Buck suddenly uttered and sat up, "lookee here." Luke and Grady cocked their heads to see. "Looks like they're pullin' out," Buck said, scarcely believing it himself.

It may be some kind of trick to get us to come out," Luke suggested. Buck nodded his agreement.

"I believe they just got tired of waiting," Grady said. No one offered anything else for a while as they watched the Indians jump on their ponies amid a chorus of war whoops and shrill yelling. Several of the young braves charged their ponies straight at the four white souls laying low in the gully, pulling up only fifty yards away to hurl insults and taunts at the survivors before turning to race back to their brothers. Buck was sorely tempted to dust one of them off his pony, but decided it might rile them enough to attack again.

When the large band of hostiles disappeared around the bend of the canyon, Grady stood up. "Hell, they're gone. Looks like we made it."

"Grady!" was all Buck managed to shout before a rifle ball ripped into the sergeant's chest. Grady staggered backward a step, staring in disbelief at the hole in his chest. No more than a moment later, another slug thudded into his stomach, and he dropped to his knees. Buck and Luke quickly grabbed him by the arms and pulled him back into the gully, but it was too late. Already dazed and weakening as blood soaked his blouse, Grady's eyes were wild and he was mumbling something so rapidly that the others could not understand. Luke tried to calm him, but Grady knew he was dying.

Horrified, Annie kept asking herself why she had been so stupid as to insist upon accompanying this patrol. Buck had advised against it, Luke had advised against it—but she had insisted that she had to personally search for her husband. Now, as she shrank back against the stone wall—not wanting to watch the dying gasps of Sergeant Grady Post, but unable to look away—she realized that Tom had not crossed her mind during these last horrible hours. Terrified for her own safety, she found herself praying that it would all go away. Whatever her life span beyond these terrible moments, she would never forget the look of horror on Grady's face as the slugs plowed into his body. So innocent looking at first, just two little puffs of dust from the sergeant's shirt, and then his very life flowed out of him in agonizing seconds. She looked down at the rifle she still held but had not yet fired. Suddenly she flung it from her, as if that might make the nightmare go away.

"Annie," she heard Luke Austen call softly, and she realized that she had been in a near trance. He crawled over to where she sat against the wall and put his arm gently around her shoulders. Without hesitating, she pressed her body close against his and lay her head on his shoulder. He held her there for a while before speaking again, letting her take what small comfort she could. Finally he made himself tell her what he felt he must, but had dreaded to impart. "Annie," he began, "we may get out of this yet . . ." He hesitated. "But if worse comes to worse, I want you to take this." He pulled his pistol from his holster and pressed it into her hand. "Save this for yourself just in case we don't make it. It'll be easier than letting the savages capture you."

The reality of what he was telling her jolted her brain and her mind suddenly became clear and lucid. Her eyes wide, she gazed directly into his and a calmness began to settle over her. Taking the pistol, she nodded that she understood and sat up again. "I'm all right," she assured him. "Maybe I won't have to use this," she added, knowing the odds were against it.

Buck glanced briefly at the lieutenant when Luke crawled back to the rim of the gully where the old scout was keeping watch. He had heard Luke trying to comfort Annie while he gave her his pistol, and he knew it wasn't easy for the lieutenant to do. Indians often took women prisoners, and most of the time they were treated kindly—sometimes even taken as wives. But he had a feeling the lieutenant was of the same mind he was—this bunch wasn't looking for prisoners.

Buck had been in many a hot spot in his long years in the mountains. But this time, he couldn't see any possible escape from the hole they were now in. The main body of Sioux had pulled out, but some had stayed behind. The Indians would keep them pinned down while some of their brothers worked their way up on the slope behind them. There was no way out. Buck's only hope was that he and Luke could make it so costly for the Sioux that they might eventually decide the cost was too dear. Still, glancing up behind him at the sheer face of the rock wall, he had to admit that, once the Indians reached that ledge above them, this little party was over. The girl might have to use that pistol after all.

The afternoon wore on, and now the sun was almost resting on the western side of the canyon. Buck and Luke sat watching in opposite directions—Luke with his back against the rim of the gully, watching the ledge above them—Buck trying to pinpoint the warriors positioned in the canyon before them. They had gathered as many rifles as they could safely recover and loaded them, preparing for an all-out assault if one came. Grady Post had collected enough canteens so they had enough water to last for a couple of days, maybe longer if they used it sparingly. Buck was not concerned about the water supply. He was pretty sure that they wouldn't be there that long. *This boil's gonna come to a head before then*, he thought. *Injuns ain't got that much patience.*

They discussed the possibility of trying to sneak out of their trap after dark. It might be their only chance. But they would be on foot, since their horses—those that weren't lying dead on the canyon floor—had all wandered toward the mouth of the canyon into the waiting arms of the Sioux. If they were successful in slipping by the Indians, then it would be a dangerous game of hide-and-seek—and with a woman it would be that much more difficult to escape the Sioux on their ponies. After some discussion, it was decided to try to make a run for it, feeling it was better than waiting where they were. So they settled back and waited for darkness, not knowing how many warriors might be on the slope above them when nighttime came.

This was a terrible time for Annie Farrior. While she had come to terms with her desperate situation, and accepted the fact that her life would probably not extend beyond this night, still she could not control the shivering that had taken over her body. For the most part, all was quiet now in the canyon, the quiet interrupted only now and then by a rifle shot or two ricocheting off of the stones behind them—just to let them know the Indians were still there, according to Buck. Then all would be quiet again.

The quiet was the worst. Annie thought about Grace Turner, waiting back in Fort Laramie. What would Grace think when she failed to return? What would Grace do without her? She had become so dependent upon Annie since their husbands had been away—and what about Tom and the others? Annie wondered if, even as she lay waiting for the slaughter that seemed inevitable now, Tom might actually be on his way back to Laramie, thinking her safe and waiting for him there.

A flicker of a smile creased the layer of grime upon her face as she realized the irony of it. As quickly as it had struck her, the spark of amusement faded away to return her to the blackness of reality. The sun was sinking. Soon it would be dark in the narrow canyon. Already the shadows had closed over the floor of the canyon, although she could still see spots of sunshine, illuminating the needles of the pines on the slopes high above them.

Buck, embarrassed, asked her to excuse him while he crawled to the end of the tiny gully to urinate. "I'm sorry, ma'am, but I can't hold it as long as I use'ta."

"It's all right," she said. "I'll watch the canyon for you." She wondered why he would even care if she saw him or not—in a matter of hours, maybe less, they would all be dead. She made a point of turning her back toward that end of the gully to satisfy him, however. She gazed for a few moments at Luke Austen, his eyes constantly focused on the dark line of pines above the ledge. He was a handsome man, she decided as she studied his profile. Then she quickly admonished herself for thinking such thoughts, and forced herself to picture her husband instead. *Tom, my Tom—I could have loved you, given time. I know I could.*

Along about dusk, the sound of a drum began, soon followed by the singsong chanting of several warriors. "Won't be long now," Buck offered, "they're callin' on their medicine to help 'em fight brave."

Luke shifted his position to ease a stiff back, and listened to the singing for a few moments. "When I first came out here, I was told that Indians never fought at night."

"Who in tarnation ever told you that?" Buck snorted, not waiting for an answer. "I ain't ever seen an Injun git slowed one bit by darkness. They'll be comin', all right, and I expect we'd best git ourselves ready to climb this here wall if we don't wanna be here to meet 'em."

They readied themselves as best they could, each of them—Annie included—hauling two rifles and two canteens plus all the ammunition they thought they could carry. When the last remnants of sunlight had disappeared, Buck placed his hat on his rifle barrel and held it up over the rim of the gully. After a few minutes, he stood up, knowing it was too dark for the Indians to see him. He stepped out of the shallow slash in the ground that had been their fortress most of the day, being careful to avoid Grady Post's body lying stone-cold before him. He peered into the growing gloom of the narrow passage they had ridden down hours before, wishing his eyes were as sharp as they were when he was young. "Damn," he uttered, looking up at the sky.

"What is it?" Luke whispered.

"There's gonna be a moon tonight," Buck answered. "That ain't gonna help."

The singing and drumbeat suddenly stopped, leaving the valley as quiet as a tomb. The suddenness of it caused Annie to gasp audibly, and without thinking, she pressed close against Luke. He put his arm around her and held her for a moment. "We've got to get going," he said, and gently turned her toward the rock wall behind them.

Their plan was the same as Private Logan and his two friends had attempted earlier. The flaw, however, was the fact that Luke was not as tall as the strapping Logan, and Buck was not as tall as either of the other two troopers. To remedy this, it was necessary to build a platform for Luke to stand on. The only materials available to them were the bodies of their own comrades, but Luke and Buck didn't hesitate a moment before building their macabre platform, stacking one body on top of another until the proper height was attained.

"Listen!" Buck whispered. After a few moments when no sound was heard, a nightbird called out, answered a few seconds later by another on the far side of the canyon. "We've got to git the hell outta here!"

Luke offered a silent apology as he stepped up on the back of a young trooper. As soon as he was steady, Buck climbed up behind him and struggled up to a standing position on Luke's shoulders. Throwing his rifles up before him, he strained to pull himself up over the edge. Once on top, he took a few moments to quickly look around him, then whispered for Annie to come up. With Luke's help, she climbed up to his shoulders and stretched her arms up toward Buck. With Buck pulling, and Luke pushing, she was lifted to the ledge. As soon as she disappeared over the top, Luke got down to retrieve the rest of their gear. One by one, he threw the rifles and canteens up to them.

Annie, frantic now for Luke to join them, whispered loudly, "Hurry!"

He climbed back upon the grisly platform and reached up to them when suddenly the darkness was split by the flash of a muzzle and a slug ricocheted from the rock beside Luke. Immediately, another rifle flashed, sending another bullet glancing off the rock wall. Buck and Annie grabbed Luke's arms and hauled him scrambling over the edge to safety—if only for a moment.

"They know we're up here now!" Buck panted. "We got no choice but to git to them trees above, and hope to hell there ain't too many of 'em."

The ledge they had gained turned out to be narrow and hazardous, consisting of a thick layer of loose shale and gravel that shifted with each step. Annie, struggling to carry her two rifles, and weighed down by the canteens and ammunition, lost her footing. Had Luke not been behind her to stop her slide, she would have certainly gone over the edge. Luke and Buck each took one of her rifles, leaving her hands free to grasp the occasional scrawny sappling or imbedded rock and pull herself up the steep slope.

"Stay with it, honey," Buck panted, his breath coming short and labored. "If you can make it another twenty yards, we'll be in the trees." *I hope to hell I can make it*, he thought, feeling the toll being taken on his old bones, his heart pounding from the exertion. He took a sideways glance at Luke Austen, young and strong, and knew it was time to give up the mountains to the younger men—go back to Promise Valley and sit by the fire in a rocking chair. Then it struck him how ludicrous the thought was—*You old coot, if them Sioux gits to them trees before we do, there won't be no worry 'bout gittin' any older.*

Ten yards before the line of tall straight pines, the severity of the slope eased, allowing them to climb without using their hands to hang onto the mountainside. Toiling to cross the last few yards of open ground before the cover of the pines, the three desperate people pushed their aching bodies relentlessly—constantly looking back, expecting pursuit by the warriors behind them. When at last the first trees were reached, they staggered up—first Luke, then Annie, then Buck—and fell exhausted against the dark trunks.

"Everybody all right?" Luke panted between gasps for air.

Before anyone could reply, the dark forest above them was seared by the sudden flashes of several muzzle blasts, and the trees around them were peppered with rifle balls, sending bark flying amid the angry whine of the bullets. Hugging the ground behind two tree trunks, Buck and Luke immediately returned fire, trying to aim at points in the darkness where muzzle flashes were last seen. As soon as they fired, they discarded the empty rifles and took up loaded ones. As anticipated, several warriors leaped up from the darkness above them and charged down upon them. Now they could see their targets.

Buck and Luke each took careful aim. The rifles barked and two warriors tumbled head over heels, crashing into the brush at the edge of the trees. There was no time to be frightened. Annie picked up the empty rifles and passed the remaining loaded ones forward. Luke and Buck fired again, killing two more of the attacking warriors.

Surprised and confused, the Sioux dropped back to

take cover behind the trees. Clearly they had assumed that, once the white men had fired, they could overrun them before they had time to reload. Buck and Luke had won this round, but it was obvious to them that their position was tenuous at best. They were still pinned down, much as they had been in the gully. In the darkness, it was impossible to estimate the strength of their assailants, for the warriors were smart enough to move to new positions as soon as they fired a shot, knowing the white men would send a lead missile flying their way immediately after. Buck and Luke had cut down four of their number, and still the dark forest was alive with random muzzle flashes. The waiting game was on again.

"You think they might reconsider charging us again?" Luke whispered. "It cost them plenty the first time."

"I don't know," Buck answered. "I'm afraid this bunch was already riled. And they ain't gonna take losing them four lightly. I expect they ain't gonna be satisfied till they take our scalps." He strained to see into the darkness, hoping to get a clear shot. "I just don't cotton much to being pinned down here when the sun comes up," he muttered softly, almost to himself. "These trees we picked is mighty skinny."

"What?" Luke whispered.

"Nuthin'," Buck replied. "I just said the moon'll be up directly. Keep your eyes skinned. Some of them devils is liable to try sneakin' round to the side." He turned then and took a long look behind them. It puzzled him that those warriors in the canyon did not follow them up the rock wall. Whatever the reason, he was thankful for it—he had no desire to be caught in a crossfire.

The hopelessness of their situation rendered Annie oblivious to the night chill that, under less dire circumstances, would have made her shiver. Lying close beside Luke, every nerve in her body alert to the danger that lay waiting for them in the forboding darkness, she still longed to simply close her eyes and make it all go away. Knowing that propriety was no longer relevant, she pressed her body closer to Luke's. Luke, understanding, reached back and gave her a reassuring pat on the shoulder.

Hearing a rustle of pine boughs several yards off to their left, Buck rolled away from the protection of the tree he had taken cover behind and crawled a few yards to a new position closer to the origin of the sound. He listened, his Hawken rifle raised, waiting for any movement from the dark shadows. There was another sound of rustling and what he thought was a low grunt. He tensed, ready to fire, but there was no assault. After another lengthy period when no further sounds were heard, Buck slowly withdrew to his original position beside Luke.

"They're up to something," Luke whispered as soon as Buck crawled back. "I heard something, like they're moving around."

"They're up to somethin' all right, and it don't take a genius to figure it out. They're moving in closer, and from the sound of it, boxing us in on both sides." He gestured with his head toward his right shoulder. "The moon's coming up. In another hour, it's gonna be bright as day on the edge of these trees. I reckon that's what they're waitin' for. I don't think they know for sure there ain't but three of us. When they find out, church'll be out for sure."

No more talk was wasted upon plans to escape. There was no place for them to go. Even had they decided to try to go back down the cliff, they would have to descend the steep open area of loose gravel—an area that was now bathed in bright moonlight. All three knew they could do nothing but wait for the end.

A strange shroud of calmness settled about Annie Farrior as she lay close to Luke. Almost like a dream, it seemed beyond belief that she was quietly awaiting her death—a death now certain. She reached down and rested her hand on the handle of her pistol. When the time came, could she do it? Her thoughts fluttered back and forth between her husband and Luke, and her fatal determination to find Tom when all advised against it. *Well*, she thought, *this is where it got you.* She could only marvel at the serenity with which she now viewed her destiny—no longer terrified, although still missing a heartbeat each time she heard the sound of a twig snapping or a rustle of boughs.

Thinking he had seen some movement in the shadows above them, Luke strained to make out a possible human form. Maybe it was his imagination. The wait was excruciating. He was impatient for the combat that would decide their fate. During the long minutes they had lain there waiting, he had examined his feelings toward the probable end of his young life. There was apprehension, he decided, but no fear. He would take as many of the warriors with him as any fighting man could. Who could say? Maybe he and Buck could drive them off. Then his thoughts turned to the girl pressing close against his leg, and he suddenly wished he had met her earlier—before she had married. He wanted to pull her in close in his arms to comfort her, but he restrained himself to an occasional reassuring pat.

Buck Ransom had never really known what it was like to be afraid. His old friend and departed partner, Frank Brown, had always maintained that Buck wasn't intelligent enough to know fear. Buck had never given it much thought. He wasn't afraid now—

but he was perturbed. It galled him to think he was to go under after stupidly following a renegade Sioux up a box canyon. What would Frank or Trace McCall think about that? They'd probably laugh at his foolishness. *Well, the son-of-a-bitching Injuns might git this old gray scalp, but, by God, it's gonna cost 'em a heap.* Further thoughts were interrupted by the sudden sound of a loud grunt no more than fifteen yards directly in front of them.

Buck immediately tensed, preparing for action. Seconds after the first sound, another sound—almost like a cough—followed. "Git ready, son," Buck warned, "I think they're gittin' set to jump us."

Luke shifted his body to get a better angle to shoot from behind the tree. Annie, without being told, pulled the spare rifles up, ready to hand them off to the two men now waiting silently for the coming attack. The total darkness that had enclosed the pines before now began to give way to random splotches of moonlight so that individual trees began to take shape. Fingers on the triggers, Buck and Luke strained to make out a target.

"Is that you down there, Buck?"

The clear, familiar voice had come from the pine forest before them. Buck, stunned at first, was not sure he wasn't hearing things. "Trace?" he called out.

"I reckon," the answer came back.

Luke and Annie watched in astonishment as Buck lowered his rifle, and with a groan for his aching joints, slowly got to his feet. Had it been a little less dark, they could have seen the wide grin upon his grizzled face. As it was, they watched in amazement as Buck left the cover of the tree and started making his way up the hill. Almost as an afterthought, he paused and called back to them. "You folks can come on out now. It's all over."

Still reluctant to abandon all caution, Luke stood up, still holding his rifle ready to fire at the first provocation. He found it hard to believe there was no gunfire as soon as he exposed himself. He reached down, extending his hand to Annie. She took it and helped herself up, and they followed Buck up the slope through the trees.

He was standing between two small trees, his feet widespread, the moonlight silhouetting his powerful frame that appeared to be taller than the pines themselves. Even in the half-light provided by a three-quarter moon, there was a detectable sense about this mountain man that conveyed a presence of strength and confidence. Waiting for them to make their way up through the trees, he stood as casually as if they had chanced to meet on a crowded street in St. Louis, instead of this dark and forboding forest amid the bodies of half a dozen Sioux warriors.

"This here's Trace McCall," Buck announced when the three of them reached the point where he stood waiting. There was a hint of paternal pride in his voice when he added, "The Blackfeet call him the Mountain Hawk—me and Trace has been partners for more'n a few years." Then he introduced his companions.

Trace shook hands with Luke and nodded politely to Annie. "Looks like you folks have had some hard luck. How'd you happen to get caught in that canyon down there?" This last he directed at Buck.

Buck was quick to stress that he had possessed some very negative feelings about riding into that canyon, but it was not his decision to make. Then he hastened to explain that it wasn't really the lieutenant's fault either—they had no notion to suspect the Sioux scout of treachery. "When you shake this blanket, I reckon more'n a few bugs'll fall out, though.

Ain't no gittin' 'round the fact that we was plumb bamboozled."

"A full troop of thirty-four men was massacred," Luke volunteered, "and it was my responsibility to take care of them. So I also have to take the blame for putting the troop in that position in the first place." His voice trailed off as he continued, "I guess I'll have to live with that on my conscience."

Buck cocked his head in surprise. This was the first expression of guilt and remorse that Luke had voiced. He had been so occupied with saving their asses that he hadn't stopped to think that the young lieutenant might also be carrying a heavy burden of guilt for the loss of his command. He felt the need to enlighten the young man on the subject of Indian warfare. "Son, don't go gittin' down in the mouth about bein' out-smarted by a band of Injuns. We got double-crossed. That's all there is to it. As far as gittin' tricked into that box canyon—why, hell—Injuns' stock and trade is pullin' tricks like that. Them Sioux warriors is some of the finest fightin' men alive. You ain't the first officer that got caught with his britches down—and you ain't gonna be the last."

"Buck's right, Lieutenant. I'd say the fault's more likely on the doorstep of the damn fool that sent you out here with less than a full regiment. This is smack-dab in the middle of Sioux, Cheyenne, and Arapaho hunting grounds, and no white man is welcome, especially soldiers. That said, I expect we'd best not linger here. When these warriors don't come back, there's bound to be somebody come looking for them."

"How many of them devils was up in these woods, anyway?" Buck wanted to know.

"Well, you and the lieutenant got four of 'em. That didn't leave but six for me."

This simple answer baffled Luke. "You killed six of

them? But we heard no rifle shots, except the ones fired at us."

"Bow," Buck answered for Trace, "bow and a knife—much quieter that way." He didn't bother to explain to Luke that Trace was as good with a bow as any Indian who ever took to the warpath. He knew without asking how Trace had silently moved through the dark forest, taking the six warriors out one by one until they had all been eliminated. Then another thought struck him, and he turned back to Trace. "How'd you know it was me down there?"

Trace smiled. "I saw that mangy coyote you call a horse with a bunch of army mounts they had corraled at the mouth of that canyon. I knew there couldn't be two like that—and I figured anybody else would be too proud to ride him."

"Huh," Buck grunted indignantly. "He'll run that paint of your'n into the ground." It wasn't necessary to express his joy upon hearing the news that his horse might not be lost to him. The two of them had been together for a long time, and Buck had always planned for them to go into retirement together. "We need to go after them horses before the rest of that band of Sioux come back here lookin' for their brothers. You say they're corraled near the mouth of the canyon?"

"I said they were," Trace replied. "I moved them to the other side of this ridge where I left my horses." Again, this was all that needed to be said for Buck to know that Trace had eliminated however many Indians were left to guard the horses. It also explained why Luke, Annie, and he were not followed up the rock cliff by the Sioux.

"I expect we'd better git ourselves out of here before that band of Sioux comes back lookin' fer their cousins," Buck said. "They're gonna be plenty hot when they find all these dead Injuns." He paused to consider which direction might be best to make good their escape. "You got any idea where this bunch's camp is?"

"Two days ago they were camped on the Belle Fourche," Trace answered. "I had to take a detour around them—Iron Pony's bunch, I think."

"If they're on the Belle Fourche," Buck said, "then I reckon we'd best head east to the Cheyenne—work our way back south from there."

Before anyone could take a step, Annie interrupted the two mountain men. "What about my husband?" In the pressing concern to escape before the band of Sioux returned, no one had given thought to the original purpose of their mission. "We've got to find Tom and the others," she reminded them.

The distress in her voice caused Buck to stop and think for a moment. In the aftermath of the slaughter of the entire troop of dragoons, he had assumed that the mission was canceled, the primary concern now was to save what hair was still growing on the few heads that survived. "Considerin' our predicament, I naturally figured the lieutenant here would say to head back to Laramie." He scratched his whiskers thoughtfully. "What do you say, Lieutenant?"

Like Buck, Luke had all but concluded that the mission was canceled. But now, seeing the look of distress on the upturned face of Annie Farrior, he hesitated, not sure what to do. "I've already lost a troop of cavalry. I think my first responsibility is to the safety of the lady, so we should probably get back to Laramie as fast as we can."

Annie, frightened into tremors hours earlier, was now in possession of her former resolve. "I'm not going back until I look for my husband. That's what I came out here for, and if Mr. McCall has found our horses, I intend to continue. You can go back without me."

"Annie," Luke pleaded, "I can't let you do that."

Buck glanced at Trace to see his reaction, but there was no change of expression on the imperturbable face of his tall friend. *Foolishness*, Buck thought, but he understood why she felt she had to say what she did. Seeing the indecision in the face of the young lieutenant, he offered a suggestion to placate the lady. "Wouldn't hurt to take a look around some of these canyons while we're headin' toward the Cheyenne—if that's all right with you, Lieutenant. There ain't but a few valleys they could be in, anyway, and we can check them out all right." He glanced quickly at Trace, aware that his friend knew there were a hell of a lot of places where the four prospectors might be. But Trace made no comment. "The most important thing right now is to git ourselves away from this ridge," Buck added.

CHAPTER 5

Of the dozen horses Trace had hobbled on the far side of the ridge, Buck's scruffy-looking bay and Luke's chestnut were recovered. Aside from Trace's two horses and three Indian ponies, the rest were army mounts. By this time, some of the other strays had probably wandered back toward the canyon, but they had no desire to be burdened with the task of driving extra horses. One of the army mounts was selected for Annie to ride, the rest were unsaddled and set free.

By the time they got underway, the first hint of dawn was upon them. They rode in single file, Trace leading, as they made their way through the narrow valleys, winding deeper into the dark green slopes that towered up on each side of them. Not until the sun was almost directly overhead did they pause to rest the horses and take time to eat something themselves. It had been almost twenty-four hours since Buck, Luke, and Annie had their last meal. So the dried buffalo meat from Trace's pack was welcome fare. To wash it down, Trace was also able to provide some coffee from his dwindling supply.

"I was fixing to head back to pick up some supplies when I came across your little party back there with those Sioux," Trace commented as he watched over his coffee kettle. This was in answer to Buck's question as to how Trace happened upon them.

Buck nodded. "I sure am proud you showed up when you did. We was gittin' down to skinnin' knives and prayers."

Annie, chewing away at a rock-hard piece of buffalo jerky, studied the soft-spoken man, dressed in buckskins. He was a tall man, taller than Luke even, with sandy-colored hair that barely touched wide, powerful shoulders. Unlike most of the so-called mountainmen—like Buck for instance—Trace was clean-shaven, Injun style as Buck would say. He carried a Hawken rifle, much like Buck's. On his back, he wore an otterskin bow case and quiver, decorated with beads and porcupine quills—a gift from a Snake maiden, Buck had said. Buck had also told her that Trace was known to the Blackfeet as the Mountain Hawk. Judging by the ease with which he moved through the wild country that surrounded them, she decided that Trace McCall belonged in these mountains—fully as much as the hawk for which he was named. For reasons she could not explain, she felt safer with him than she had before when escorted by a whole troop of soldiers.

Following old game trails for much of the time, they worked their way up into the hills, scouting out any streams they chanced upon for signs that the four white prospectors had passed that way. There was no evidence that anyone other than Indian hunting parties had been there. Trace and Buck were careful to cover their tracks whenever possible. They figured the Sioux war party was sure to be trailing them. The country was rugged and the riding hard. Still they continued to search until sunset found them close to the Cheyenne River.

"We'll strike the river 'bout noon tomorrow," Buck said, as he and Trace sat by the fire, discussing the next day's march. "I reckon that little gal is gonna be mighty disappointed we didn't find no sign of her husband. But I don't see much future in hangin' around this territory any longer. You know that dang party of Sioux is gonna turn this country inside out, lookin' for us."

Trace nodded and glanced toward the horses where Annie was talking to Luke as he checked the condition of the girth strap on Annie's saddle. He thought for a moment more before making a suggestion. "I know a place that might be a likely spot to check. It ain't far from here, but we'll have to backtrack about half a day." Before Buck could ask why he hadn't mentioned it a half a day ago, Trace explained. "I don't know why I didn't think of it before. I guess I just forgot about it. It's a little hard to find, so I doubt they would have stumbled on it. The only reason I know about it is because I followed a deer there last fall."

Buck called Luke and Annie over to discuss a decision to backtrack or to continue to the river. If they continued, he explained, they would be out of the hills the next day, and should probably have the best chance of getting back to Laramie before being overtaken by a Sioux war party. In spite of the danger, Annie urged them to continue the search. It seemed obvious to Luke that they could spend weeks searching every draw and valley before finding a trace of the missing four. Concern for Annie's safety was foremost in his mind, and his better judgment told him to get the hell out of there while they still could. He was already burdened by his failure to prevent the massacre of his patrol. On the other hand, he found it hard to deny the young lady's wishes.

In the end, the three men gave in to the lady. They decided that Trace should start back immediately, since there were still a couple of hours before dark. The others would start back in the morning. He could make much better time alone, perhaps enough to scout the area and intercept them before they backtracked the entire distance. Once it was decided, Trace wasted little time saddling his paint pony, and leaving his packhorse with Buck, started back the way they had come. He had drawn a little map on the ground to show Buck how to find a large column of stone that stood like a chimney near the foot of the ridge that hid the stream where he had followed the deer. If things went as he expected, he would be on his way back before Buck and the others got to that ridge.

Early the next morning, Trace reached the long tree-covered ridge that ran like a high wall above the old game trail he had been following. Leaving the trail where it looped around the chimney-like stone column, he guided the paint up through the pines. Upon reaching the top of the ridge, he had to pause for a few moments to get his bearings. Looking off toward the east, he spotted the mouth of the narrow draw that led down to the stream.

As he descended the slope into the little valley, his eyes constantly scanned back and forth, alert for anything that looked out of the ordinary. There was a heavy silence hanging over the dark slopes that surrounded the valley. It seemed to amplify the gurgling sounds of the noisy stream that cut like a scar through the grassy bottom. He thought about the first time he had seen this tiny valley, and recalled how peaceful it had seemed to him then. On this day, however, there was an ominous feeling about the place. He couldn't explain why—the grass was high, still with some scattering of wildflowers that defied summer's end—the stream was strong and clear. It was just a feeling he had, but he had learned to pay attention to those feelings, for they had often forewarned of something the eye had not yet detected.

Urging the paint forward again, he crossed over the stream and climbed up the other bank. That was where he found the first one. Lying parallel to the rushing water, the sun-bleached skull seemed to stare vacantly up at the cloudless sky from its grassy tomb. Trace dismounted and knelt to examine the skeleton. It had been a white man—he could tell by the clothes. The fact that they were torn and shredded was a clear indication to Trace that the body had been found by wolves or buzzards—or both. He reckoned the worms had cleaned up what was left.

He found the other three close by, almost hidden in the tall grass. The position of two of the skeletons, with their arms flung out and legs spread or bent under, led Trace to conclude that it had most likely been a wolf pack that devoured the corpses. There were no signs of injury on any of the skulls but one, and that one had a neat bullet hole in the forehead. He considered this for a moment. If the men had been attacked by a band of Indians, there would have been much more evidence of broken skulls and bones. If he had to guess, he would say they might have been murdered in their sleep. Apparently, Annie's husband and his partners were murdered soon after they first arrived in the Black Hills. And from the lack of sign, no one had been here since. It was a hard thing to have to tell the young lady, but there was little doubt that these four skeletons were the men they searched for.

It would not be a pleasant thing for Annie to see, but Trace decided after some serious thought that it might be important to the girl to know which skeleton was that of her late husband's. So he left the bones where they lay, figuring she could identify her husband by his clothes, if she decided that's what she wanted to do. After looking around a little while longer to see if there were any clues that might shed more light on the murders, he decided there were a few signs that didn't seem right. He determined to make a closer search of the area later after Buck arrived.

Shortly before midday, Trace spotted the three riders as they approached the rock. He walked out on the flat surface of the giant stone and signaled. Annie, upon seeing the tall mountain man, urged her horse ahead of the others, anxious to know what Trace might tell them. Buck already knew that Trace had found something, since he had waited for them instead of meeting them farther along the trail. And he had a pretty good idea that the news wasn't good since Trace was waiting alone.

"Did you find anything, Mr. McCall?" Annie yelled long before her horse pulled up to a stop.

"Yes, ma'am, I'm sorry but I did."

"Oh," was all she responded. She had dreaded this moment, knowing deep inside that Tom had in all probability met with some disaster. In spite of telling herself for months now that Tom could take care of himself, there had been a nagging lack of faith in his return. He would have gotten a message to her somehow—and none had come. She waited for Trace to explain.

"I found 'em," he began. "I don't know any way to make this any easier . . ." He paused, groping for some words to soften the message he had to give her.

"I know," she interrupted, "they're dead." Feeling suddenly weary, she dismounted and walked off a few yards to shed her tears in privacy.

Trace felt a deep compassion for the young woman, but he was not good in situations like this, so he was greatly relieved when Luke Austen quickly dismounted and moved to comfort her. Buck shook his head sadly and nudged his horse up beside Trace.

"Injuns got 'em?" he said, his voice soft enough to keep Annie from hearing. Whereupon Trace related the scene of the murders that he had discovered.

"I ain't so sure it was Injuns, Buck," Trace answered. "It just doesn't look like the work of Injuns. They ain't nothing but bones now—and rags—but I left them where they lay till I find out if she's up to looking at 'em. Then we can put them in the ground." He glanced over at the grieving woman, her head now buried against the lieutenant's chest.

Buck's curiosity was up. "Well, I'd like to take a look. You think they might have been murdered by white men?"

"Well, I don't know for sure, but right now it appears that way to me."

Annie regained her composure after only a few minutes, and when she again exhibited a calm demeanor, Trace described the scene he had found by the stream. "I didn't bother 'em, ma'am. I mean, I left 'em lay as I found 'em in case you wanted to try to identify your husband's bones."

"Annie," Luke said, "it might not be a good idea for you to see them. Why don't you let us bury them and then you can take a few minutes alone to say goodbye."

"What if it's not Tom?" Annie quickly responded. "No, I've got to see for myself. It could be any four men—we don't know for sure."

"Ain't likely it's anybody else, ma'am," Buck commented. "The lieutenant's right, it might be somethin' you don't need to see."

Her composure recovered and her resolve firm, Annie insisted. "I need to know if it's my husband or not. Mr. McCall, will you lead us to the place?"

Trace glanced at Buck before answering. "Yes'm, I'll take you there."

                    *   *   *

Gazing down, unblinking, at the bleached white skull whose empty black sockets stared up at her, Annie found that she could not picture Tom's face even though she tried to focus her mind on it. Cheerful and cocky, he had kissed her farewell and stepped up in the saddle, promising to return with enough gold to build her a fine house in Oregon. Young and boyish in his enthusiasm for this great adventure, he and his three equally inspired partners rode out of Fort Laramie more than four and a half months ago. Now as she felt a tear creep slowly down her cheek, she found it difficult to believe that these cold bones were once the warm and caring man who had shared her bed, albeit briefly. Although the only remaining possessions were his shirt and pants, she knew that it was Tom lying there. She had made the checkered shirt for him herself, and the trousers were the same he had worn on the last day she had seen him. Suddenly she felt a heavy blanket of guilt descend upon her shoulders—guilt born from knowing she had not loved him as passionately as he had loved her. *I would have, Tom. I was learning to.* Tasting the salt on her lips, she realized that her tears were now flowing freely. She turned as a shadow fell across the skeleton, and a voice gently woke her from her reverie.

"We'd best put these poor souls in the ground and be on our way, ma'am," Buck softly urged. She nodded and turned toward Trace who was already scraping out a shallow grave for one of the others—Ned Turner, she guessed, although she could not be sure.

"I'm sorry there don't seem to be no keepsake for you to take with you," Buck said. "They was stripped pretty clean."

"His watch," Annie spoke softly, not really meaning to say it out loud, "I wish I could have kept his watch."

"Ma'am?" Buck asked.

Realizing then that she had spoken loud enough to be heard, Annie explained. "I gave Tom a silver watch for a wedding present. I had his name inscribed on it. I just wish I could have kept it."

"Oh—Well, I'm sorry, ma'am."

The rest of the afternoon was spent burying the remains of the four prospectors. There were still several hours of daylight left before the shadows would close in on the valley, but Trace and Buck agreed that they wouldn't find a better campsite than where they stood. After making sure that it wouldn't be too painful for Annie to spend the night at the scene of her husband's massacre, they decided to wait until morning to start back to Laramie. While Buck and Luke gathered wood for a fire, Trace took a closer look at the area where Tom Farrior and his partners had been slain.

The sign was several months old, but there were still enough clues to enable Trace to get a pretty fair picture of Tom Farrior's final hours. According to Annie, each of the four men had led three packhorses. Based on this, Trace concluded that the four had no more than two or three visitors to their camp. There were not a great number of prints, and all but a few of them came from shod horses. It would be impossible to determine the exact number of horses—dependent upon the comings and goings of the party, and how many days they spent at this campsite. But Trace was confident that the number of tracks definitely ruled out a large war party. In addition to the four skeletons, there were bones from a large animal—probably a deer from the size and shape of the bones.

"Whadaya think happened here?" Buck asked when Trace came over to the fire.

"Hard to say," Trace answered. "Ain't no way to know for sure, but if I had to guess, I'd bet they were visited by two or three strangers pretending to be friendly—probably murdered them in their blankets."

By the time night's heavy veil had lifted from the deep-shaded valleys, Trace was halfway down the back side of the ridge, working his way carefully toward the chimney rock. He figured the others were still in camp, probably getting packed up to ride by then. Trace had felt a need to scout the way back to the old game trail before the four of them started out again. He didn't like surprises, a trait that had contributed to his longevity in hostile territory. He also had a healthy respect for the tracking ability of the Sioux warrior.

When he spotted the towering rock below him some two hundred yards away, he dismounted and tied his pony to a pine bough. Moving quickly but silently, he made his way farther down the ridge, his eyes alert to every movement of the wind in the pine needles that whispered a muted warning. Below him, a bird suddenly fluttered from its nest, screeching an angry protest for having been disturbed. Trace froze, his eyes searching. Then he saw them—two Sioux scouts, kneeling to study the ground where Trace and the others had left the trail the day before.

The discovery of the two warriors caused no sense of fear in the Mountain Hawk but served to alert every fiber of his mind. He dropped slowly to one knee and carefully scanned the forest below him. The decision to be made now was whether to fight or run, depending upon the number. His decision was easily made, for only seconds later, the two scouts were joined by two others, with the rest of the war party on their heels. Trace counted fourteen more that he could see through the trees—he couldn't say how many more were hidden from his view.

Moving quickly, carefully placing each foot so as not to dislodge a stone or limb that might alert the warriors of his presence, Trace climbed back to where the paint was waiting. Still on foot, he led the pony back over the crest of the ridge before climbing in the saddle and starting down the slope toward the stream.

When he rode into camp, his companions were ready to leave and only awaiting his arrival. "Where the hell you been?" Buck demanded, "We've been ready to ride for half an hour."

Trace couldn't help but smile. Noticing that Luke was still adjusting Annie's saddle for her, Trace estimated it to be more like five minutes. "I expect we're gonna have to find another way out of here."

No more needed to be said as far as Buck was concerned. "They found where we left the trail, I reckon."

"They did," Trace confirmed.

"How close?"

"Thirty minutes, maybe."

Buck looked around him, at the slope they had originally come down, to the even steeper opposite wall of the valley, then back at Trace who had already determined their escape route. "Don't look like much choice, does it?" Buck quickly determined. "Down the stream for as far as we can." He would have told Luke and Annie to get ready to ride, but he glanced back to discover they had already mounted and Luke was checking his rifle. Glancing back at Trace, Buck asked, "You have any idea where this stream comes out?"

"Nope," Trace answered, "but this is as good a time as any to find out."

"I reckon," Buck snorted and climbed up in the saddle.

With Trace leading, they rode down the middle of the stream for approximately a quarter of a mile until the slope steepened and the stream became narrower and deeper, making it too difficult for the horses to find solid footing. Leaving the water, they made their way through the trees that hugged the coursing waterway, and detoured around a flume of solid granite, picking up the stream again some distance down the mountainside. As the slope continued to steepen, it became more and more hazardous, with the riders almost laying on their horses' rumps in some places. And in even steeper areas, it was only possible to keep from tumbling head over heels by sidling along the slope, back and forth, gradually working their way down.

Annie could feel her heart pounding against her ribs as she held onto the army saddle for dear life, the muscles in her legs almost cramping from pressing so tightly against the horse's sides. It seemed to her that she was about to fly over her horse's neck at any moment. In spite of the threat of pursuit, she was too afraid of tumbling down the mountainside to worry about the Indians behind them. She could see the valley a quarter of a mile below and no apparent access to it. The tiers of tall pines stood like rows of sharpened spears, waiting to impale the horse that made the first misstep.

Ahead of her, Luke Austen laid back in the saddle, trying to help his horse maintain its balance—his concern for her safety apparent in his frequent glances back at her. Leading Luke, Buck's horse hit a patch of loose shale and started to slide sideways. The horse, a mountain horse like Trace's, recovered, finding solid footing after a slide of some seventy-five feet, coming to a stop in front of Trace.

"I swear, Buck," Trace deadpanned, "if you wanna lead, just say so." Then he looked back to make sure Luke and Annie avoided the soft spot Buck had hit.

Buck held his horse back to let Trace lead. "For a minute there, I thought I was gonna take the shortcut down," he said. "You go right on ahead. I'm kinda interested to see how you plan to git us offen this dang mountain."

"I'm kinda anxious to find out myself," Trace returned. "We'll just keep sidling till we come across a gulch or a draw that leads down from here."

"We better find somethin' pretty soon before we have a pack of Sioux warriors slidin' down on top of us," Buck said as Trace's paint passed him. He continued to hold back to let Trace's packhorse by. Usually hitched by a lead line to the back of Trace's saddle, the packhorse was no longer tied. It was not as surefooted as the paint, and Trace didn't want to risk having the packhorse lose its footing and drag him down the mountain with it.

Buck waited for a few minutes until Luke and Annie caught up, then continued the treacherous descent toward the trees below. After what seemed a painfully long time, Trace disappeared into the pines that formed a thick ring around the mountain, and it appeared that the four of them might gain the cover of the trees before being spotted by the warriors pursuing them. Buck was about to call back to Annie and Luke to hurry when he heard a sharp cry of alarm high up the mountain above them.

"Damn!" he uttered, looking up to search for the source of the war cries that now rang out from above. In a few moments he spotted them. Several hundred feet above, he could see them scrambling over the boulders, trying to find a place to get a clear shot. Moments later, he saw an eruption of tiny puffs of black smoke, like mushrooms suddenly sprouting forth among the rocks, and the sounds of lead balls rattling through the trees followed immediately.

"Hurry!" Buck called, as he herded Luke and Annie into the thick pine forest. As soon as they reached the cover of the trees, the shooting stopped, but the war cries increased. They hurried to catch up to Trace, the ground having leveled out to form a ridge at last. Making better time now, Annie and Luke followed Buck as he weaved his way through the thick forest, still mindful of the red horde wildly descending the mountain behind them.

The easy going was short-lived, for the three of them had gone no more than fifty yards when they found Trace waiting for them. There appeared to be an opening in the trees beyond him which was immediately interpreted as a bad sign by Buck. Just as he feared, the ridge they had been following ended abruptly before a cliff. Trace had dismounted and was looking over the situation when the others pulled up.

"Well, now ain't this somethin' to write in your diary," Buck cracked when he joined Trace at the edge of the granite cliff and peered down at a lower ridge two hundred feet below. "How we gonna git down there? Fly?" He paused to give Trace a mischievous glance. "'Course, you bein' the Mountain Hawk, that might be what you had in mind."

"We'd better find some way outta here or we might have to find out if we can fly." He turned to

face Luke and Annie. "Lieutenant, we ain't got a lot
of time, so we'd best split up and look for a way
down from here. You and I can follow the cliff line
along the slope ahead. Buck and the lady can follow
it in the opposite direction. That all right with you,
Buck?" Buck nodded. "All right, then, let's get to it."

Closer now, the war whoops rang from the mountainside above them, only muted slightly by the thick
stand of trees that hid them from sight. Trace knew
that the Sioux braves would abandon all caution in
an effort to overtake them. Half of them might end up
sliding and tumbling down the slope, but the other
half might be enough to rub the four of them out.
Moving as fast as they could, he and Luke led the
horses along the rocky ledge, searching for some
means of escape. If worse came to worst, they might
have to abandon the horses and climb down the face
of the cliff. Trace sought to avoid that if at all possible.

Luke and Trace soon came to the eastern limit of
the ledge, only to find that it ended at the face of another cliff that ascended straight up—a dead end.
They turned around, retracing their steps, when they
heard Buck sing out.

"It ain't exactly the St. Louie turnpike, but I expect
it's the best we'll find."

It proved to be little more than a gully that slashed
across the face of the mountain. But plenty of sign
showed that it was an old game trail, so Buck was
confident that it had to be a way down the mountain.
"We ain't got a helluva lot of choice," Trace commented dryly. "At least they're deer tracks and not
goats, but I reckon we'd better go down on foot,
though."

"I reckon," Buck agreed. "That nag of mine ain't
exactly no deer."

Buck led the way, followed by Annie, then Luke. Trace stayed behind to make sure everyone got a headstart on the angry mob pursuing them. Calling to Buck, he said, "I'm gonna see if I can slow 'em up a little." It would be slow going for at least fifty yards until the rude trail disappeared around an outcropping of granite. If the Sioux caught them on the open face of the mountain before they reached that point, they'd be sitting ducks for even the poorest of shots.

After tying his packhorse on a lead line once more so it wouldn't stray, Trace left his horses at the head of the gully, grabbed his Hawken and an army rifle that he had picked up from one of the dead troopers, and made his way up through the pines. As he had figured, the Sioux warriors were still on the open mountainside, but they had nearly reached the belt of pine trees. Scrambling wildly in an effort to overtake the white men, their ponies sliding and stumbling, the warriors drove recklessly on. Lying on his belly at the base of a medium-sized pine, Trace paused a moment to determine the range. Then he carefully lined his sights on the leading Indian and squeezed the trigger. The warrior threw both hands up in shocked surprise when the lead ball tore into his naked chest, rolling him backward over his pony's rump. There was only a few moments' pause by the warriors behind him as they sought to avoid the confused riderless horse. Trace picked up the other rifle and took deliberate aim. A second warrior cried out in alarm when the lead ball found its target.

While the startled Sioux scrambled for cover among the rocks, Trace reloaded his rifles and waited for a clear shot. Certain that Buck and the others had now had time to reach the bend in the gully, still he waited, thinking that if he could convince the Sioux that they were making a stand, he might gain ample time to make good his own escape. He had to wait no more than a minute before the first impatient warrior showed his head from behind a jagged piece of granite. Even at that distance, Trace could clearly see the look of profound surprise when the slug created a neat hole just above his eyes. This last casualty created the span of time Trace hoped for as the Sioux drew back to powwow over a plan of attack. Trace moved a few yards farther to his right and fired another shot just to make them think there was more than one of him. Then he quickly withdrew and started back down through the trees at a dead run.

Just as he had hoped, when he reached his horses again, there was no sign of the others—they had safely reached the outcropping. *At least I can't see any bodies at the foot of the cliff*, he thought as he led his horses down into the mouth of the narrow gully. Making his way down the steep defile, placing each foot carefully and mindful of the tons of horse flesh immediately behind him, Trace hoped like hell he wouldn't round the bend past the outcropping and find three frustrated souls staring over a sheer drop.

About three quarters of the way to the bend, the gully broke down to form a ledge barely wide enough for one horse to negotiate. Peering over the side of the ledge, Trace looked straight down at the valley floor, eight hundred feet below. It caused him to worry more about the heavily loaded pack on his packhorse behind and above him. He glanced back then, but the animal appeared to be balancing the load adequately.

There were only a few yards to go when the war party spotted him on the face of the cliff. Suddenly shots rang out as rifle balls whined and ricocheted from the rock above his head. Shielded by the horses, the Indian marksmen could not get a clear shot at him, so they began to concentrate their fire on the horses. Due to the steepness of the incline, the paint was also shielded, the packhorse catching the brunt of the attack.

Trace hurried as much as he could, but it was impossible to go any faster without chancing a misstep that might result in an eight-hundred-foot fall. The hail of slugs from the Sioux rifles soon found their target. The packhorse screamed in agony as shot after shot impacted, and Trace saw that his horse was mortally wounded. Afraid the wounded animal would go over the ledge, dragging the paint with it, Trace squeezed between the paint and the face of the cliff and managed to cut the lead rope. Only a few steps away from safety now, Trace led the paint around the bend in the trail. Past the rock outcropping, he discovered that the trail was still no more than a narrow ledge. But it was not as steep and it did widen enough to get around his horse, so he left the paint there while he went back to check on the wounded packhorse.

On his hands and knees, he inched his head around the edge of the granite wall to determine the fate of his horse. The poor animal had been riddled with bullets and was dead, but it had not fallen from the ledge, having simply dropped against the face of the cliff, its legs folded under it. Trace realized at once that the dead animal had performed one last service for him, for the narrow ledge was now effectively blocked. Trace crawled along the ledge until he reached the carcass. Using the horse for cover, he managed to reach an extra bullet pouch and a sack of buffalo jerky from the pack before being forced to retreat by the constant barrage of rifle fire from the Sioux, still gathered at the mouth of the gully.

Making his way carefully back to safety, he led the paint down the ledge until the narrow path began to level off and widen, finally leading off the face of the cliff and into the trees. Here he found Buck and the others waiting for him at the head of a ravine that led down to the valley.

"Where's your packhorse?" Buck asked as soon as Trace appeared.

"He decided to stay," Trace answered.

"Heard all the shootin'. I was just fixin' to go back to see if you needed help," Buck said. "Are they still on our tails?"

"I think they'll be held up for a while, but I expect we'd best waste no time, anyway."

CHAPTER 6

Old Broken Arm suddenly released the water he had just scooped in his cupped hand, letting it trickle through his fingers as he strained to listen. His warrior's instincts confirmed the faint sound he thought he had heard—like that of a moccasin treading upon a small pine branch. Forgetting his thirst, he rose to his feet, looking all around him, aware also that a sparrow lark singing noisily moments before was now silent.

Looking across the wildly swirling waters of the wide stream, to the lodges of his small party, arrayed in a half circle—fourteen tipis in all—he saw nothing out of the ordinary. Still, he had a feeling that something was wrong. It might be a good idea to alert the young men and take a look around the camp. This country was familiar hunting ground for both the Sioux and Cheyenne, and Broken Arm's band was small, mostly relatives, numbering only twenty-eight warriors and thirty-two women and children. Unaware of the Sioux warrior behind him, he turned, too late to avoid the heavy war ax that buried in his chest, knocking the wind from his lungs and driving him backward into the stream. Unable to give a warning cry, or defend himself, Broken Arm was set upon by the grinning warrior, the old Shoshoni's blood already tinting the rapidly running water.

Twenty yards downstream, a Snake woman paused in the process of filling her water skins to puzzle over the crimson streaks flowing past the rock she knelt on. At almost the same instant she realized it was blood, the eerie war cries of the Sioux raiding party rang out across the little valley, and suddenly the peaceful camp was shattered by an explosion of cracking rifles and war whoops. Dropping the water skins, she ran for her life, only to be tumbled to the ground by an arrow between her shoulder blades.

In the confusion of the surprise attack, Broken Arm's young men ran to get their weapons in an attempt to repel the hated Sioux. But Iron Pony had planned his attack well. Outnumbering the unsuspecting Snakes, his warriors converged upon the camp from all sides, slaughtering men, women, and children—even the dogs were slain. Most of the Snakes were killed within a half hour. The few that had managed to avoid the dreadful sweep through their camp scurried to take refuge in a rock-strewn pocket of willows and brush. Of these, only four were warriors, while the remaining seven were either women or children.

Working frantically to help dig firing pits for the men, Blue Water called to her son. White Eagle heard his mother's calling, but he did not come to her. Instead, he had taken a place beside the four warriors, facing the attacking Sioux, his bow ready to shoot as long as he had arrows. Though little more than eleven summers, he was ready to fight for his people.

It was a hopeless defense, as the four warriors had very little ammunition. After an initial volley, they were forced to retreat back to the cover of the pocket to reload. Amid the storm of rifle balls and arrows, the boy stood firm until his last arrow was shot. Then he scrambled to the cover of the streambank where his mother still clawed at the rocky soil with her bare hands. He tried to shield her with his body, a knife now his only weapon.

"We cannot stay here!" one of the warriors shouted as the hailstorm of Sioux arrows began to find the range, and the whine of bullets was almost constant. "Run for the gully on the other bank!" The words had barely left his lips when a rifle ball split his forehead, and he sank to his knees.

Blue Water screamed in horror as the warrior tried to get to his feet. No longer in control of his limbs, he took two wobbly steps before collapsing helplessly on the rocky soil. Grabbing White Eagle by the arm, she scrambled over the side of the sandy pocket after the other fleeing survivors. Spotted immediately by the Sioux warriors, the remaining Shoshoni men turned back to meet the overpowering numbers of their assailants in an attempt to give the women and children time to escape.

White Eagle turned to stand with the men, but Blue Water yanked him around and dragged him after her. "It is hopeless," she cried as she pulled the reluctant boy along behind her. "Live to fight another day."

The mouth of the gully was no more than a few yards away now, as they made their way up the bank of the stream. Behind him, White Eagle heard the death moans of the three Snake warriors as they were overrun by the bloodthirsty Sioux. Looking straight ahead, his eyes fixed on his mother's back, he was aware of the stinging bullets spitting in the sand around her feet as she ran. Just as Blue Water reached the mouth of the gully, she fell. White Eagle thought that she had stumbled, only noticing the dark stain spreading between her shoulder blades when he tried to help her up.

"Mother!" he cried, but she only gasped as her

lungs began to fill with blood. Frantic, he took her wrists in his hands and dragged her into the gully. Safe for a moment, he tried to prop her up in an effort to keep her windpipe clear of the blood that was choking her. Her eyes fluttered wildly as she struggled to breathe, but it was becoming more and more difficult, and he knew that she was dying. Looking back down the gully in the direction of the pursuing warriors, his eyes were captured by an image that would burn in his mind forever. It was the leering face of a white man, staring straight at him. As White Eagle knelt frozen for an instant, the man laughed and started to reload his rifle.

"My son," Blue Water suddenly said, calm for a moment, "you must get away from here." She groaned from the effort required to form the words. "We are too far from Washakie and the others. Go back to Fort Laramie and look for the old white trapper called Buck. He is a good man. He will help you find our people."

"I can't leave you here," he cried, his gaze shifting frantically from his mother back to the evil white face under the flat-crowned black hat. The man's horse, frightened by the shooting close behind it, reared and jumped, causing the man to fumble with his rifle, unable to reload it quickly.

"Go!" Blue Water commanded. "I am dying." Then she smiled at her son—her only child—the son of the Mountain Hawk.

Blue Water did not slip peacefully into the spirit world. The rifle ball that tore into her lungs and damaged her internal organs caused a massive flow of blood that literally strangled her to death. It was not of a long duration, but the agony his mother endured before she finally lay still in death would remain in White Eagle's memory, a vivid and lasting picture.

Even as he lay her gently back on the sand, he could hear the footsteps of the swarming Sioux warriors as they splashed through the stream and charged up the bank toward him. There was no time to run. He thought of leaping from the gully to meet them, to die like the warrior he sought to be. But his rational mind told him his mother was right. He must try to survive and live to avenge his mother's death. With no chance to run for it, he did the only thing he could think of. Smearing his mother's blood on his face and neck, he lay down next to her, hoping the Sioux would think him dead.

Moments later, they were there, pouring over the sides of the gully, chasing after the few terrified survivors who were running in a desperate effort to reach the hills beyond the stream. Two Sioux warriors paused briefly to stare down at the woman and boy in the bottom of the gully. Satisfied that they were dead, and anxious to participate in the slaughter of the final survivors, they raced after their brothers. There was no sign of the white man in the black hat. Had it been an illusion, brought on by the terrible slaughter going on around him? At that moment, he was not sure.

Lying next to his dead mother, White Eagle breathed once again. He knew he had been lucky, and he also knew he didn't have much time. When the Sioux had completed the massacre, they would be back to take scalps. He had to find a better place to hide until dark. Then he could make his escape. Cautiously raising his head above the edge of the gully, he peered after the warriors who had just passed him. They were intent on overtaking the Snake women running toward the hills. Looking back toward the camp, he saw the main body of the war party busily scalping and plundering among the tipis. Behind him were the open plains and no chance for escape until darkness could hide him.

His eyes darted back and forth frantically, searching for a safe place. He had to hurry, the warriors would be back soon! Finally his gaze fell upon a hollow cottonwood. Larger than the others, it had been struck by lightning sometime in the past, and now it was no more than a shell, hollowed out by the fire that had resulted. The opening on one side looked just big enough for a boy his size to squeeze through. There being no better choice, he crawled the length of the gully, and keeping low behind the bank of the stream, made his way back toward the riotous band of Sioux, now whooping and laughing in celebration of their victory.

With more difficulty than he had at first anticipated, White Eagle was able to force his body through the opening in the hollow trunk, leaving some of his skin in the process. Once inside, he found he had room to stand, though his chamber was extremely confining. There were splits and cracks large enough for him to see through, but his hiding place was not obvious to anyone who might not suspect it. It was through one of these cracks that he saw the white man ride into the center of the plundering Sioux.

"Don't give me that ol' evil eye, you heathen son of a bitch," Booth Dalton warned—a wide smile on his face as he said it, knowing the warrior didn't understand a word of English. He prodded his horse past the sullen brave and made his way through the throng of noisy Indians to sidle up beside Iron Pony. "It was just like I told you, Chief, just ripe for the pickin'."

Iron Pony was pleased with the overwhelming victory his warriors had earned that day. He would have been more pleased if the Snakes had possessed greater amounts of powder and flints, but a good many rifles were captured, just as Booth had promised. Some of his warriors were suspicious of Booth's intentions. Although he and his friend, Charlie White Bull, had brought them many things to trade their hides and horses for, there were many in Iron Pony's camp that did not trust them.

Iron Pony sneered at the thought of the peace treaty just completed. He felt contemptuous of his Sioux and Cheyenne brothers who attended the conference with the white soldiers, sitting to smoke with the Snakes. He would never smoke with the hated Snakes, nor with the soldiers who sought to cheat the Lakotas and push them back from their ancestral hunting grounds. His scouts had told him of the large band of heavily armed Snakes that had made the journey to Fort Laramie. They were too many and too well armed for Iron Pony's band of Sioux. But then Booth came, claiming to be a friend of the Lakotas, and told him that a smaller group of Snakes had broken off from the main body and was traveling alone. This was when Iron Pony knew the spirits were smiling in his direction. He glanced over at the grinning white man who had just ridden up beside him and smiled. *You are my friend, white man, but only until you cross me. Then I will tie your scalp to my lance along with those of these Shoshoni dogs.*

Booth Dalton was corrupt, godless, and completely without morals, but he was also a sly fox who considered himself a shrewd conniver. At this particular moment, Booth was feeling justifiably smug for the successful massacre of the unsuspecting Snakes. He grinned unabashed as his witless partner, Charlie White Bull, joined in the looting and mutilating with Iron Pony's Sioux warriors. It struck Booth as rather humorous that the whole bunch might jump on ol'

Charlie if they knew he was really half Flathead. Like most Injuns, Charlie derived great satisfaction from the mutilation now taking place—it was supposed to make it harder for their dead enemies to find their way in the spirit world, and render them incapable of doing them any more harm. A foolish belief in Booth's opinion, mutilation of those he had killed never held any interest. So he sat on his horse and watched the savage rituals, a disinterested spectator.

Booth figured his stock with the Sioux chief was bound to go up after leading him to the small band of Snakes heading back from the treaty talks. The bitter hatred between the Sioux and Shoshoni was well known, and even though the Sioux greatly outnumbered Chief Washakie's warriors, the Snakes held a superiority in firepower—having been well armed by their friend, Jim Bridger. Consequently Booth had figured that Iron Pony would jump at the chance to catch a small band of Snakes out of their territory. Maybe now Booth's stock would be so high that he could influence the Sioux chief to use his warriors for other purposes beneficial to Booth.

The boy hiding in the burnt-out hollow tree now knew that the white man he had seen leering at him had not been an illusion. He felt his blood go cold and his body tremble with rage as the murdering white man rode up to talk with the Sioux chief. White Eagle made an effort to sear in his mind the image of the slender man in the black coat and flat-crowned hat. He memorized everything about the man, knowing that the Great Spirit must surely provide him an opportunity for revenge. No matter how far in the future that might be, he would recognize this evil man. He studied his movements and gestures, as the man took a round silver object from his coat pocket, opened it, and peered inside before returning it to his pocket. What it told the man, White Eagle could not guess, but the man looked at the sun before he stared at the object, then looked up at the sun again after he had put it away—so it must hold some strong medicine from the sun. *I will remember you*, he thought. *Someday I will find you and kill you.*

Stiff and shivering, his limbs aching from standing motionless for hours, White Eagle began to wonder if the celebrating Sioux were ever going to sleep. He had to fight the almost overpowering urge to break from his confining prison and take his chances in the glow of the many campfires. The one thought that prevented him from taking such foolish action were the words of his mother, *Live to fight another day*. In spite of his thirst for revenge, he knew that if he were caught trying to escape, he would be no more than an added amusement for the Sioux warriors. If he had any arrows left, it would be different. He could make the price of his death expensive for the hated Sioux. But with only his knife to fight with, he would be easily overpowered and his death would be for nothing. So he waited.

It was long after the moon had risen directly overhead before the last of the dancing and singing finally stopped and the Sioux camp was quiet. When he could see no one walking around the dwindling campfires, he decided it was safe to make his move. Straining as before, he squeezed his body through the narrow opening in the tree trunk, standing for a few moments on legs weak from lack of circulation. Walking unsteadily for a few steps, he quickly regained his balance and was once again his nimble self.

White Eagle made his way carefully between sleeping warriors, exhausted from their celebration and strewn randomly like dead bodies—some with blankets hastily wrapped around them, some lying half naked in the cool night air. It would have been an easy thing to sink his knife in a belly filled with the white man's firewater, but he resisted the temptation and made his way quickly toward the stream.

Out of the camp now, he crossed the stream to the place where the horses were grazing. As he searched for his own spotted gray pony among the Sioux horse herd, he heard a grunt behind him. Whirling at the sound, he raised his knife, ready to defend himself, only to find a sleeping sentry, groaning in his slumber. His heart started beating again and his muscles relaxed when he realized he was not about to be attacked. He started to walk around the sleeping guard when he hesitated, looking down at the helpless man. Here was one of the men who had murdered his people, lying vulnerable at his feet. There was a great temptation to extract some measure of revenge. He considered the possible consequences. The body would probably not be found until after sunup, by which time he should be hours away. But if he left the sleeping man alone, no one would pursue him. It was a hard decision to make. His heart was filled with grief and outrage over the death of his mother and grandfather. To steal away quietly unnoticed? Or to strike a blow for his people? He fingered the blade of his knife, his mind in a panic of confusion while he stared down at the snoring warrior. The man lay helpless before him, but what if he struck and he didn't kill the Sioux? The sleeping man shifted slightly, causing his blanket to fall slightly away. White Eagle started in fright, but the warrior did not awaken. A strange token attached to a rawhide string around the warrior's neck caught White Eagle's eye. As he stared at it in the moonlight he realized that it was a human tooth. White Eagle looked up at the warrior's face again. Suddenly the warrior's eyes popped open, and White Eagle took a step backward, staring horrified at the Sioux.

"What is it?" the warrior asked, still half drunk and groggy with sleep. He reached for the edge of his blanket to pull it over his shoulders.

There was no time to think. Acting on instinct alone, White Eagle quickly knelt down and grabbed the blanket as if to help cover the sleepy man. Then he whispered, "Die, Sioux dog." The confused warrior did not understand the words, but there was no mistaking their meaning when, a moment later, the blanket was stuffed over his face and White Eagle's knife opened his throat.

The eruption that followed was almost more than the boy could handle. As soon as he had severed the warrior's windpipe, White Eagle tried to sit on the man's head to keep him from throwing the blanket off and yelling an alarm. But the panicked Sioux rose up violently, tossing the boy aside. Staggering to his feet, the Sioux stumbled around in blind confusion, one hand holding his throat, the other swinging wildly in an attempt to defend himself. He could not make a sound other than a choking cough. Finally his stunned brain focused on the boy kneeling before him in the moonlight, and he stumbled unsteadily toward him. Terrified, the boy's will to survive took over. His heart racing, he managed to avoid the wildly swinging arm. Slipping under it, he struck as hard as he could, sinking his knife in the warrior's belly. Horrified when the man did not fall down dead, White Eagle backed away as fast as he could, eyes wide as he watched the last moments of the Sioux warrior. His chest glistening in the moonlight with the blood from his throat, the man frantically pulled the knife from his belly and flung it aside. Then he released a long sigh and crumpled to his knees. He remained in that position for a long moment, his eyes wide but seeing nothing. Finally he fell facedown in the grass.

Frozen in shock, White Eagle was unable to move for a long minute, staring at the body only a few feet from him. The realization that he had just killed a man struck him, an enemy, and in close combat. What he had just done was overwhelming, and his mind was in a confusion of shock, fear, and disbelief—but also pride. He might have stood there longer had he not felt a sudden nudge at his back. Startled, he turned to discover that his pony had found him. Awakened to action, he briefly hugged the pony's neck before picking up a coil of short rawhide line that lay near the body of the Sioux horse guard. He quickly made two half-hitches in the middle of the line, looping them around the pony's lower jaw for a bridle.

In minutes, the scene of the massacre was far behind him as he urged the gray across the prairie, retracing the trek his people had made the day before. It crossed his mind to circle the Sioux camp and try to continue on the long journey to find the rest of Chief Washakie's people in the Wind River Mountains. But it was closer to ride back to Fort Laramie—one day if he didn't stop that night, and this was where his mother had told him to go—to find the white trapper named Buck.

He wondered if Buck was his real father. He had known since he was a small child that Eagle Claw was not his real father. There had been no attempt to keep his white blood a secret. At one time he had hated the fact that he was not a pure-blooded Shoshoni like his mother and grandfather. But his mother had told him that he was not born the son of a typical white man— he was the son of the Mountain Hawk—a man who was feared by the Blackfeet, traditional enemies of the Snakes. After that, he was no longer ashamed to be half white. As he made his way across the moonlit prairie, he tried to recall the white man's name his mother had called his father. In fact, he couldn't remember if his mother had actually told him, but Buck didn't sound familiar. What if this man, Buck, was not at Fort Laramie? He decided to worry about that after he reached the fort.

The day was clear and unseasonably cool when four weary riders approached the outer buildings of Fort Laramie. Most of the many bands of Indians that had attended the peace talks had been gone for almost a week, with only a few smaller groups lingering on outside the walls. Trace and Buck had set a ground-eating pace from the Black Hills, with no complaints from Lieutenant Austen or Annie Farrior. After the disastrous encounter with Iron Pony's Sioux, Annie was especially anxious to put hostile country behind her, although she was not looking forward to her reunion with Grace Turner. Burdened with her own grief for the loss of her husband, she now had the sorrowful task of telling Grace of Ned's death.

To further trouble her mind, she found her thoughts constantly straying toward the slender young lieutenant with the reddish-brown hair and the finely chiseled features. Though it made her feel guilty, she found she could not help herself. Poor Tom's bones lay in the ground no more than a week, and already there were long periods when he did not cross her mind. She hoped Tom would forgive her, for she had no desire to betray his memory. Even now, as anxious as she had been to reach the safety of the fort, there was a definite feeling of dread that she would no longer see Luke Austen after they got back.

As for the young lieutenant, Luke had a great load on his mind upon reaching Fort Laramie. Foremost

was the burden of responsibility he shouldered for the
loss of his entire detachment of troopers—and this at a
time when the post was dreadfully understrength. He
knew he would have to answer for decisions that resulted in such a devastating massacre at the hands of
the very tribe the committee was negotiating a peace
with. He feared a court-martial might even be called
for. In spite of the ominous cloud of concern, there was
one thing he was certain of. As soon as it seemed
proper to do so, he was going to call on Annie Farrior.
It might be callous of him to think of such things with
her husband only recently killed, but there wasn't always time to do things the proper way in this country.

Captain Henry Leach got up from his desk and
went to the open door. Moments earlier, his orderly
had informed him that four riders were approaching
and one of them was plainly Lieutenant Austen. As
Leach stood there, he could feel his whole body tens-
ing as the anger rose in his veins. *So it was true*, he
thought. *The whole damned troop was wiped out*. It further infuriated Leach that his Sioux and Arapaho
scouts knew about the massacre long before any offi-
cial word reached his ears. *The damned Indian telegraph*,
he fumed, unable to understand how news was able to
travel so rapidly throughout the Indian nation.

Now, as the four crossed the empty yard of the fort,
the captain could readily identify the riders. Austen,
Ransom, the woman—but who was the other? Leach
had never seen the tall buckskin-clad sandy-haired
mountain man before. As he watched, Annie pulled
her horse up short, and after a few words with Luke,
turned back toward the river to seek out Grace Turner.
Good, Leach thought, *I don't have to be bothered with the
female*. Finding it increasingly difficult to contain his
anger, Leach turned on his heel. "Private, escort the

lieutenant and the scout in here." Then he returned to his desk and awaited their arrival.

"Sir, Lieutenant Austen," the orderly announced and stood aside to let the three men enter.

Leach could not wait to sail into his subordinate. Ignoring Luke's salute, he rose to his feet and demanded, "Thirty-four men! Maybe you can explain to me how you lost your entire troop, mister!" Luke blanched, but before he could open his mouth to explain, Leach railed on. "With thirty-four dragoons, you should have been able to defend yourself against any size Indian force. I'll have your explanation, sir!"

Luke, stunned at first by the hostile reception, steeled himself to meet the captain's angry tone. "We were led into a trap, sir, and attacked by a superior force of Sioux. There was no way we could hold out against the overwhelming odds."

"How in hell could you be foolish enough to be led into an ambush? Maybe they didn't teach you that at West Point, but out here any shavetail junior officer knows that you don't go chasing after a few Indians into a blind draw."

Before Luke could respond, Buck figured it was time to butt in. He didn't particularly care for the direction Leach was taking. "Beggin' your pardon, Captain, but none of this was Lieutenant Austen's fault. It was that damned double-dealin' renegade Bull Hump. He damn shore set us up for that massacre—led us right into that box canyon."

Leach cocked his head at the old trapper, squinting his eyes as if annoyed by Buck's intervention in the captain's dressing down of his subordinate. "Are you suggesting we put the blame on a trusted Sioux scout?"

"Trusted, my ass," Buck responded. "I'd like to know who decided he could be trusted. Oh, I ain't sayin' I don't take part of the blame. He pulled the wool over my eyes, too. I just thought he wasn't too smart—wanderin' away from the rest of us for half a day and more—actin' like he didn't know one canyon from the next. He was smart enough all right—led us right to the slaughter. I caught a glimpse of him when we was runnin' for cover at the end of that canyon. He was right in the middle of 'em."

Leach paused to consider this. He was still inclined to place at least part of the blame for the tragedy upon the broad shoulders of Luke Austen. There was going to be hell to pay for this when word got back to Washington. If the massacre of thirty-four soldiers by hostile Sioux got into the papers back east, then there was going to be a public outcry for justice. And Leach was smart enough to know that wasn't going to please the generals. For one thing, the peace talks were not even a week old—and another, the army didn't have enough manpower to go against the Sioux nation at the present time. Leach was going to have to leave it to his superiors as to what action, if any, should be taken against Lieutenant Austen. Somebody back East was going to have a hell of a job keeping this one quiet, especially when they had to explain to *The Chicago Herald* how their reporter got killed.

"Who the hell is this?" Leach suddenly demanded, glaring at the tall clean-shaven man in buckskins who had stood silently in the background while Buck and Luke gave the captain the details of the attack.

Buck glanced back at his friend briefly. "This here's Trace McCall. If it wasn't for him, you might be standin' here talkin' to yourself."

Trace remained silent, his expression unchanged. Luke hastened to explain Buck's flippant response to the captain's question. "Mr. McCall managed to dispatch a body of hostiles that had us pinned down with our backs to a cliff. Mr. Ransom's right. We might not have made it without Mr. McCall's help."

"Well, then," Leach began reluctantly, "I expect the army owes you a word of thanks."

Leach's manner irritated Trace. He gave the belligerent officer a long look before answering. Then he said, "Thanks ain't necessary. If the army owes me anything, it's a horse."

"That's right, sir," Luke said. "Mr. McCall's packhorse was killed while he was holding off the hostiles during our escape. I expect he lost more than the horse—there were supplies, too."

While Luke related the events that led up to their escape along the narrow precipice, Leach kept his eyes on the tall mountain man. *One of the real wild ones*, he thought, *more Indian than white*. Being a military man, Henry Leach held no particular admiration for the brand of men like McCall who roamed the prairies and mountains. It was his opinion that most of them were hard-drinking, squaw-loving rascals whose greatest attribute was the ability to tell colossal lies about their exploits. Now he was thinking that he might have to change his opinion about this one at least. There was a quiet confidence in Trace McCall's bearing that conveyed a sense of strength, and Leach knew that here was a man to be reckoned with. He glanced at the old scout for a moment, a true mountain man, too. But the contrast was impossible to miss for someone as perceptive as Henry Leach. Buck was old, of course, but he was as noisy and rowdy as a prairie thunderstorm. McCall, on the other hand, was like the deadly flight of an arrow—silent but lethal.

"All right," Leach said, when Luke finished his account of Trace's part in their escape, "Mr. McCall can pick a replacement horse from the army's stock—

maybe pick up some things at the post trader's store to replace his lost articles."

"Obliged," Trace said.

Leach turned back to Luke. "As for you, Lieutenant, you can report back to duty. But make no mistake, you're not off my shit list just yet. I'll file my report on this incident, and we'll see what disciplinary action is called for."

"What are you aimin' to do now?" Buck asked as he and Trace led their horses toward the sutler's store.

"I don't know for sure, but I don't reckon I'll stay around here for longer'n it takes to replace some of what I lost on my packhorse."

"I swear," Buck snorted, "you're gittin' so you can't stay around people for more'n two or three days before you go hightailing it back up in them mountains."

Trace laughed. "Now, that ain't exactly so, Buck. I've been hanging around with you for the most part of a week. 'Course most folks wouldn't call that the same as hanging around with people."

Buck snorted again and spat to show what he thought of Trace's humor. "I thought you might wanna ride on back to Promise Valley with me. It's been a while, and there's folks there who'd like to see you."

"How *is* Jamie?" Trace asked.

"Last I saw her, she was workin' that little farm of her daddy's like a man. I swear, she can outwork ol' Jordan any day of the week. You mighta made a big mistake not marrying that gal." He cocked an eye at Trace, his tone almost wistful. "I thought the two of you would end up together."

"And do what?" Trace replied. "Settle down in Promise Valley and raise young'uns?"

Buck wiped his mouth with the back of his hand

while he studied his friend's face for a moment. "No," he said finally, "I reckon not. You'd hear the call of a hawk before the first year was out. Jamie'd turn around and you'd be gone."

"I expect so," Trace replied softly, his mind drifting back years ago to a young Shoshoni maiden on the banks of the Green River. She remained fresh in his mind even after all this time, and he wondered if he ever entered her thoughts. There was a time, years ago, when he was inclined to look for her. But things got in his way, and before he knew it, years had passed and he finally decided it was not in the cards for the two of them. He often reminded himself that it was she who slipped off in the night, leaving him no word of her whereabouts. Still the smoky fragrance of her raven-black hair lingered in his memory, to surface occasionally in moments like this.

CHAPTER 7

Sergeant Michael Barnes, sergeant of the guard on the night just past, walked out of the orderly room holding a cup of steaming black coffee. He stood on the wood stoop for a few moments, evaluating the coming day as he looked out toward the east to catch the first rays of light on the silent prairie. First light, it was his favorite time of day, while the post was still and peaceful, before the first blasts from the bugler. He glanced back toward the bakery and almost spilled his coffee when he discovered an Indian boy quietly sitting on his horse no more than fifty feet from him.

"Damn," Barnes swore. Turning to the sentry standing by the orderly room door, he asked, "I swear I didn't see that boy when I came out the door." Looking back at the Indian boy, who remained silent as he stared at the door of the headquarters building, Barnes spoke again. "How long has he been settin' there starin' like that?"

"Can't say for sure, Sergeant," the, sentry replied. "It was awful dark out here. I didn't see nothin', didn't hear nothin'. Then, first light, and there he was. Kinda spooky, ain't he? Scared the shit outta me at first, I can tell you that—till I seen he was just a boy."

"Well, what does he want?"

"I don't know. I asked him what he wanted, but I

reckon he don't understand American. He just sets there starin', so I just let him be."

Barnes shrugged his shoulders and returned his attention to the cup of coffee he was sipping. One of the privileges that came with guard duty was having the following day free from fatigue details, and the sergeant was taking his leisure to enjoy a morning cup before catching up on a little of the sleep he had lost the night before.

The sergeant stood outside the door until he had finished the bitter black brew, leaning against the wall, occasionally glancing at the stone-still Indian boy on the gray spotted pony. Finally his curiosity got the best of him. Tossing the last few swallows from his cup, he stepped off the stoop and walked toward the boy. The boy did not move as Barnes approached, but his eyes followed the sergeant's every step until Barnes stopped two paces from his pony's nose.

"Somethin' I can do for you, son?"

"Buck," the boy replied.

"Buck?" Barnes echoed. The boy nodded solemnly. "Whaddaya mean, Buck?"

"Buck," the boy repeated.

Barnes shook his head, puzzled. "Do you speak any white-man talk?" He could see by the boy's confused expression that he didn't. "Well, now, that makes things a little harder, don't it?" He pulled at his whiskers, thinking. "Buck, you say?"

"Buck," was the quick response.

"Well, I'm afraid I can't help you, boy." He glanced up then to see Lamar Thomas walking to the sutler's store. "Mr. Thomas," he called, "you know an Injun word that sounds like Buck?"

Lamar stopped and turned around to look at the boy, who promptly uttered, "Buck." Lamar thought for a minute trying to recall his limited Indian vocabulary. He couldn't think of any word that sounded like that. "Maybe it ain't Injun. Maybe he's looking for somebody named Buck. Buck Ransom's still here if he didn't cut out this morning. At least Buck can talk his lingo." He motioned for the boy to follow him. "Come on," Lamar said and started walking. The boy appeared hesitant, but when Lamar didn't turn around again and just kept walking, he nudged his pony and followed.

Lamar found Buck behind the stables, where the old trapper had spread his blankets the night before. Now he was busy packing up in preparation for the trip back to his cabin in Promise Valley. He looked up to see Lamar approaching on foot followed by the Indian boy on a pony. As soon as he came close enough, Buck recognized the boy.

"Well, I'll be . . ." Buck muttered. He looked beyond the two, expecting to see the boy's mother. "What are you doin' back here all by yourself? Where's your mama?" From the quizzical expression on the young boy's face, Buck realized he didn't understand English, so he repeated the questions in Shoshoni.

There was immediate change in the boy's expression. His face lit up at the familiar sound of his own tongue. Without further hesitation, he told Buck of the massacre of Broken Arm's band and the death of his mother. Buck's heart went out to the boy. *What a shame*, he thought, *that pretty little Snake woman.* For a brief moment, he pictured the young Indian maiden who had captivated Trace McCall's adolescent heart—then left as quickly as she had appeared. That brief encounter had resulted in this precocious young boy standing before him now—looking for his daddy, and Trace didn't even know he existed. The news would most likely hit Trace McCall pretty hard. He never mentioned it, but Buck suspected that Trace still carried a special memory of the young girl called Blue Water.

"Are you called Buck?" White Eagle asked when he had related the details of the tragedy that befell his people. "My mother told me to come here and find Buck."

"Yeah, I'm Buck. I'm the one your mother sent you to find." He paused to nod to Lamar Thomas who excused himself, saying he had to open the store, leaving the two talking. Buck was puzzled at first as to why Blue Water had sent her son to find him instead of making his way back to the Snake village. But after thinking on it for a few minutes, he figured that the main band of Snakes must have been too far ahead of Broken Arm's band. And rather than have the lad ride alone through Sioux and Arapaho territory, she knew it was closer for him to run back to Laramie. It was Trace she wanted the boy to find, but she had no idea where Trace might be—so she sent him to Buck, hoping Trace's friend could find him.

White Eagle was studying the old mountain man intensely, wondering if this old graybeard could possibly be the Mountain Hawk his mother had talked about. He had pictured a younger man. "Are you my father?" he finally asked.

Buck smiled. *So she did tell you about your daddy, did she?* In the boy's tongue, he said, "No, your father left here yesterday, heading for the Big Horn country."

There was a discernible change of expression on White Eagle's face, a mixture of relief and disappointment—relief that the grizzled old trapper was not the legendary Mountain Hawk he had been told of—disappointment that he had missed seeing his real father by one day. He was now at a loss as to what he should do. He couldn't stay there in a strange land, a land where there were many enemies of the Shoshoni. His only possessions were the pony he rode, a knife, and a bow with no arrows. He was not without the courage to fight, but he knew he was in no position to defend himself if it came to that.

Reading the concern now etched in the boy's face, Buck made a quick decision to change his plans to return to Promise Valley. After all, this was Trace McCall's son, even if Trace had no notion of the boy's existence. He knew Trace well enough to know that he would feel responsible for the boy—at least responsible enough to see White Eagle safely back to Chief Washakie's village.

"Your mother told you the right thing," Buck said. "I'll take you to find your father. He's not but a day ahead of us and he's not in any particular hurry." Again, he read relief in the boy's face. "We'll catch him," Buck assured him.

White Eagle nodded and expressed his thanks, trying hard to disguise the concern that had worried him moments before. Buck could not help but marvel at the resemblance to Trace. *The spittin' image of Trace McCall*, he thought. *I could have picked him outta a crowd to be Trace's son.* He thought back to the time when he first met Trace. Trace wasn't a great deal older than this half-Shoshoni boy before him now when Buck caught him stealing beaver from his traps. Buck almost laughed when he thought about it. Trace, left on his own in the mountains, was robbing Buck and Frank Brown's beaver traps for food. Buck shook his head and chuckled, *He was a damn sight ways from a Mountain Hawk back then.*

Annie was sitting on a long cottonwood log by the water's edge, a place she came to when she needed a few moments alone. It was approaching evening and she would have to go back to the cabin soon to help

Rose Thomas with supper. There was a chill in the air, but the old log still felt warm from the sun it had absorbed during the afternoon. It made a pleasant seat for her, hard by the water's edge, and away from Grace Turner's sorrowful countenance for a while. Most of that first day back at Fort Laramie had been spent consoling Grace. Grace and Ned had been childhood sweethearts, and had been married for four years when he and Tom first started talking about the expedition to the Black Hills. The news of Ned's death was devastating to Grace, making Annie feel even more guilt for her own lack of grief.

Annie didn't mean to avoid Grace. It was just that she needed some time for herself to think private thoughts. So after they had finished the wash, and Grace felt the need for a short nap, Annie slipped quietly out the door and headed for the creek.

After checking both sides to make sure there was nothing crawling under it, she parked herself on the warm old log and let her mind flow with the rapid current that tickled the sandy stream bottom.

Gazing around her, up and down the streambank, she realized how much she enjoyed the privacy of this little spot. She could hear the sounds from the Thomases' cabin, but she could not see the house through the cottonwoods and willows that bordered the stream. This was her spot, well upstream from the cabin. She learned soon after coming to stay with Rose and Lamar to avoid the trees directly behind the cabin. For this was Lamar's favorite spot to relieve himself, disdaining the privy he had built for his wife.

Grace was taking Ned's death extremely hard, still weepy and feeling faint after three days of mourning. Annie had known about Tom's death several days before Grace learned of Ned's. It was natural that she should be thinking about getting on with her life while Grace was still deep in sorrow.

Grace was going to have to pull herself together pretty soon, though. There were decisions to be made. Annie feared that the Thomases might be wondering when their guests were going to depart. A few times Grace had mentioned a desire to return to her father's place in Ohio. Annie knew Grace assumed that she would accompany her, but Annie was not sure she wanted to go back east. There was a little money left, an emergency fund that Tom had left with her when he rode off in search of gold. She was glad now that he had insisted upon it. More and more lately, she had entertained the notion of using the money to continue the journey to Oregon as originally planned. Seated upon her cottonwood log, she thought about Oregon and what wonderful country it must be. A woman alone couldn't think of taking the trip, but she might be able to pay her way on one of the wagon trains that would come through in the spring. Grace might be upset if she decided to go on to Oregon; Annie would have to give it serious thought.

"Annie . . ." Her thoughts were interrupted by the sound of her name. It was a man's voice. Annie could not identify it at first—it was not Lamar's nasal twang. When she heard it again, this time several yards closer, she recognized the voice as that of Luke Austen. At the same time, she felt a definite quickening of her pulse, a sensation that almost made her blush in embarrassment. She had not seen Lieutenant Austen but once since their return to Fort Laramie, and that was only a brief exchange of greetings. Though he had been removed from her sight for a while, she had to admit to herself that he was seldom gone from her thoughts for large portions of the day.

"I'm here," she called out, getting to her feet and

quickly shaking the wrinkles from her skirt, after a cursory effort to smooth her hair back from her face. A moment later, the tall slender figure of Luke Austen emerged from the trees.

"Evening, Annie . . . Mrs. Farrior . . ." he stumbled. "Mrs. Thomas said I'd find you down here."

"Annie," she corrected. "Yes, I guess my special spot wasn't so secret after all." She smiled warmly and extended her hand. "What brings you over here from the fort?"

He took her hand eagerly, making an effort to be gentle. "I just wanted to check on you—to see if you were getting along all right." Still holding her hand, he fumbled in his brain for a legitimate reason to explain his visit, unable to tell her that he had come because he had been unsuccessful in ridding her from his thoughts. "I mean, that was quite an ordeal you went through. I just wanted to make sure you were all right—if there was anything I could do . . ."

"How very thoughtful," she said. "I'm fine . . . I mean, under the circumstances, of course."

"Of course," he echoed, just then realizing that he was still holding her hand. Embarrassed, he released it. "Mrs. Turner—is she all right?" He thought it polite to ask, even though he had to admit that he had given Grace Turner's loss very little thought.

She invited him to sit on the cottonwood log beside her. Then he fashioned his most attentive expression while Annie told him of Grace's difficulty in adjusting to the loss of her husband. Hearing her words, but not really listening, he instead filled his mind with the image before him. Though wearing a simple cotton dress, with a knitted wrap to ward off the evening chill, in Luke's mind she might have as well have been wearing a ballroom gown. He was smitten by the angelic image facing him. He fully realized it, at the same time feeling a portion of shame, knowing the woman should be in mourning for her late husband. *What kind of crass dog are you, Luke Austen?* he asked himself, fully realizing that deep down he didn't really care.

"I guess you'll be thinking about heading back east," he said, trying hard to hide his concern.

In spite of his efforts to conceal his feelings for her, she was certain that she detected an interest deeper than a polite concern for her well-being—and the thought caused a flutter of excitement in her heart. She didn't express it, but her decision was made at that moment to remain at Fort Laramie, at least until spring. She said, "I haven't made up my mind yet. I think Grace will definitely go back. And of course, she would expect me to go with her."

"Oh . . . I expected as much," he replied.

She was pleased to see the disappointment in his face, and she quickly added, "As I said, though, I really haven't made up my mind. I guess there's really nothing to keep me out here."

"Why, sure there is," he blurted, almost forgetting discretion. "I mean, there are lots of reasons to stay out here." He tried to think of some but could not at the moment.

Forgetting her own discretion, she said, "I guess I only need one good one."

Glancing up quickly, he found her eyes gazing deeply into his, and he suddenly lost all composure. "I don't want you to go back." As soon as he said it, he knew he had taken liberties that were outside the boundaries of common etiquette. At once, he started to apologize, but she quickly pressed a finger to his lips to silence him.

"It's all right," she whispered softly, "I don't want to go back, either." She continued to gaze warmly into his eyes, transmitting a message that could not be conveyed with words.

Luke Austen was treading on unfamiliar ground when it came to the uncertain terrain of emotion and affairs of the heart. But as an officer of mounted dragoons, he had never been lacking in courage under any circumstance, and he was never reluctant to charge into the breech when it was necessary to save the day. Now he was sure Annie had provided the opening with her eyes. So throwing all caution to the wind, he charged in to exploit it.

Taking her hand again, he said his piece. "Annie, I don't want you to leave . . . ever. I know I'm being a little bold—and I don't mean to show any disrespect to your late husband—but I just wish you'd stay out here a while—long enough to get to know me a little better." The incredulous look on her face caused him to pause, but he was determined to finish what he had started. "I apologize if I'm being insensitive. I don't mean to be, but there isn't time for propriety. If you even feel half of what I feel for you, then it's a solid basis for giving it a chance."

He paused, waiting for her response, but she was not sure how to answer him. "Luke, I don't know if I understand what you are saying. Are you proposing to me?"

Totally confused by his own emotions, Luke stopped to consider, then said, "Well, yes, I guess I am." This seemed to stun her, and when she did not respond right away, he began to retreat. "I'm sorry if I stepped out of line. If I've insulted you, I'll go now, and you won't ever be bothered by me again." He fumbled for words to repair the damage he felt he might have done. "I don't know what got into my head. I shouldn't have opened my mouth. It's just that I'll be going out on patrol in a couple of days, and I was afraid you might be gone when I got back. Please, won't you consider staying a while?"

Annie, certain now of what she had found too incredible to believe upon first hearing his declaration, was quick to reassure him. Placing her other hand upon his, she said, "I'm glad you spoke your feelings, Luke. I understand your concern and I appreciate it." She smiled. "I do care for you, Luke—and I'll stay. Let's take a little time to know each other, before we talk of more serious things."

The cloud of doubt was lifted immediately from the love-struck lieutenant's face, replaced by a glow of unbounded joy. Releasing her hands, he took her by the shoulders. "Annie," was all he could think to say, as he gazed hopefully into her eyes. Seeing his longing, she smiled and turned her face up to him, waiting to receive his kiss. When their lips first met, it was a tender union, her mouth warm and soft, sending his senses reeling. And then the fire of passion consumed them both, a fire that had grown in the dark and uncertain nights in the Black Hills when she had pressed close to him, seeking protection from the Lakota war party that pursued them. He kissed her hard then, hard and long, while once again she pressed close to his body, this time openly and unafraid.

Luke's rapture was abruptly interrupted when Grace Turner made her way down to the creek, calling Annie's name. The lovers quickly parted, leaving a respectable distance between them as they sat waiting for Grace to appear. Annie had thought it best not to make public their affection for each other for a while yet, so Luke did his best to effect an impersonal countenance for Grace's sake.

"It was so thoughtful of you to come by, Lieutenant," Annie said loud enough for Grace to hear. "We're doing fine under the circumstances."

Taking his cue from Annie, Luke responded, "It was my pleasure, ma'am." Then he added, "If it's all right with you and Mrs. Turner, I might call on you again. Captain Leach thought it a good idea if I kept a close eye on you, especially you, Mrs. Farrior, after the ordeal you suffered." He figured it highly unlikely that Grace might have an occasion to confirm his statement with Leach, so he manufactured an excuse to call again.

The faintest hint of a smile tugged at the corners of Annie's mouth as she replied that she and Grace would be happy to have him call. He rose to his feet. "Well, I guess I'd better get back to the fort." He nodded politely to Grace as he walked by. "Mrs. Turner."

"Lieutenant," Grace replied, stopping to watch his departure, a puzzled look upon her face. When he had disappeared beyond the trees, she turned her gaze toward Annie, her natural female suspicions aroused. "Well, you two had quite a little visit. What was that all about, anyway? Check on us? Is that one of the duties of an army officer on the frontier? To check on poor widows?"

Annie hoped she wasn't blushing. "I don't suppose so, but it was awfully nice of him—and his captain—to be concerned for our feelings."

Grace smiled—the first time in three days, Annie noted—a hint of mischief showing in her face. "Seems like he spent a great deal more time being concerned for you than he did for me."

Annie definitely felt herself blushing then. "Well, he does know me a little better than he does you. Anyway, you were taking a nap when he called."

"He is kind of handsome," Grace replied, an eyebrow raised accusingly.

"Why, Grace Turner!" Annie gasped, pretending to be shocked, even though she feared that Grace had seen right through the charade performed by Luke and herself.

Grace just laughed and said, "Come on, it's time to put supper on the table."

It was good to see Grace laugh again. Maybe she could begin to put the sorrow of Ned's death behind her. Like Annie, she was still a young woman with a lot of life yet to live.

As chilly as the night air had become, Luke could still feel the clammy dampness under his arms from the nervous sweat that had been spreading just minutes before. His emotions were in such disarray that he wasn't sure if he should be elated or depressed. He tried to replay the scene in his mind, leaving out no detail, no matter how small. Looking back, he could not help but feel a little foolish for stumbling bluntly into a proposal of marriage. *She must have thought I was insane.* He squeezed his eyes tightly shut in a grimace for an instant. *She didn't answer yes or no, just 'Let's get to know each other before talking of more serious things.' But she did say she cared for me.* And he had kissed her. That had to mean something to her. "Jesus," he swore aloud, "I couldn't have been more the buffoon."

He would have to construct some pretense to call on her again right away. Maybe he could salvage some of his dignity before he took to the field. There was so little time. Captain Leach was still furious over the loss of Luke's patrol and the frustrations it had caused. According to the treaty signed with the various tribes at Laramie, the army wasn't supposed to send patrols into what had been decided upon as Indian lands. While his superiors thought it best to keep the massacre quiet, Leach felt that such action by Iron Pony's band of Sioux could not go unpunished. Consequently, Leach had decided to lead a detachment of sixty of his mounted troopers on a patrol to find Iron Pony's band. He had ordered Luke to ride with them.

CHAPTER 8

Trace McCall pulled gently on the reins, and the paint pony stopped immediately, turning his head to look back at the tall mountain man gazing up at the sky. A redtail hawk turned random circles high above the hills that rolled into the Bighorn Mountains. The ghostly image formed by the peaks of the Bighorns as they reached heavenward never failed to strike a spiritual chord in Trace's soul. There was something mystical about the silent peaks when the sun began to sink behind them, outlining each spire with a fiery gold brush. It was little wonder that the Sioux and Cheyenne thought this to be a special place.

Trace kicked his feet out of the stirrups and stretched his legs, looking up again at the hawk still floating on the late-afternoon breeze. There was a special bond between the hawk and the free spirit of the mountain man that had existed since Trace was a boy, living with a band of Crow Indians. Patiently, the paint stood there, waiting for his master's signal, only tossing his head slightly and whinnying softly when Trace's packhorse pushed alongside. Although the late afternoons had become quite chilly, there had been no frost yet, so the buffalo grass was green and high. The paint pulled at the grass, grazing unhurriedly as his master continued to fill his lungs with the crisp air. The pony tossed his head impatiently then. It was not the first time they had followed the flight of a hawk, and anxious to slake its thirst, the horse was impatient to reach the valley before them and the river that flowed through it.

Finally, Trace placed his moccasined feet back in the stirrups and made a soft clicking sound out of the side of his mouth—all that was necessary to put the swift Indian pony in motion. They descended the grass-covered knoll, following a treeless ravine down into the valley. "We'll just ride on down to the river to get a drink, then we'll double back to see who's been in such an all-fired hurry to catch up with us," he told the horse.

Buck pushed the horses as much as he thought reasonable in his effort to overtake Trace. Once he had determined the trail Trace had taken when he left Laramie, he was able to make pretty good time, having ridden the same trails with his younger friend many times in the past. He had a pretty good notion where Trace was heading, anyway. There was a double bend in the river that Trace favored for a campsite whenever he rode through the Bighorn country and so far the trail pointed to that spot.

Occasionally, Buck glanced back at the young Shoshoni boy riding silently behind him on the spotted gray pony. Trace Junior. Buck laughed to himself, marveling at the resemblance to the boy's father every time he looked back at White Eagle. Each time he was met with the same stoic stare. *He shore knows how to look Injun*, Buck thought. If there was any fear in the boy, he didn't show it, even though they were alone in the country of the Snakes' most dreaded enemies.

Just as the sun dropped below the peaks of the Bighorn Mountains, the two riders pulled up at the head of a ravine that led down to the river. Buck waited for White Eagle to pull up beside him. "See that thicket of willows and brush," he said, pointing toward the banks of the river. "On the other side of that, in that stand of cottonwoods, is where I'm thinking we'll find Trace McCall. But we'd best go down there with our eyes open—Trace ain't the only one that uses this place as a camp."

White Eagle nodded his understanding and followed Buck down the ravine at a slow walk. Shadows were long and fading as they cleared the ravine, now looking at fifty or more yards of open flat before the trees along the riverbank. Buck signaled for quiet as he dismounted and led his horse toward the willow thicket. White Eagle followed his lead, and when they reached the cover of the brush, they tied the horses to a willow and proceeded on foot.

Making his way cautiously through the bushes that bordered the thicket, Buck suddenly held up his hand and stopped. Dropping silently to one knee, his rifle cocked and ready to fire, he peered through the tangle of brush and willow shoots. After a moment, he smiled. There, hobbled in the trees, was Trace's paint Indian pony and the packhorse he had just acquired from the army's remuda at Fort Laramie. Buck looked all around him, to both sides. Trace was getting a mite careless, he thought. *He's lucky I ain't a Sioux war party.*

With White Eagle following in his footsteps, Buck moved closer to the river's edge until he could see a small fire burning in a gully and the outline of a man sitting with his back against a tree. "It's him all right," he whispered to White Eagle. "Keep close behind me and don't make no noise." Buck always enjoyed an opportunity to let Trace know he could still learn a thing or two from this old trapper. "We'll just let him know how easy it is to catch a Mountain Hawk."

Placing each foot carefully so as not to make even

the slightest sound, Buck made his way around the brush so he could come up behind Trace. Patiently stalking his friend, ready to yell out when Trace finally became aware of him—he didn't want to take a chance on getting shot—Buck sneaked right up behind the cottonwood in the near darkness of the shadows. Having to restrain himself to keep from chuckling, he stepped up to the tree and said, "I don't know how you kept your hair this long, partner." He thought to poke Trace in the back with his rifle as he said it, only to discover he had prodded Trace's saddle pack, propped against the tree. "Damn," he uttered, knowing he'd been outfoxed and at the same time hearing the soft pad of horses' hooves behind him.

"Evening, Buck," Trace casually greeted his visitors, as he rode into the camp on Buck's horse, leading the boy's pony behind him. "Figured you might want to bring your horses on in and hobble 'em with mine."

Buck was too flabbergasted to say anything for a moment. He had been certain no one could have seen him approach that thicket. "Well, dang," he finally sputtered, "I had to be shore it was you."

Trace laughed. "Is that why you came sneaking up here like that?"

"I wasn't sneakin'," Buck shot back. "If I'da wanted to sneak up on you, you'da never knowed I was there."

"I reckon you're right," Trace allowed, a twinkle in his eye as he slid down from Buck's horse. "Looks like you got yourself a new partner," he said, nodding his head toward the boy.

White Eagle, a silent spectator of Buck's attempt to get the best of Trace, stood in awe of the tall sandy-haired man who was said to be his father. Standing next to Buck's slightly stooped and blocky body, the man seemed as tall as a lodgepole pine, with shoulders broad and powerful. He could understand now why his mother had told him that his father was a mighty warrior, even though he was white—and why such a man might be called the Mountain Hawk by the Black-feet.

Remembering the purpose of his mission, Buck turned to face the boy as if examining him for the first time. "This young feller is the reason I come after you." This piqued Trace's curiosity and he took a closer look at the boy. Buck went on. "This here's White Eagle and I reckon he needed to find you."

"Oh?" Trace replied, speaking to the boy. "Why did you need to find me, son?"

"He don't speak no American," Buck answered for him. "He's a Snake—leastways his mama was, his daddy's white." Buck deliberately held back, curious to see if Trace would see the resemblance to himself.

Trace was still puzzled. "I thought he looked more white than Injun." He shrugged, "Well, what does he want with me?"

Buck got real serious then. "Trace, this here's Blue Water's son."

Buck saw the dawn of realization breaking in Trace's eyes, but his tall friend said nothing, continuing to stare at the boy standing wide-eyed before him. Then Trace looked at Buck and the old trapper answered the unspoken question with a nod of his head. Trace shifted his gaze once again to the boy, his face a mask of amazement. "Blue Water?" looking quickly back at Buck. "Where is she?"

Buck shook his head slowly. "Gone under. They was at the treaty talks at Laramie—got jumped by a band of Sioux on the way home. Accordin' to White Eagle here, ever'body but him got kilt."

The news of Blue Water's death hit Trace with the impact of a boulder. He took a step backward as if to maintain his balance. This could not be. Somehow, he had always thought that he would someday find the young Shoshoni girl who had taken his heart captive over a decade ago. It was this belief that had sustained him over the long winters that had passed since his one moment of supreme passion on the banks of the Green River. The image of Blue Water that had burned brightly in his mind ever since was the reason he had been unable to commit himself to Jamie Thrash in spite of his tender feelings toward her. Over the years, he had been able to call Blue Water's face to mind whenever he felt melancholy. And though it was only a dream he had carried hidden away in the deep recesses of his thoughts, still it was a dream that he hoped would someday come true, even though a small part of him knew he was destined to ride the lonely ridges with no one at his side. But he had held onto her in his memory, where she would always be as young and beautiful as she had been when he last saw her. Now the dream was gone, snatched away like a thistle in a windstorm.

Buck watched Trace's reaction with confused concern. Trace was visibly stunned by the news. A fact that came as a mild surprise to Buck. He knew that Trace was a serious and responsible man, but he had no notion of the depth of the mountain man's feelings toward this Snake maiden. He wished now that he had been a little more compassionate instead of bluntly announcing Blue Water's death. Buck had known many a trapper who had taken a squaw for a time—he had himself at one point in his life. But most of them left the Indian women to return to their villages when the trappers moved on—usually without a backward glance. That's just the way it was in the high mountains.

Buck scratched his head and glanced at White

Eagle, then back at Trace. He didn't know what to say.
The only reason he brought the boy here was because
he knew Trace would feel responsible to take White
Eagle back to Snake country to find his people—a mission Buck had no desire to undertake. He was getting
too damn old to risk his hair anymore, while Trace
seemed to prefer living a knife blade away from danger.

Suddenly the awkward moment was over, and
Trace seemed to bring his focus back to present company. It had been a show of emotion that Buck had not
seen since Trace was a boy not much older than White
Eagle. He was relieved to see the calm, unperturbable
demeanor return.

Trace spoke to the boy in Shoshoni. "I am deeply
sorry to hear of your mother's death." A single nod of
the head was White Eagle's only response. "What did
she tell you about me?"

"She said you are my real father," White Eagle answered. Searching Trace's face intently, he asked, "Are
you my father?"

One look at the boy's features would answer that
question for any casual observer. Trace answered,
"Yes." As he said it, the realization of it began to dawn
on him. But it would be some time yet before he felt
the full impact of his new status as a father. "Tell me
how Blue Water died."

White Eagle told them of the murderous attack by
the large Sioux war party, of how his people were
taken by surprise, not suspecting an attack after the
peace talks at Laramie. From the description of the war
party, Trace suspected it was Iron Pony's band.

"A white man killed my mother," White Eagle said.
This captured Trace's attention at once. He glanced at
Buck to see if he had heard, certain now that it was
Iron Pony's band. White Eagle went on, "I think he

was some kind of medicine man. I saw him talking to the sun, then he took out a shiny object and opened it and looked inside. It must have told him something because he talked to the sun some more before he put the medicine thing away."

This was mighty curious as far as Buck was concerned. He scratched his beard and tried to picture what the boy had just related. He couldn't make any sense of it. "I don't know what in thunder he could be talkin' about," he confessed.

"Pocket watch," Trace said. "Coulda been looking at the time." It was just a notion that had come to him. They had pretty much decided that it was a white man who had participated in the killing of Annie Farrior's husband and his partners. And Annie had lamented the fact that the silver pocket watch she had given her husband had been taken. "Just a notion," Trace continued, "a lot of men carry pocket watches. But it ain't something a lot of men in this part of the world carry. I wouldn't be surprised if this white man White Eagle saw was the same one that murdered those four young fellows up in the Black Hills."

"I kinda figured that myself," Buck said. "A coyote like that leaves a wide track."

While speculation upon the identity of the white man who had crossed their paths was of more than passing interest to Buck and Trace, there was a more pressing issue to be resolved at the moment—and that was what to do with young eleven-year-old White Eagle. The boy had been sitting quietly while the two mountain men talked, understanding not a word spoken. Realizing this, Trace changed the conversation by asking Buck, "What are you aiming to do with the boy?"

Buck jerked his head back as if surprised. "What do

I aim to do with him? Hell, he's your son. What do *you* aim to do with him?"

My son—the thought was almost too much to believe. Trace was not prepared to be anybody's father. But what Buck said was true, he was the boy's father, and he guessed that pretty much made him responsible for his welfare. He looked at the youngster, staring back at him with the dark eyes of his mother, and the image of Blue Water filled his mind once again. Quickly, before he began to dwell on it, Trace pushed it from his mind. He would think about it later, when he could be alone with his thoughts. Now was not the time. "I was planning on doing some trapping and hunting in the Bighorn country, but I suppose I could take him to find his mother's people. He must have aunts or uncles in Washakie's village. Even if he doesn't, they'll take him in."

Buck shrugged. "I reckon. That's why I brung him after you. I'm gittin' too damn old to go tearing off after a band of Snakes. I've been away from my place in Promise Valley too long already. I told Reverend Longstreet I'd be back before the end of summer, and here it is gittin' close to winter."

Trace understood. His old friend's blood was getting too thin for the cold winters in the high mountains. Buck's aches and pains were multiplying every day, and his eyesight was fading. It was time to retire to settlement life. It was a sad thought, but a fact of life that no man could escape. It just seemed to Trace that old age settled upon those who chose to wade the icy mountain streams a lot sooner than the folks who stayed by the hearth.

When Trace sought to assure White Eagle that he would see that he reached the camp of Chief Washakie, he was surprised by the boy's reaction. "I do not wish to return to the land of the Shoshoni,"

White Eagle stated calmly. He had been thinking hard about the white man who had murdered his mother and grandfather. Now that he had escaped the massacre, he had begun to feel the burden of his conscience and his obligation to avenge the deaths. After studying his new father closely while he talked with the older man, White Eagle was favorably impressed that this man's medicine was indeed as powerful as his mother had told him. With such a man as the Mountain Hawk to ride with him, he might be able to seek out the murdering dogs that killed his mother. "I don't want to return until I have taken the scalps of those who killed my mother and grandfather."

This statement was met with undisguised incredulity on the faces of both white trappers. Buck was the first to reply. "Well, now, that's a mighty tall order for a pup your size. Just how do you plan to go about it?"

White Eagle was not discouraged. He turned to Trace and asked, "Are you not the one the Blackfeet call the Mountain Hawk? My mother told me of your great medicine, that the Blackfeet could not kill you. If this is so, then you must go with me to avenge the death of my mother."

Trace shot an accusing glance at Buck. *What in tarnation have you brought me?* Already he was beginning to regret letting Buck catch up to him. He and Buck had just narrowly escaped having their hair lifted by Iron Pony's band of warriors, leaving the Black Hills running for their lives. Now this young'un expected him to go back to fight the whole bunch. Trying his best to be patient and understanding of the youngster's state of mind, Trace responded to White Eagle's questions.

"I think we'd better get a few things straight right away. First, the Blackfeet can kill me just like any other man that gets careless around 'em—same goes for the Sioux, the Snakes, the Cheyenne, anybody else. I don't have any special medicine. I'm just careful. It's true the Blackfeet call me the Mountain Hawk, but that's their doing. I'm just a man—like Buck or your grandfather. Is that understood?"

"Yes, I understand," White Eagle answered, but there was a doubting gleam in his eye. His mother, Blue Water, was not one to exaggerate, and she had told him of Trace's special medicine.

"Tomorrow, we'll start for the Green River, see if we can find Chief Washakie's village and some of your kin." To Buck he said, "We can ride together over South Pass as long as you're set on going back to Promise Valley."

Buck grunted his approval, and they settled in for the night. White Eagle made no protests over Trace's refusal to ride with him to wipe out Iron Pony's warriors. The boy remained in the background, listening to the two men talk until it was time to turn in. But if they thought he was that easily dissuaded, they did not know White Eagle very well.

Buck awoke the next morning to find Trace already up and saddling his horse. "You're in kind of a rush this mornin, ain'tcha?" the old trapper muttered as he threw his blanket back and started rubbing some of the stiffness out of his legs. "I swear, one of these mornin's these old bones are just gonna stove up solid." Realizing then that Trace's mind was fully occupied with readying his horses for travel, he looked around him for some sign of potential danger.

"The boy's gone," Trace said, "lit out during the night." He continued packing up his belongings.

"Well, I'll be . . ." Buck muttered, astonished. "What in hell would he wanna do that for?" When there was no immediate response from Trace, he continued to speculate. "I reckon he was in a bigger hurry than we were."

"He didn't head out for South Pass," Trace stated unemotionally. "He's on his way back toward the Black Hills, judging from the trail he took out of here."

Buck detected a hint of irritation in Trace's tone. "I reckon he's still got a notion of revenge in his head." He paused before adding, "A fool notion that's gonna cost him his scalp."

"That's exactly what he's got on his mind—the damn little fool." Trace turned to face Buck who was still sitting on his blanket, rubbing his legs. "The little coyote took my bow case and arrows with him."

Buck couldn't help but smile. This was the main reason for Trace's irritation. It wasn't the fact that White Eagle had taken his quiver as much as it just naturally got Trace's goat that the boy had been able to steal it without waking him. "Well, ain't that something now? You aimin' to go after him?"

"I reckon—I sure as hell ain't gonna let him run off with my bow."

Trace didn't voice it, but Buck knew that the bow case and quiver that White Eagle had taken was a gift to Trace from the boy's mother. Blue Water had made it from otter skins and decorated it with colored beads and porcupine quills. Trace would never admit it, but he'd probably just as soon lose his rifle as that quiver. Buck got up and poked around the ashes of the campfire, until he generated a spark of life. "I don't reckon I'm gonna go with you, Trace. I need to be gittin' on back to Promise. I ain't as young as I used to be, and I don't wanna git caught up in them mountains by an early snow. Hope there ain't no hard feelin's."

Trace looked at his old friend, a faint smile on his face. "Ah, hell no, Buck. Like you said, he's my son. I'll go after the young scamp, maybe warm the seat of his britches for him." He laughed, the first sign that he had gotten over his initial irritation. "I'll bet that's something he's never had before, growing up in a Snake village."

So the two friends parted—one toward South Pass, the other to the east, toward the Powder River. Buck had been away from Promise Valley all summer and he was ready to sleep on a bed for a change. He thought about his longtime friend as he skirted the Bighorns. There would come a day when Trace would be forced to give up his wild and free existence. Buck wondered if Trace would ever be prepared to face that day—a hawk didn't thrive too well in captivity. Then he thought about the boy, probably on his way to getting killed. Buck suspected there was another reason for going after the boy—it wasn't for the bow case alone. He had caught Trace intensely studying the boy a couple of times, no doubt seeking to find just how deeply his blood ran in White Eagle's veins. Buck was convinced that the boy had exposed a new side of Trace McCall, a serious side that maybe Trace himself wasn't aware of. But Buck had suspected a deep sense of decency and responsibility in his longtime friend. In a way, Buck envied him. Thinking back over his past, when he was Trace's age, there had been several periods when he was living with an Indian woman. He might be a father himself for all he knew—he never stayed around long enough to find out. And he was a little ashamed to admit that he might have run sooner if he had found out that he was. On the other hand, a conscience was a mighty hard thing for a man to live with—maybe he didn't envy Trace so much after all.

CHAPTER 9

Luke Austen sat on his horse at the edge of the parade ground waiting for the formation to be assembled. In a few moments, the bugler sounded "Boots and Saddles" although most of the men already had their horses saddled and were standing around waiting. Sergeant J. C. Turley, a thirteen-year veteran, pulled his horse alongside Luke's.

"The captain," Turley commented, "he sure loves to go by the book when he leads a patrol."

Luke only smiled in response, but he had been thinking the same thing. Most officers on frontier duty relaxed garrison regulations when in the field. Luke supposed Leach didn't feel he received the respect he deserved from the men, and that probably accounted for his passion for military courtesy. At the command, *"To horse"*, Luke and Turley moved to their assigned places in the formation while each trooper stood at the head of his horse. When Leach was satisfied that all were standing ready, the commands, *"Prepare to mount"*, followed almost immediately by, *"Mount"*, were given. Leach paused for a long moment to make sure no one anticipated his next commands, then he instructed Luke to have Sergeant Turley put the detail in motion. Turley sang out, "Right by twos," and the column was underway. This was not going to be a pleasant patrol. Luke was sure of that. Ordinarily, he would have led the detail himself, but Leach decided to lead this one, apparently to demonstrate to Luke that the captain did not have confidence in his ability to lead—Leach's form of punishment for the loss of the patrol in the Black Hills. Since it had been decided not to publicize the massacre, it prevented Leach from court-martialing Luke. Deprived of that pleasure, Leach obviously sought to punish his lieutenant through a constant campaign of demeaning orders and comments.

The patrol was strictly a search mission, an effort to find Iron Pony's band and punish them for the massacre in the Black Hills. Leach had ordered grain and rations for fifteen days, and the line of march was to be north to intercept the Belle Fourche River, where the trapper Trace McCall had reported Iron Pony's last known camp. In Luke's opinion, this was a useless patrol. It was highly unlikely that Iron Pony was still camped on the Belle Fourche. More than likely, he would have grazed off most of the feed for his ponies, depleted the game, and moved his village to a new site. Even if they were lucky enough to find Iron Pony, he might not choose to fight a force of sixty soldiers armed better than his braves. If that was the case, he would simply disappear into the prairie, leaving the patrol to scout endless gullies and coulees, and in constant fear of ambush.

Luke dropped back to ride beside Sergeant Turley. Turley said nothing, but his expression was enough to tell Luke what he was thinking. Luke smiled and shook his head. He wondered himself when Leach would give the command to march at ease. The fort was a good two miles behind them already, and the men were still in a close formation. Finally Leach decided discipline was firmly established, flankers were sent out, and the Indian scouts were sent on ahead.

"Looks like the captain learned something from your last patrol, sir," Turley remarked, a wry smile on his ruddy face, "not to send Sioux out to find Sioux."

"Looks that way," Luke agreed. Leach had taken six Pawnee scouts to search for Iron Pony. They were bitter enemies of the Sioux. In fact, one of the major problems Leach had been faced with when he arrived at Laramie was to keep the Pawnee scouts away from the Sioux scouts in order to keep them from killing each other.

Captain Leach called a halt after making thirty miles the first day. Due to a late start from Fort Laramie, the customary short march on the first day of a campaign— usually about fifteen miles—was extended. The troop went into camp by a small stream that cut through a wide grassy draw. A picket line was set, guards were detailed, and individual cookfires allowed. There being no readily available wood for the fires, the men were sent out to collect buffalo chips.

After a tour of the perimeter to check on the pickets, Luke returned to prepare his dinner of salt pork and hardtack. In a show of relaxed discipline, Leach invited Luke and Sergeant Turley to eat with him. Luke and Turley shared the fire with Leach's orderly while the three of them fried the salty meat.

Leach smoked a cigar while he waited for the orderly to prepare his meal.

"I want to make the fork of the Cheyenne River by tomorrow night," Leach informed them.

"I expect the Cheyenne's a good fifty miles from here," Luke answered, exchanging quick glances with Turley.

"I know how far it is, Lieutenant," Leach snapped.

"Yessir, of course you do. I was just pointing out that it was a long day's march."

A thin smile etched Leach's face as his eyes riveted

on Luke's face. "It only seems long to you, Lieutenant. That's one of the things I intend to correct about this outfit. There's been too much mollycoddling of the men in this troop. They've gotten too complacent, too soft. That's one of the reasons for the loss of thirty-four men under your command, sir. I intend to return to Fort Laramie with sixty hardened fighting men."

Luke said nothing in his defense, biting his tongue until it almost bled. No matter what Buck Ransom and Trace McCall had reported to the contrary, Leach was still intent upon placing the entire blame for the massacre squarely on Luke's shoulders. Sergeant Turley fixed his gaze steadily upon the coffee cup he held in his hands, embarrassed for the lieutenant being chastised before an enlisted man. The balance of the meal was finished in stony silence until Luke excused himself to check on the guards again. Turley took the opportunity to withdraw also, saying it was time to see to the men. Leach smiled to himself as he watched the two men depart, confident that he was instilling long-needed discipline.

Thoughts of Annie Farrior occupied Luke's mind when the column was underway again early the next morning, driving out the unpleasantness of Leach's cutting remarks. The captain's attitude toward him had caused Luke to wonder if it was an opinion shared by the rest of the personnel at Fort Laramie. Was he now branded as an officer the men were reluctant to serve under? The thought worried him as he had made his rounds of the pickets the night before. But if the men shared the captain's feelings toward him, they showed no evidence of it, each picket offering a polite greeting as he passed—some even pausing to pass a few words of conversation.

But now, in the early-morning light, when a soft mist lay on the dark ribbon of water that parted the knee-high buffalo grass, Luke thought of her. She would still be sleeping, or maybe not—maybe she rose early to start breakfast for the Thomases. He decided not. He'd rather picture her sleeping, her dark hair laying touseled around her face, her lips full and soft—lips like a heady wine, sweet and intoxicating. *Damn!* he suddenly thought. *This patrol will seem like eternity. What if she's not there when we return? But she said she would stay, dammit!* He shook his head to rid it of such thoughts lest he drive himself mad before the patrol was over.

"What's the matter, Lieutenant?" Sergeant Turley was suddenly at his side.

"Nothing, just a little chill, I guess—made me shudder," he lied. *You'd best keep your mind on your business, mister,* he scolded himself.

"Yessir, it is gettin' a little chilly. I expect we'll see some snow before much longer. At least, that's what Mr. Thomas back at Laramie says." Like Luke, Turley was new to this part of the country. He had campaigned in Mexico in '48, but had no experience with the Sioux or Cheyenne. Actually very few of the troopers assigned to Fort Laramie had been *blooded*. Luke thought of thirty-four dragoons who had been blooded—and didn't live to tell it. *Well, with Pawnee scouts, we won't have to worry about being led into a Sioux ambush.*

It was almost dark when the scouts rode back to report the Cheyenne River ahead. Leach had made his fifty miles, but not without a grueling strain on horses and men. Like it or not, he was going to be forced to shorten the next day's march—he could drive the men till they dropped, but the horses had to be rested. Otherwise they would be useless in the event the hostile Sioux were sighted. The larger, grain-fed horses the army rode were no match for the faster Indian ponies when the soldiers' mounts were well rested. Fatigued and footsore, they were in no condition to flee or pursue.

Even Leach was not immune to the irritable mood of his men. Realizing that morale was an extremely important factor in the performance of a fighting unit, he endeavored to instill a sense of pride in the detachment. "My compliments," he began in a hastily called formation. "You men have shown what a highly motivated unit of dragoons can do when conditions demand. You should be proud of yourselves. We'll rest here until ten o'clock tomorrow morning. Then I intend to find this murdering band of savages and teach them what it's like to face a real fighting unit." Expecting a rousing cheer for his remarks, Leach was disappointed when he was met with stony silence. He ordered Luke to dismiss the formation and set the picket line.

The following morning, the Pawnees were sent out to scout the river up ahead while the troop cooked their breakfast. After making his rounds of the men, Sergeant Turley dropped down beside Luke, who was intent upon removing the worms from a piece of salt pork he was about to cook.

"It's just more meat, Lieutenant," Turley said with a chuckle.

"You're welcome to add 'em to your breakfast. I'm afraid they might not mix with the bugs in the hardtack," Luke returned. Some of the men didn't bother to pick the worms out of the salty meat, but Luke couldn't stomach them.

Turley graciously accepted the cup of coffee Luke offered after first glancing over at the large cottonwood under which Captain Leach had set up his command tent. Leach frowned upon the fraternization between enlisted men and officers, thinking it only permissible upon special occasions, as when he had invited Turley to join him for supper two nights before. The sergeant was about to comment on the quality of the coffee when there was a flurry of activity at the far end of the camp. He and Luke both stood up to see what had caused it.

Three of the Pawnee scouts had ridden into camp, quirting their ponies hard. One of them was leading a pony with the body of a fourth Pawnee draped across the saddle. Luke and Turley hurried to the crowd of soldiers that had already gathered around the Pawnees, joined a few seconds later by Captain Leach.

The Pawnee had been scalped, his arms and legs slashed, his groin mutilated, and his eyes gouged out. Some of the men, upon seeing the ghastly sight backed away in horror. Along with Leach, Luke and Turley pushed through the crowd to the wildly ranting Pawnees. After a few minutes of inflamed raving in a tongue that none of the whites understood, the scouts finally calmed down enough to talk in broken English. They said that the dead one had crossed the river to scout the other side and disappeared for a long time. Worried about him, these three went looking for him and found him where he had been jumped by several Sioux—how many, they were not sure. The other two, of the six scouts, were about a mile ahead of them and these three were uncertain about their safety.

"Well, looks like we've found our Sioux," Turley said softly.

"Or they've found us," Luke replied.

Turley shook his head slowly. "Wonder why they mutilate 'em so damned much?"

"Buck Ransom says they do it so that their enemies can't find their way in the spirit world," Luke answered.

"All right, men," Leach sang out, "we've found

them. By God, they've made their first mistake in alerting us of their presence." He raised his hat over his head and waved it as if to rally his troops. "Bugler! 'Boots and Saddles'! Mr. Austen! I want to be ready to ride in fifteen minutes. I want to catch them before they have a chance to run."

Luke hesitated. "Sir, we don't know where they are or how many. Shouldn't we send the scouts back out to see what we're dealing with?"

He received a cold hard stare in reply, then Leach said, "I'll tell you what I'm dealing with—I'm dealing with a lieutenant that hasn't learned yet how to carry out orders." The two officers stood glaring at each other amid the frantic hustle of a camp breaking up with men and horses running in all directions, shouting and cursing under the blaring notes of the incessant bugle. "It doesn't make a damn how many there are," Leach shouted. "With sixty mounted dragoons, I can take any Indian village."

"Well, one thing's for certain," Luke said, his voice laden with disgust, "they damn sure know where we are, and how many. So, if they don't run, God help us."

"I already have you marked for insubordination, Austen. Do I have to add cowardice to that?"

Luke had had a bellyfull of the sarcastic captain. "I don't give a damn what you have marked down—write it on a piece of paper and stick it up your ass."

Leach blanched and took a step backward, his face a twisted mask of fury. "Consider yourself under arrest, mister. You'll answer for this when we get back to Laramie." He turned to Turley, who was standing dumbstruck during the brief confrontation. "Sergeant, you are a witness to this officer's insubordination."

Luke turned on his heel and headed for his horse. "Damn fool," he muttered to himself. "With him in command, we'll be damn lucky if any of us get back to Laramie."

While the troopers scurried to get mounted and underway, the three Pawnee scouts painted themselves and their ponies for war. When they rode to the front of the column, ponies prancing, feathers flying in the wind, they were singing war chants and songs of vengence. At this time, their two missing brothers had not shown up and it was feared they had met with the same fate as the first one.

The column moved upriver to the point where the slain Pawnee scout had been found. There the scouts covered the area, looking for tracks that would tell them what size force had killed their brother. Then the three of them parlayed over what they had found and reported to Captain Leach.

"Eight ponies, no more, go that way," he pointed toward the northwest.

"Let's get after them," Leach commanded, and the column was underway again, the Pawnee scouts leading them out across the rolling prairie.

They had been in the saddle for less than fifteen minutes when they sighted buzzards circling on the far side of a rise back in the direction of the river. As Luke suspected, they found the mutilated remains of the two missing Pawnees. Unfortunately, the buzzards had been at work for a good while, leaving very little but bones and a few rags to bury. This latest discovery set the remaining three scouts off in a death song again, a loud mournful chant that seemed to try Leach's patience.

"Sergeant," he barked, "get some men with shovels and get them in the ground. We're wasting time."

One of the scouts, a short sturdy-looking Pawnee named Bad Horse, was a cousin of one of the slain men. He was visibly upset at the hastily scratched

graves, protesting that his cousin should have been
buried with more dignity befitting the warrior that he
had been. Bad Horse complained that the first scout
killed back near the river had been rudely covered
with sand and stones. Now he wanted time to properly prepare his cousin for his journey to the spirit
world. Leach had little patience with him. In his mind,
he had already shown more than ample compassion
when he delayed the column for even the short time it
took to cover them with dirt. After all, they were Indians. His plea rejected, Bad Horse threatened to take
the other two scouts and return to Laramie, leaving the
soldiers to find the Sioux themselves. Leach did not
take kindly to threats, especially from savages.

"By God, I'll blow a hole in that heathen head of
yours if you quit my command." He pulled his pistol
and pointed it at Bad Horse's forehead. "Do you understand?"

Bad Horse recoiled in anger, but he thoroughly understood that the captain was serious and would not
hesitate to kill him. Luke saw the muscles in Bad
Horse's arms tightening and he stepped forward,
ready to interfere if the Pawnee decided to act. But Bad
Horse held his anger. Still seething, he suddenly
turned away and moved back to stand with the other
scouts. While the column was forming up to ride, the
three Pawnees talked quietly among themselves. They
didn't look any too happy about the treatment Bad
Horse had received. Luke wondered if there would be
trouble from the scouts before this campaign was completed.

But, as before, the three scouts rode out ahead of the
column, flankers were sent out to the sides, and a
trooper took the point five or six hundred yards in
front of the main body. Leaving the Cheyenne River
behind them, the detachment moved up a dry coulee

to a grass-covered flat beyond. The flankers rode the rims of the coulee, their eyes peeled for any sign of Indian activity. Using a crude map, drawn for him by Jim Bridger, Leach calculated that the direction the Pawnees had started out would eventually lead them to the Powder River.

Although Bridger certainly knew the country well enough to draw an accurate map, Luke would have felt a good deal more confident if a seasoned scout like Buck Ransom or Trace McCall had accompanied them. He had his concerns about the Pawnee scouts. Leach should not have insulted them. One thing Luke had learned in the short time he had been assigned to this country was that an Indian had a great deal of pride as well as a sense of dignity. Leach apparently had not learned that yet, or simply didn't care. In any case, his treatment of the Pawnee scouts certainly wasn't going to help matters.

There was a definite sense of wariness throughout the whole detachment now that it was known that hostiles could not be far away. Each soldier had been provided with a vivid picture of the Indian's capacity for butchery, as witnessed by the condition of the three Pawnee corpses. The flankers especially were alert as they scanned the rolling hills around them, knowing that they would probably feel the first thrust in the event of an attack.

After a two-hour ride, with no sign of the Sioux, the tension began to lift among the troopers and pretty soon the normal banter began among the soldiers. Leach, expecting to have made some sighting of the Sioux almost immediately, was now frustrated, his patience waning with each mile that was void of sign. It soon became apparent to him that the column had continued on the same course since leaving the Cheyenne, with no variance in direction.

"Recall the point man," Leach finally ordered. When the private had galloped back to join the column, Leach questioned him. "Are the scouts still tracking the Sioux? We seem to be making no progress in catching up to them."

"I don't know, sir," Private Orwell replied. "I ain't had no contact with 'em for an hour."

"But you can see them ahead of you, can't you?" Leach prodded impatiently.

Orwell hesitated. "Well, no, sir, not for 'bout an hour. When we first started out, I saw 'em. They'd signal once in a while. It was always the same, just kept waving me on toward them hills in the distance. Then, when I didn't see 'em for a while, I figured I was supposed to keep going—figured if I was supposed to change direction, they'd show up again to tell me—so I just kept going."

Leach was flustered. He didn't know if he should chew Orwell out or not. One thing was clear, however, the detachment had been marching for the better part of two hours in a straight line for what even Leach knew to be highly concentrated Sioux country. Ignoring his second in command, he turned to Sergeant Turley. "What do you think, Sergeant?"

Turley glanced apologetically at Luke before answering. The sergeant recognized the obvious slight by Leach. Luke acknowledged Turley's concern with a faint smile and a nod. Like Luke, Turley had witnessed the threat Leach had made toward Bad Horse. "Captain," he said, "what I think is that we're riding on a wild goose chase. I think them Pawnees took off and left us out here with no scouts. They ain't coming back."

There was no apparent reaction in Leach's eyes as he received Turley's opinion. He stared, unblinking, at his sergeant for a long moment, realizing that what

Turley said was probably true. His confidence slipped, but for only a moment, then his arrogant sense of superiority returned. "Well, no matter, we should be able to do our own scouting. Sergeant, send two men out to scout the country ahead. We'll continue on until we find the enemy or until we strike the Belle Fourche."

It was getting on toward the middle of the afternoon when a small party of Sioux riders were spotted on a rise off toward the west. One of the troopers serving as scout rode back to alert the captain. "By God, I knew we would find them," Leach exulted. "How many?"

"We counted eight of 'em, sir."

"Eight, huh?" Leach smiled. "That's got to be the party that killed our scouts. Good work, Private! Go on back and don't let them get out of your sight." He paused to watch the private wheel his horse and gallop off again, then he turned to Turley. "Sergeant, we're going to catch that bunch. Turn the column out toward that rise . . at a canter."

Luke watched Turley drop back to pass on Leach's orders, then gave voice to his concern. "Captain, don't you think we should find out if these eight Sioux are part of a larger band? They could be decoys."

Leach blistered Luke with a gaze filled with contempt. "Mister, I don't believe I requested your opinion on this matter. But since you insisted on giving it, I'll respond. I imagine this small party of Sioux is just that, a small party out to cause mischief—eight hostiles, the same eight horses the Pawnee scouts tracked back at the river." His eyes flashed fire as he added, "I hope to hell they are part of a larger band. It'll be an excellent chance to teach the bastards a lesson in modern warfare."

Luke fell in line behind the captain and Sergeant Turley as the column moved out smartly toward the low hills to the west. The pace seemed a bit strained for horses that had still not been properly rested, but Leach spurred them on. *We're not going to be able to give much chase if we do spot them*, Luke thought as he held his mount to the pace. Cresting a slight rise that led to a flat a half mile wide, they were met by the two men who had been sent out as scouts. Riding hard, they slid to a stop before the captain, waving their arms excitedly.

"They're still there!" Private Orwell blurted, struggling with the reins in an effort to prevent a collision with the captain's mount.

"Where?" Leach demanded, standing in his stirrups to get a better look.

"Yonder," Orwell responded, pointing to the far side of the flat.

Luke pulled up beside Turley. They were there all right, eight Sioux warriors, sitting on their ponies, calmly watching the approaching soldiers. Turley spoke. "Hell, they're just settin' there. They don't look like they're worried about us, do they?"

"They probably aren't," Luke answered. "We better look out for something fishy."

Overhearing Luke's remark, Leach gave him a quick glance, then turned back to Orwell. "Any sign of any more hostiles in the area?"

"Nossir, just them eight—for as far as we could see."

"Very well," Leach replied, "let's get after them, then."

The eight Sioux warriors remained on the far edge of the flat plain and watched the advancing military column. Motionless, save for the occasional flutter of a feather in the light breeze or the stamping of a pony's hoof, they seemed almost unconcerned that the soldiers were of any danger to them. In one line, side by side, they continued to sit there until the troopers had cut the distance between them in half. Then, as if on a signal, they raised lances and bows, shaking them defiantly at the oncoming soldiers, and calling out insults and war whoops. When the troopers broke into a gallop, the Sioux wheeled and sped away toward the low line of hills to the west.

Knowing his tired horses were no match for the Indian ponies, Leach nonetheless spurred his command onward, fearing the hostiles would escape into the rolling prairie. Just as the galloping army mounts seemed to be closing the distance, the hostiles disappeared down a narrow draw. Leading the charge, Leach galloped into the draw behind them only to discover the Sioux were nowhere in sight.

With a signal of his hand, Leach halted the column, which was by this time strung out rather thin as the weaker horses had become unable to keep up with the stronger mounts. Realizing that he was blindly following the small party of Sioux into a possible ambush, Leach shouted, "Flankers! Sergeant Turley, get flankers out! Be alert now. I don't want to lose these savages." He frantically scanned the grass-covered slopes on either side.

Luke dismounted to try to give his weary horse a rest. Most of the men followed suit, causing the captain's anger to flare. "Dammit! I didn't give the order to dismount!" Sheepishly, the guilty troopers climbed back aboard their winded mounts.

Luke couldn't hold his tongue any longer. Leading his horse up beside Leach's, he said, "If we don't rest these damn horses, we're gonna be chasing those Indians on foot."

Leach's eyes narrowed, his face contorted in rage. "By God, Austen, I won't tolerate any more of your . . " The sudden thud of an arrow in the ground a few yards in front of his horse caused him to bite off his threat. In the next few moments, several arrows landed near the first. Leach pulled his horse back.

"There!" someone shouted. "On the ridge!"

Luke looked in the direction now being pointed out by several of the men behind him. The hostiles had crossed over the rim of the draw and were kneeling in the high grass. It seemed a useless gesture, shooting at the soldiers. The range was too far for their bows. Luke decided it was just a form of harassment.

"Sergeant," Leach ordered, "bring some rifles to bear on that ridge. Let's see how they like a little hot lead."

"Yessir," Turley replied and signaled for the first twelve men to advance. After they were in place, he ordered a volley fired at the hostiles still kneeling in the tall grass on the ridge. The heavy silence of the valley was split by the roar of twelve rifles discharging simultaneously. Luke watched the ridge intently as a thin cloud of blue rifle smoke floated above the line of troopers now reloading in anticipation of a second order to fire. Leach held up his hand, ordering them to wait. He wanted to evaluate the effect of the volley. It was not as he had anticipated. The eight Sioux warriors yelled defiantly, waving their weapons in the air and making insulting gestures. Leach was furious. "Sergeant, aren't there any marksmen in this company?"

Turley didn't reply immediately, but Luke knew what the sergeant was thinking. One of the first things Turley had complained about when assigned to this regiment was the poor quality of recruits. Green and inexperienced, most of them foreign-born, some had not fired their rifles since their induction into the army. It was a source of frustration to professional soldiers like Turley that, due to the lack of ample supplies of lead and powder, there was no allowance for target practice. Consequently, no one should have been surprised by the poor marksmanship exhibited by the troopers.

After the ineffective volley that sprayed the tall buffalo grass around them, there was little wonder that the eight Sioux warriors expressed their open contempt. Turley was about to order a second volley when the eight hostiles let fly another flight of arrows—this time, some of the missiles landed close to the mounted soldiers.

"Gimme that!" Turley barked, taking the rifle from the soldier nearest him. He checked the load then spurred his horse a few yards in front of the column. Taking careful aim, he pulled the trigger. An instant later, one of the hostiles yelped in pain as the rifle ball imbedded itself deep in his shoulder. This prompted the Indians to retreat to their ponies, and with two of them helping the wounded man, they leaped on their horses and disappeared over the far side of the ridge.

"After them!" Leach shouted, encouraged by the wounding of the hostile. And the column was off again, pushing their exhausted horses up the side of the ridge. At the top, the soldiers halted momentarily while Leach looked frantically over the rolling hills before them, searching for signs of the hostiles.

"There they go!" Turley shouted, pointing to another rise a few hundred yards off to their left. Luke followed Turley's outstretched arm and saw the eight Sioux as their ponies scampered up the slope. At the top, they paused to once again hurl defiant gestures at their pursuers.

Leach was off again immediately, leading his troopers down the grassy slope toward the next ridge. "Come on, boys," he shouted in encouragement, "their horses are as tired as ours. Don't give 'em a chance to rest."

Having no choice in the matter, Luke followed his captain's lead, but it seemed to him that Leach was embarking upon a foolhardy endeavor. Luke remembered something that Buck Ransom had once told him—that the smaller, faster Indian ponies could run the army's horses into the ground. Their horses were already near foundering, but Leach had blood in his eye and an overpowering desire to punish the Sioux. He was determined not to let the Indians escape. Luke wondered how far Leach would go before he realized they might all be afoot.

By the time the heavy army mounts had gained the base of the next rise, the hostiles were on their ponies and gone again, disappearing down the far side. Charging up to the top of the ridge, the troop halted once more and searched for the fleeing Sioux. Someone spotted them galloping toward a stream, lined with heavy brush and a few cottonwoods—a good half mile away.

"Dammit," Leach muttered when he realized that he was no closer than before—the Sioux had actually increased the distance between them. Without hesitation, he signaled the column forward. Down the side of the ridge they went, some horses beginning to stumble as they struggled to maintain their footing. Leach spurred his mount mercilessly, while constantly waving his men onward. Into a narrow defile they galloped, only to be brought to a stop by the sudden appearance of a lone rider standing squarely in their path.

Holding his horse back to keep from colliding with Turley's, who was fighting to keep his horse from plowing into Leach's mount, Luke was startled to recognize the solitary figure of Trace McCall, casually biding his time in the middle of the trail, patiently waiting for them to approach.

Leach was mystified. "What the hell . . ?" was all he managed to utter.

While the surprised troopers stacked up behind their officers, Trace nudged his pony gently with his heels, and the paint moved obediently forward to meet the column at the mouth of the draw. Before he could speak, Captain Leach demanded, "McCall, what in hell are you doing here?"

"Well," Trace began, taking his time to reply, "figuring on saving you a heap of hurt, I reckon." He glanced at Luke and nodded, then looked at the column of soldiers behind Luke, taking note of the spent horses and drawn faces of the troopers. Turning back to Leach, he asked, "Where are your scouts?"

"They deserted," Leach snapped back.

Trace considered this for a moment. "I guess that explains why you're letting that bunch of Sioux run you all over the territory."

Leach was at once incensed and not about to be chastised by this half-wild individual. "We were about to overtake those murdering savages when you got in the way."

Trace fixed the bristling captain with a look of contempt. "You weren't even close to catching up to those warriors—and you never will, that is, until they're ready for you to catch 'em—which would be pretty damned soon now—as soon as you can drag your wore-out horses down to that creek."

"What do you mean?" Leach demanded impatiently.

"It's just a guess on the number, but I'd say there's about two hundred Sioux warriors waiting for your soldierboys to come riding down to that water."

Leach was stunned, but after a moment he recovered enough of his arrogance to retort. "Good! I believe sixty well-armed mounted dragoons are more than enough to handle two hundred savages." He pulled on his reins as if to go around the mountain man. Trace moved to the side to block him again.

"Captain, I'm trying my damnedest to save your ass. You've been slickered by one of the Injuns' favorite tricks. They sent that small bunch of warriors out to lead you all over hell and back—wear your horses out so you can't run. Now they're gonna lead you right into an ambush."

Leach finally received the message, but he was still stubborn enough to make protests. "I still like the odds—sixty rifles against their bows and arrows."

His impatience clearly defined in his face now, Trace nevertheless responded calmly. "Captain, there's at least fifty rifles in that bunch. You go riding in there and there's gonna be another massacre."

Leach hesitated, his resolve finally broken when reminded of the massacre of the thirty-four troopers under Luke's command in the Black Hills. For the first time, the sobering possibility of a second disaster penetrated his feeling of invincibility. He looked behind him at his detachment of weary mounts and men, as if just then noticing their condition. Calmer then, but still unwilling to acknowledge any careless actions on his part, he reluctantly thanked Trace for the warning. "You're right, McCall, they have a superiority in numbers. It's best to let them go this time. But I hate to miss an opportunity to fight the bastards."

The hint of a smile parted Trace's lips. "Oh, you're gonna be in a fight, all right. It's just a question of where, and on whose terms. Your horses are spent. Ol' Iron Pony already knows that and he's waiting for you. As soon as he figures out that you ain't coming no more, he'll be after you like bees after a bear."

"You're saying we'd better set up a defensive position?" Luke asked. He had been silent up until then, and only spoke because it appeared Leach was undecided as to what he should do.

Trace nodded, then said, "But not here—they'd be above you on both sides here. If you can make it about a mile and a half back over the ridge, the creek winds back below that butte. You can dig rifle pits on both sides of the stream and have a clear field of fire before you."

"Very well, McCall," Leach said, "lead us out."

Very well, indeed, Luke thought, knowing Trace had just saved their necks, even though they were not out of the fire as yet. He filed in behind Trace as the tall scout Buck Ransom had called the Mountain Hawk led the column back the way they had come. When he reached a shallow draw that led off to the west, Trace followed it for a few hundred yards until he found a place to climb up the side that would be easier on the weary horses. Turning south then, he set a course that would intercept the stream.

As soon as they reached the banks of the stream, Turley began positioning his men on either side and ordered them to start digging. At Trace's suggestion, the horses were herded into the middle and allowed to drink. To most of the men, young and inexperienced, Trace McCall remained a mysterious figure as the buckskin-clad mountain man rode slowly up and down the line of frantically working soldiers, his eyes taking in the defensive preparations as well as occasionally checking the hills they had just recently deserted. Seeing Luke Austen striding over to meet him, Trace dismounted and let his horse drink from the stream.

"Howdy, Lieutenant," Trace said.

Luke smiled broadly, offering his hand. "Trace Mc-

Call—you do seem to show up when you're most needed." Trace only shrugged in response. Luke went on, "How do you happen to be out here, anyway? Looking for us?"

"No," Trace answered. "I just stumbled on you boys. I'm looking for somebody else. I saw that big party of Sioux hiding back there by the water, and I knew they were planning a little reception for somebody. So I decided to have a look-see." Trace thought it unnecessary to say that he had come in search of Iron Pony's band himself, and the half-Shoshoni boy who had set out to take revenge for his mother's death. Trace continued, "I watched those eight bucks when they crossed the ridge back there. It wasn't hard to figure what they were up to."

The quick smile faded from Luke's face as the seriousness of their situation returned to prompt him to ask, "What are our chances of getting out of this without a fight?"

"None," Trace quickly replied, nodding toward a low hill off to the north. Luke turned to follow Trace's gaze and saw a lone Sioux warrior in the distance, obviously scouting them. "They've already found us. Now that they know what we're gonna do, they'll be coming, all right."

Captain Leach joined them at that point and immediately asked, "Are you sure of the number of hostiles? I'd hate to think you exaggerated the count and they're getting away while we're busy digging in here."

Trace turned a cold gaze on the arrogant officer, thinking carefully before he answered. He didn't like Leach—not since the first time he laid eyes on the little martinet—and his inclination was to tell him to go scout them for himself. Leach was about to repeat the question when Trace spoke. "Captain, you're gonna get all the Injuns you can handle in the time it takes that scout on the hill over yonder to go tell Iron Pony you ain't riding into his ambush. Your sergeant did the right thing, having the men dig in and get ready. The Sioux are fighters—born to it—and these men of yours look pretty green to me. The best chance you've got of coming out of this thing with most of your men is to stay dug in here to make your fight. You've got your horses protected and plenty of drinking water. You can hold out here for a long time. If you can keep your head down, and kill off a good number of his warriors, Iron Pony might decide his losses ain't worth staying on the attack."

Leach cocked a skeptical eye at the tall man in buckskins. "I'm not so sure we couldn't dispatch this band of savages with one concentrated volley. I doubt if they've ever faced a disciplined line of dragoons."

Trace was rapidly losing his patience. He shot a quick glance at Luke Austen to see if the young lieutenant agreed with his captain. Luke showed no emotion one way or the other, staring unblinking at the mountain man. Shifting his gaze back to the captain, Trace said, "I don't know about the moral effect of a disciplined volley, but I do know about Sioux warriors. If you stand your soldiers up in a line to fight, Iron Pony ain't likely to line his boys up against you. He'll just lay back and snipe away at your soldiers till he's rubbed them all out. Then he'll likely thank you for lining up another bunch."

Leach didn't say anything right away, but Luke could see that the mountain man's obvious contempt for him was raising the captain's bile. Irritated, but reluctant to chance serious casualties in the event Trace knew what he was talking about, Leach swallowed his pride, the bitter taste of which caused him to screw his face into a deep frown. "We'll make a stand in these emplacements until I can evaluate the hostiles' fighting capability. Then we'll see."

The first sighting was not long in coming. The lone Sioux scout that Trace had spotted on the ridge had been gone for no longer than half an hour when a long line of mounted warriors suddenly appeared along the ridge line. Silent and motionless except for the occasional feather that fluttered in the gentle breeze ruffling the long buffalo grass, they presented a foreboding promise of what was to come.

After a lengthy wait with no show of action by the Sioux, Turley uttered, "Damn, how long are they gonna just sit there?"

"Long enough to make sure we see how many of them there are." Trace answered. "Iron Pony is trying to intimidate us with his superior numbers," Trace answered. "If he didn't have the advantage in numbers, he wouldn't be showing his strength. We don't have to worry yet. He ain't gonna come charging down here and take a chance on losing a lot of his warriors. Right now, he's deciding how he's gonna attack. My guess is he'll come at us from the sides, up and down this creek."

Captain Leach moved up beside Turley and Trace, his field glasses in his hand. "They're still sitting there," he said. "I believe they're having second thoughts about attacking us." He stood up, brazenly exposing himself while he scanned the seemingly endless line of warriors. "Hell, they know damn well we'll cut 'em to pieces. They've lost their stomach for a fight." He turned an accusing eye on Trace. "One attack en masse from us and they'll scatter to the wind."

Trace held his tongue. He had no more patience to waste on the arrogant officer. Looking around him at the nervous troopers, crouching low in their rifle pits and staring at the painted hostiles, he could see that

Iron Pony's intimidation ploy was successful. Unlike their bullheaded commander, the men appeared none too anxious to mount any kind of assault. Eyes wide and mouths dry, even though there was a swiftly running stream right at their backs, they nervously checked their rifles again and again. *What the hell am I even doing here?* Trace wondered. Looking for the boy, he had found Iron Pony and the soldiers, but no White Eagle. *Holed up here with a bunch of green troopers and a damn fool officer who seems hellbent on committing suicide. It ain't my job to keep the damn fool from getting scalped.* Still, he felt an obligation toward Luke and the rest of the innocent souls that Leach seemed so anxious to sacrifice. He shrugged his shoulders and moved over beside Luke.

"Lieutenant, I'm tired of trying to talk some sense into that hardheaded son of a bitch. You seem like a levelheaded young man and I hate to see you get yourself scalped because of him. I know he's your captain and he's the one supposed to be in charge. But if he orders you boys to charge up there after those Injuns, ol' Iron Pony'll just give way in the middle then close up around you and eat you up. He's just praying that you'll come after him." Having said his piece, Trace left Luke to think it over and went back to the edge of the water where his horse was waiting.

Luke was left with a desperate decision. He looked beyond the kneeling figure of Sergeant Turley and focused on Captain Henry Leach, still standing defiantly on the upper ledge of the creekbank. Luke did not doubt that what Trace McCall had told him was true—if they mounted an assault on the line of Sioux, it would result in serious losses, perhaps even total annihilation. Luke had already experienced one massacre, he wasn't anxious to be involved in another. He had been in the army too long to even think about disobeying a command from his superior. Still, did he not have an obligation to protect the men from being sacrificed for the sake of one officer's stubbornness?

Luke did not want to make the decision. He prayed to God that Leach would take Trace's advice and stay put. Suddenly thoughts of Annie popped into his mind, and he realized that he wanted desperately to see her again. He tried to form a picture of her face in his mind, but found he could not. *No matter what happens here*, he thought, "I will get back to you."

"Sir?"

Sergeant Turley's question brought him back to the present. He had been unaware that he had spoken the last part of his vow aloud. Recovering his senses quickly, he responded. "Nothing, Sergeant, I was just thinking out loud." He looked again at Leach. The captain had turned and was staring at his men, crouching in the pits. Luke knew Leach was making up his mind. "Sir," Luke said, hoping to sidetrack Leach's thinking, "I think McCall is right. We're in the best defensive position here by the stream."

Leach jerked his head around as if he'd heard a pistol shot. Glaring at his lieutenant, he barked, "I didn't come out here to go on the defensive against a ragtag mob of savages. This might be a good opportunity for you to learn what it takes to command." He turned to Turley. "Sergeant, pass the word to prepare to mount. It's time we showed these savages what it means to defy the United States Army."

"You ride out of here and they'll cut you to pieces on both flanks," Trace warned.

Leach smiled contemptuously. "They'll play hell, trying to turn my flanks if I'm charging straight into them."

"They've already done it," Trace answered calmly.

Leach snorted his disbelief, his obvious dismissal of

Trace's opinions apparent in his eyes. Displaying his impatience with those whom he regarded as fools, he extended his arm in the direction of the stoic line of Sioux on the ridge. "Unless my eyes have betrayed me, the enemy is standing in a line, waiting to be routed, and apparently showing no stomach to join in battle with a disciplined troop of cavalry."

"Maybe you need some glasses," Trace retorted, his tone low and even. "You better take a closer look at that line of warriors—a good third of 'em ain't there no more."

Trace's remark brought Leach up short, and he jerked his field glasses up again to scan the formation of Sioux more closely. The line of warriors *was* spread out a little more than before, with slightly more space between the ponies. While Leach had been contemplating a move to attack, every third or fourth warrior had slowly backed his pony unnoticed from the solid line, disappearing from view below the crest of the ridge.

Immediately leaping to the wrong conclusion, Leach exulted in what he interpreted to be a confirmation of his initial assessment of the situation. "By God, they're starting to withdraw." Turning an angry leer in Trace's direction, he spat, "Damn you, McCall, I should have never listened to you. If these savages escape, I've a good mind to put you in irons for aiding the enemy."

"That might take a little more doing than you're figuring on," Trace answered calmly, his gaze locked on that of the captain's.

A tense moment followed, while the two men glared into each other's eyes, neither man blinking. Leach was the first to break the eye contact when he suddenly turned to Sergeant Turley. "Get 'em mounted, Sergeant, we're gonna ride right over that bunch on the ridge." Running for his horse, Leach called out, "Bugler!"

Holding his horse steady in the midst of sudden confusion, Trace stood there watching the frenzied actions of the troopers as they scrambled from their rifle pits to collar their reluctant mounts. Looking across the stream to the point where the first soldiers were forming up behind their captain, Trace's gaze met that of Luke Austen's. Luke simply stared back at him, expressionless, obviously contemplating what Trace had told him before. *What a waste*, Trace thought when he perceived that Luke was not going to be able to bring himself to countermand the captain's orders—he had been a soldier too long to disobey. He glanced back at the ridge where Iron Pony's warriors remained, motionless, waiting. *Get ready, boys*, Trace said to himself, *here comes another serving of soldierboys*. Climbing on his horse, he walked the pony slowly across the stream to a point out of the way.

To the brassy blare of the bugle, Leach led his company of men up out of the creekbanks. His pistol drawn and held high overhead, he forced his tired mount into a gallop, charging straight up the rise toward the waiting Sioux. Sixty men strong, the troopers galloped, intent upon breaking the center of the hostiles' line and scattering them with their rifle fire.

Upon first seeing the soldiers' advance, the Sioux retreated slowly as if to give ground. Encouraged by this, Leach rallied his men to push recklessly onward. As the last trooper cleared the brush beside the stream, and the whole detachment was in the open, the staccato notes of the bugle were suddenly swallowed by an eruption of rifle shots. Caught in a blistering crossfire, Leach was the first man killed as Iron Pony's warriors rose up from the gullies on both sides of the troop. His tunic rent by numerous bullet holes, his eyes wild with disbelief, he fell heavily in the grass as his horse charged on, arching and bucking.

Luke looked around him, horrified to see more and more saddles suddenly empty as his men were trapped in the crossfire. "Back!" he shouted, trying to be heard over the roar of the battle, now joined by the Sioux before him on the ridge. "Back!" he continued to shout. Out of the corner of his eye, he saw Sergeant Turley trying to lead a group of troopers back toward the stream, fighting desperately to cut his way through a swarm of hostiles that had closed in behind the soldiers. With no time to reload his pistol and rifle, Luke drew his saber and hacked his way through to join Turley. Together they led what was left of Leach's command back to the stream.

Desperate and panic-stricken, the surviving troopers stumbled into the previously dug rifle pits, most of them letting their horses run free, intent only upon escaping the hail of lead balls and arrows. Ignoring a grazing wound that soaked his sleeve with blood, Luke reloaded and fired as rapidly as he could. Gradually, the attacking Sioux were driven back, thanks in large part to the efforts of Sergeant Turley, who could be heard throughout the encounter, cursing and threatening as he moved up and down the line of men until every man was firing his weapon.

As suddenly as it had started, the assault ended, and the Indians withdrew, taking their dead and wounded wherever possible. Still close to a state of shock, Luke forced himself to get up and check on the condition of his men. Upon seeing the lieutenant get to his feet, Turley made his way over, still keeping an eye on the retreating hostiles.

"Damn, Lieutenant," was all Turley could manage at first.

"How many did we lose?" Luke asked.

"Well, I can't be sure till I go back and get a careful count, but I think we're missing a good half of the patrol."

"Damn," Luke swore. "It's my fault. I knew Leach was making a big mistake. McCall tried to warn me, but I didn't have the guts to face Leach down." He paused and looked around him then. "Where is McCall, anyway?" In the chaos of the ill-fated charge, no one took notice of the mountain man's whereabouts.

Turley looked quickly around him then. Like Luke, it had not occurred to him until that moment that there was no sign of Trace McCall. "I don't know. I thought he stayed behind when we rode out of here. I reckon he took the opportunity to light out while the shooting was going on."

"Can't say as I blame him," Luke said. "He really didn't have any obligation to stay. I sure like it better when that man is around, though." With no time to waste further thought on the whereabouts of Trace McCall, Luke called his mind back to the situation at hand. After moving up and down the line of troopers now firmly entrenched in the sandy banks of the stream, giving instructions and encouragement where needed, Luke and Turley returned to discuss the possible intentions of the Sioux.

"You think they've had enough?" Turley wondered aloud. "McCall said they wouldn't stay with it if they lost too many warriors—we must have killed five or six."

Luke shook his head, never taking his eyes from the band of painted hostiles now reassembled on the ridge. "I don't think five or six casualties will be enough to drive them off, especially with the prospect of gaining sixty rifles and ammunition." He turned then to look Turley directly in the eye. "Besides, McCall said this was the same band that ambushed my patrol in the

Black Hills. They've had a real taste of blood already. I think they'll want more."

Turley was thoughtful for a long moment, thinking over the predicament they found themselves in. "I reckon we just kind of got our asses kicked real good."

"I reckon," Luke replied soberly.

Turley turned to look out across the grassy slope where the bodies of several horses still lay. Scattered among them he could see the faded blue lumps that were once troopers under his command. "I swear, Lieutenant, I wish we could bring our boys in before them savages get to 'em."

"I know. I don't like leaving them out there, either, but I don't want to lose any more men. We'll just have to leave them for the time being."

Most of the battlefield was a no man's land now with a good portion of the slope within rifle range from either side. Luke couldn't take a chance on sending a detail out to recover their dead. Near the top of the slope, where Leach had fallen, a party of Sioux brazenly stripped the captain's body. One of the warriors took Leach's scalp and held it up so the soldiers could see. "Filthy bastards," Turley spat angrily and took a shot at the jeering hostile. The ball fell harmlessly short.

"Save your ammunition, Sergeant, we're gonna need it later," Luke said. He looked back at the sun, sinking ever closer to the distant hills. In a matter of two or three hours it would be dark and then the real danger would begin. Movement upon the ridge caught his eye and he turned to see the Indians split off in two groups and disappear from his sight.

"I don't reckon they've decided to go home for supper," Turley said sarcastically.

"Looks like they're getting set to hit us from the sides—probably wait till dark. Sergeant, you better

have the men get some sleep now because there won't
be any tonight."

Turley nodded and left to follow Luke's orders.
Confirmed by a headcount, the detachment was reduced to twenty-eight men, four of whom were
wounded, though still capable of performing their duties. Twenty-eight men, he had lost over half of the
troop. The waste of it was highly grating upon Turley's
sensibilities, feeling it his responsibility to protect his
men whenever possible. He silently cursed Leach for
his arrogant foolhardiness as he moved down the line
of rifle pits, instructing every other man to rest while
the others stood guard. Before nightfall, he would
have to set a picket line before the emplacements. It
was going to be a long night.

CHAPTER 10

Little more than a mile from the embattled soldiers, a lone figure also waited for darkness. Resting comfortably in a willow thicket, his pony tethered safely out of sight, Trace McCall patiently chewed on a tough strip of buffalo jerky while he considered the events that had taken place that afternoon.

He wasn't totally surprised that Captain Leach had decided to go charging up that hill in the face of all common sense. He had pegged Leach for a fool from the beginning. But it was a damn shame to sacrifice the lives of so many men. If Trace had been in Luke Austen's place, he would have taken command—shot Leach in the head, if it took that to prevent the slaughter. But he reckoned it wasn't fair to fault the young lieutenant for refusing to mutiny. After all, Luke had been trained to obey orders without questioning.

One thing Trace had known for sure: He had better sense than to go galloping up that slope with the soldiers. So he took advantage of the commotion to slip out, down along the stream, until he was well clear of the battle. *Wasn't much of a battle, he thought, more like a turkey shoot.* He hoped Luke Austen had survived the assault, he felt a fondness for the young lieutenant. *I oughta go on about my business, and let the army go on with their hurry to get killed.* But he knew he couldn't. He also knew that he could be a hell of a lot more ef-

fective by himself behind the Sioux. If he had stayed
back at the creek, he would be just one more rifle. On
his own, he could do a lot more damage, especially
after dark. So he settled back and waited. While he
waited, he thought again of the boy, and he wondered
if he was too late to find him. White Eagle, *his son*—it
was a strange thought to him, one he was not yet comfortable with. While he had never considered the possibility of being a father, still there was a strong sense
of duty within him to find Blue Water's son—his son.
He shook his head, amazed that it was so. What
should he do with the boy, if he did find him? The sensible thing to do would be to take him to Chief
Washakie's village as he had meant to do before White
Eagle ran off.

Although it had been difficult, he had followed the
boy's trail toward the Powder River until losing it only
hours before stumbling onto the Sioux war party and
the soldiers. White Eagle had to have found Iron
Pony's camp. Had he already made some suicidal attempt to avenge Blue Water's death? Maybe common
sense arrived in time to prevent him from trying such
a foolhardy thing. Trace could only hope. One thing he
now knew, however—he was determined to find out.

Night fell with a deadly softness. Deep and moonless, the chill night air filled the coulees and draws
until the prairie around him dissolved into a vast inky
sea. It was a night made to order for his purposes. *I
wish to hell that boy hadn't took my bow*, Trace thought as
he made his way up from the willows. The work he
had to do that night called for a silent weapon. *Well, I'll
just have to borrow me one.*

If he was to be of any value to the embattled soldiers, he had to find out exactly what the Sioux war
party had in mind to do. To do that, it would be nec-

essary to work his way in close to the Sioux camp. Finding the camp would be no problem because he could already hear the singing and dancing, and the rosy glow in the dark sky beyond the ridge was indication enough that Iron Pony's warriors were already getting worked up for the battle. First, however, he decided he would scout the flank of the soldiers' position down along the creek banks to determine if a sizable force of hostiles was planning a night attack. If this turned out to be the case, Trace had no choice but to give some form of warning. It was his guess that there would be no more than a small party of scouts positioned to keep an eye on the soldiers. In all likelihood, the Sioux warriors would want to dance and make medicine for a big victory the following morning.

Leaving his horse behind in the willow thicket, he climbed up the bank and started upstream at a steady trot. Unencumbered by his rifle and bullet pouch, carrying no weapon but his knife, he was able to make good time. The rifle would be of no use to him on this night—one shot might have accounted for one dead Sioux, but it would have announced his presence to close to two hundred other warriors. He wished again that he had his own bow, a weapon he had fashioned from mountain ash, backed with sinew, made like his adoptive Crow father, old Buffalo Shield, had taught him. He was almost as confident with that bow as he was with his Hawken rifle. The bow was silent, and he could reload much faster, especially on horseback although the rifle was a hell of a lot more powerful and accurate, especially at a distance.

When he was within a few hundred yards of the embattled troopers, he slowed down to a gait between a fast walk and a trot, sharpening his senses to take in everything around him. Cautiously, he made his way closer to the water's edge, where he stopped and dropped to all fours. There on his hands and knees, he waited and listened. Looking back up toward the Sioux camp, the dark outline of the ridgetop was just barely blacker than the moonless night sky. Hearing nothing but the sound of dancing on the far side of the ridge, he started to rise again. Halfway up, he froze. A slight movement in the grass behind him caused him to tense, ready to react. It was no more than the sound a whisper of wind might make in the tall grass, but Trace instantly threw his body to the side, rolling as he hit the ground. A split second later he heard the impact of a body on the ground as a Sioux warrior barely missed him. With reactions quicker than a lightning strike, Trace was upon the dark form, his long Green River knife thrusting with deadly impact under the ribs of his would-be assailant. Thrashing violently, the two bodies rolled over and over in the tall grass in desperate struggle until the warrior was finally still.

When sure of his kill, Trace released his hold, allowing the Sioux to settle lifelessly on the ground. Moments before, with no time for thoughts beyond fighting for his life, Trace had no opportunity to determine if his attacker was a lone scout. Now he paused to listen for sounds of other warriors, making a determined effort to quiet his own rapid breathing. Satisfied that there was no immediate danger, he turned his attention back to the body before him. As the powerful adrenaline rush slowly receded, he turned the corpse over to take inventory of the warrior's weapons. There was a quiver of arrows strapped across his back, but no bow. Fortunately, it only took a few moments of searching around in the grass for the bow to turn up. He tested it and was relieved to learn that it was a good one. Armed now with the weapons he needed, he quickly moved away from the water in case one of the warrior's friends had heard sounds of the struggle.

Finding better cover in a stand of low brush that bordered the creek, he stopped to listen. Although he could not see into the soldiers' position, he detected an occasional whispered command or comment. He wondered how many of the original sixty had survived. He was about to leave the brush when he heard the soft tread of a moccasined foot upon some loose pebbles along the creek bank. Sinking back down in the brush, Trace waited until a shadowy form appeared, obviously intent upon pinpointing the source of the same whispered comment Trace had just heard. With an arrow notched on his bowstring, the Sioux strained to see through the darkness, hoping for a lucky shot at a careless trooper.

Pulling an arrow from the quiver that was now strapped to his own back, Trace took careful aim with his bow. The arrow's flight was swift and true. An instant later, a sharp cry of pain and surprise broke the heavy silence along the creek, followed almost immediately by a volley from half a dozen army rifles from the sandpits by the water. *Jesus Christ*, Trace thought as the random hail of rifle balls whistled through the brush around him. *I'd better get my ass out of here before I get killed!*

Satisfied that there was no massing of warriors to attempt to overrun the soldiers' defensive position, Trace decided to vacate the area before he ran into any more scouts. He wanted to scout the Sioux camp on the far side of the ridge, anyway. Retreating back along the stream, he paused when he came to the body of the Sioux scout. Kneeling down beside the body, he discovered that the man was still hanging onto life, although it was obvious he was rapidly losing the battle. It had been a lucky shot to have disabled the scout so quickly. At such close range, Trace's arrow had been powerful enough to penetrate the warrior's ribs, puncturing his lung, and he was drowning in his own blood. Trace decided to speed the man's departure to the spirit world, and one quick slice with his knife abruptly ended the warrior's suffering.

Trace was about to rise again when a faint glimmer of starlight reflected on a shiny object by the warrior's side. Curious, Trace paused to examine it. It appeared to be a long knife of some sort. He rolled the corpse over to reveal an army saber. *An officer's sword*, he thought. The warrior had obviously taken it from one of the two officers during the ill-fated charge. But which one? Luke or Captain Leach? *I hope to hell it was Leach*, Trace thought. *The world could get along just fine without that arrogant bastard. It would be a shame if young Austen was killed because of Leach's stubbornness.* He took the saber and headed toward the ridge.

Making his way up the rise, he passed the grim evidence of Leach's folly. As he neared the top of the ridge, it seemed there was a body every few yards—pasty white forms in the blackness of the night, stripped bare, every one mutilated. Trace did not pause but pressed on until he reached the crest where Iron Pony had originally sat, surrounded by his warriors.

Following a gully down to the base of the ridge, Trace moved quickly to a point no more than a hundred yards from the large Sioux camp. Crawling through the grass, he made his way closer and closer to the edge of the camp, stopping just outside the glow of the many campfires. He had been fairly accurate in his estimate of the number of Sioux. Chanting and dancing around one large fire, many of the warriors prepared for battle, their shadows casting long, impish forms that bobbed and darted in eerie patterns over the ground. There were no women or children in this camp, no tipis—this was strictly a war party. And it didn't take long to determine that they were not content to settle for their victory over the soldiers that day. Leach and his men were in for a total campaign of annihilation. There was no way to avoid it, unless the Sioux losses were so high that Iron Pony decided it best to call off the assault. Trace turned it over in his mind for a few moments while the incessant chanting of the dancers drummed away at his brain. There were too many of them, there was no way he—one man—could kill enough warriors to cause Iron Pony to abort the attack.

There might be another way, he thought, *if I can get close enough*. There had been times in the past—when one tribe battled another—when the leader of one of the tribes was killed, it was taken as such an ill omen that his warriors lost their confidence to fight. The plan had merit, but the problem to be solved was how to get close enough to Iron Pony without losing his own scalp—a loss that Trace planned on avoiding. *This might take a little doing*, he thought as he slowly backed away from the edge of the firelight.

Working his way around the perimeter of the camp to try to find a point where he might get a better view of the center, and the probable location of the chief, he almost stumbled into a mounted sentry circling the camp. Dropping flat on his belly, he held his breath while the Indian pony snorted a couple of times to announce the presence of a stranger. Luckily for Trace, the rider was more intent upon the activities going on around the campfire, and ignored his pony's warning. They passed no more than six feet from each other in the dark.

Trace made his way completely around the Sioux camp, stopping occasionally to lie low in the grass when one of the mounted sentries came too close. Even though it was impossible to get near the dancers without exposing his presence, it was not difficult to identify the chief. Iron Pony was easily picked out as he sat off to the side, observing the ritual. Trace watched him for a long time as warriors came to exchange brief words with him, some lingering a while to smoke with the chief.

Later in the evening, Trace suddenly tensed when he saw a white man approach Iron Pony. He had to be the man in the flat-crowned black hat that White Eagle had spoken of—the man who killed Blue Water. Trace rose to one knee, unconsciously fingering the sharp edge of the cavalry saber in his hand. He could feel the blood boiling in his veins at the mere sight of the murderer, and he forced himself to remain calm, knowing a foolish act of rage would spoil any hope of preventing the massacre of the surviving troopers trapped by the stream. *I'll settle with you later*, he promised himself and lay back close to the ground.

The chanting and dancing were still going strong when Iron Pony retired to his blankets. Trace watched as the Sioux leader excused himself and went to a small lean-to consisting of a buffalo hide propped up by a section of tree limb. There were many such shelters scattered about, although most of the warriors simply wrapped themselves in hides to sleep. Iron Pony's bed was in the center of a large circle of these makeshift beds and tents. If he was to eliminate the Sioux leader, Trace was going to have to make his way through this circle of warriors without being detected. More than dangerous, he decided it was probably stupid as well, but he was already committed to it. So he waited and watched, trying to determine how he could safely run the gauntlet of warriors between him and their chief.

Finally he decided that boldness would provide his best chance for success. He pulled his buckskin shirt off and removed his hat. With a short piece of rawhide from his shirt, he tied his hair in a tight ponytail. Even though there was still a trace of suntan on his bare torso from the warmer days of the recent summer, he scooped up some dirt and powdered himself with it to dull the skin even more. This would have to do, he thought.

Very slowly, he got to his feet and stood there motionless for a short while, looking around him to see if he had attracted anyone's attention. Satisfied that the few warriors who might have noticed him were intent on the ceremony around the huge fire, he started toward Iron Pony's bed. Carefully avoiding the light from the smaller cookfires, he walked slowly, but boldly, through the maze of hide sleeping tents—some occupied but most empty. His heart pumping heavily, looking neither right nor left, he made his way into the center of the hostile camp, relieved to find that no one paid him any notice. He held the cavalry saber tight against his leg so it would not catch anyone's eye.

He was almost there. Just as he stepped around an empty bedroll next to Iron Pony's, the chief suddenly appeared, getting up from his lean-to to relieve his bladder. He took a few steps away from his bed to do his business. Trace stopped stone-still when the chief emerged from under the hides. When it became apparent that Iron Pony had not seen him, he quickly followed the chief, looking from side to side to make sure no one else was watching.

Iron Pony stopped, suddenly sensing someone behind him. Unconcerned, he turned to see who approached. Not recognizing the tall figure striding toward him, he calmly asked, "Who is it?"

Trace held one hand up in greeting. With the other, he brought the saber up in one powerful thrust that pierced Iron Pony's belly, running him through like a piece of meat on a spit. Before the mortally wounded Sioux chief could utter a sound, Trace quickly clamped his hand over Iron Pony's mouth, stifling his cry for help. Trace caught the slumping hostile before he crumpled to the ground, supporting him with one arm. "This is for the Shoshoni women and children you slaughtered," he whispered in the dying man's ear.

When Iron Pony's eyes stopped fluttering and closed for the final time, Trace carried his body back and laid him under the lean-to. He started to withdraw the sword, but decided it might be more distressing to the rest of the Sioux to find their chief as he now was. To further work on their minds, Trace took Iron Pony's scalp. When it was finished, Trace stood over the dead hostile for a few moments, looking down at the man responsible for so many murders. If ever a man deserved killing, it was this one, but it would have been more satisfying for Trace if it had been the white man in the black hat. He ached to settle with the man who had taken Blue Water's life. But if he had killed him instead of Iron Pony, the Sioux would probably have cared very little—certainly not enough to call off their siege.

While he stood there, thinking of Blue Water, he suddenly realized that the chanting had stopped. Snapping back to his senses, he quickly looked around to see the mob of warriors around the fire beginning to disperse to take to their beds. There was no time to waste. Forcing himself to walk slowly, even casually, he retraced his steps, weaving his way through the small campsites, until he eventually dissolved into the darkness. Wasting no time, he picked up his shirt and hat and started back toward the willow thicket on the far side of the ridge.

*   *   *

Daylight was still no more than a promise when Strong Bow threw his robe aside and stood up to see the first rays of the sun crawl across the prairie. It was going to be a good day to fight, he decided. At the council of the wise ones the night before, his chief had petitioned passionately for a total victory over the remaining soldiers dug in by the stream. Iron Pony had told them that his medicine was strong and the soldiers would fall before them like they had that afternoon. Strong Bow was convinced that Iron Pony's medicine was more powerful than all the soldiers at Fort Laramie.

Soon the sun edged up over the rolling hills to the east, rapidly spreading its light over the prairie. Strong Bow looked around as other warriors emerged from their beds. It was time to prepare for battle. He turned to look toward the hide lean-to of Iron Pony's and smiled to himself. His chief was slow in rising this morning. Perhaps he had too much of the dance last night. Strong Bow would derive much satisfaction from being awake and ready to fight before his chief had stirred from his robe.

Joined by several others who were equally eager to fight, Strong Bow strode up to Iron Pony's tent. "Iron Pony," he called, "it is time to kill the soldiers." When there was no answer, he smiled to the others with him. "Iron Pony," he called his chief's name again and pulled the hide cover aside.

The small gathering of warriors gasped as one at the sudden exposure of the ghastly picture before them. Recoiling with the shock of finding their chief with a saber run through him, his face sagging as a result of his missing scalp, they stepped back in horror. Dumbfounded at first, they stared in disbelief. How could this happen right in their midst? The cry went out and soon the whole camp was alert and running toward the gathering of warriors. At once loud wailing and cries for revenge were heard. After a few chaotic minutes, calmer heads called for order, and the elder warriors of the band gathered around the body of their chief to counsel.

While the initial reaction from many of the warriors was to immediately take their vengeance from the soldiers, some of the older heads, Strong Bow among them, had other thoughts.

"This is a bad sign," Strong Bow warned, after thinking on it for a moment. "And I think maybe Man Above is not pleased with us. Iron Pony made medicine before fighting the soldiers. And though he felt his medicine was strong, someone—perhaps a spirit—came unseen into the middle of our camp and killed him." Looking around him, Strong Bow saw many heads nodding in agreement. "It is also a bad sign that he was killed with the dead soldier-chief's long knife. I cannot think for every man, but for me, I think it is a sign that our medicine is not strong for this fight. We have already killed many of the soldiers. I say we should go now and leave the others alone."

There was a great deal more discussion among the warriors, but Strong Bow's words rang a sober warning that most of the Sioux feared to be true. In the end, they decided it best not to tempt the spirits after they had sent such a clear message. The one voice that continued to protest the decision was that of the thin white man, pleading for the Sioux to continue the attack upon the soldiers. He was angrily shouted down.

Booth Dalton signaled Charlie White Bull with a subtle nod of his head, and the two quietly sidled away from the crowd toward the edge of the camp where Booth had pitched a small shelter made of two buffalo hides roughly sewn together. "I don't like the way some of them braves is lookin' us over all of a sudden," Booth said, once they had a little room between them and the large crowd of warriors milling around Iron Pony's body. Charlie nodded rapidly. Even the dullwitted half-breed had noticed the suspicious, unfriendly looks thrown his way.

Both men knew that they were only tolerated in the Sioux camp because of the guns and supplies they had been able to steal from the Montana gold fields. True, Booth and Charlie had ridden with Iron Pony on the last two raids against the soldiers from Fort Laramie, but it was through no special effort on their part that Iron Pony's braves were able to get army rifles. Booth knew that some of the young men in the camp had been grumbling for some time over the presence of the two outsiders. But Iron Pony, though generally sharing his brothers' feelings about white men, insisted that Booth and Charlie should remain—partially because Booth had led them to the small party of Snakes on their way back from Laramie, and also because Booth had convinced him that Charlie was a Santee Sioux.

Now Iron Pony was dead, and old Strong Bow was already giving them the evil eye, or so Booth thought. Booth prided himself in the ability to remove his hind end from an explosive situation before someone lit the fuse. This sense of survival was the prime factor that had allowed him and Charlie to be long gone when the Montana vigilantes rode into his camp. Now it was time to make themselves scarce around here. Booth had been dealing with Indians long enough to see trouble brewing. He knew they would chew over this omen—Iron Pony with a dead soldier's saber through his belly—until they worked it up to where Booth's presence was making their medicine bad. It always ended up that way, Booth thought.

"We'd best git our possibles together and ride on outta here while they're still arguing about it," Booth said. "No need to wait till they decide to carve us up. I can't make a red cent offen 'em anyway. They're gittin' their own damn guns theirselves—and they got more'n a few yesterday."

Charlie White Bull saddled their horses, as well as a spotted gray pony hobbled next to Booth's, all the while shooting nervous glances toward the mob of Sioux warriors still gathered around Strong Bow. He wasn't sure what Booth said was true, that they would be blamed for Iron Pony's death, but he knew the two of them were not welcome in the camp as far as most of the warriors were concerned. "You leavin' the tent?" he asked Booth when the horses were saddled.

"Hell no, I want them skins. Go fetch the boy."

"You takin' the boy? Whadaya want him for? He ain't no good to us—want me to kill him?" The thought of a few moments of pleasure was enough to crack Charlie's usual stoic expression.

"No, dammit," Booth replied, "I don't want him kilt."

This was hard for Charlie to understand. The boy had tried to kill Booth—would have, too, if Charlie hadn't been taking a crap behind those berry bushes. He had been squatting on his hauches, taking his comfort, when Booth came striding down to the crick. Charlie didn't answer when Booth had yelled for him to come load up the packhorse. *He can load the damn horse hisself*, Charlie had thought. Because Booth was smarter than he was, he thought Charlie should do most of the work. It wasn't the first time Charlie hid from him when there was work to be done.

So Charlie stayed real quiet, hunkered down behind the bushes while Booth passed within fifteen feet of him. A wide smile slowly spread across Charlie's face when Booth passed him by. Moments later, he jerked his head back in surprise when a form suddenly rose from the bushes on the other side of the narrow trail. Puzzled, Charlie stood up to get a better look, and discovered a boy, with bow drawn and aimed, about to send an arrow into Booth's back. There was little time to think, but Charlie's reactions were swift enough. Charging across the trail, into the brush on the other side, he bowled the boy over just as White Eagle released his bowstring, causing the arrow to fly wide of its mark.

Recalling the incident, Charlie unconsciously fingered the otterskin bow case and quiver now strapped to his back. The boy claimed he was Shoshoni, but he looked more white to Charlie. He still couldn't understand why Booth had stopped him from cutting the boy's throat.

The horses saddled, Charlie walked over and, reaching under the buffalo hide, grabbed an ankle and dragged White Eagle out in the open. Booth grinned. With the boy's hands tied behind his back like that, it had to hurt like hell the way Charlie dragged him over the roots and dirt. But the kid never uttered a sound. In fact, he hadn't made so much as a whimper ever since Charlie captured him. Like Charlie, Booth's first thought was to put a bullet between the brat's eyes. But unlike Charlie, Booth fancied himself a businessman, and he never destroyed any commodity that had trade value. The kid showed a lot of spunk, giving Booth a hard eye. He might be Snake like he claimed, but there was a hell of a lot of white in him, too. And Booth knew a band of Gros Ventres where he was pretty sure he could trade the boy for maybe five or six good horses. He had kept the boy out of sight while in Iron Pony's camp. They knew he had the boy, but the damn Sioux were sometimes softhearted about children, and they would more than likely want to adopt him—maybe for some old woman who had lost a son—and he wouldn't get anything for him in trade. For that reason, he had kept White Eagle under cover—to give the Sioux less to think about. Besides, he said to himself, *I might like havin' me a slave for a while—and a nice little spotted gray pony to boot.*

"Put the boy on his pony," Booth said, his voice low so as not to attract any attention. "Then let's you and me lead these horses on down across the crick nice and easy. We don't wanna disrupt the powwow goin' on." He watched with interest as Charlie struggled with the boy, who tried his best to resist. "Crack him on the head if you have to, but don't kill him, dammit."

Charlie obliged with a sharp thump of his rifle butt, and White Eagle slumped to the ground, his head reeling. Losing the will to resist further, he was barely conscious when the stoic half-breed threw him up over the saddle. Unnoticed by the congregation of warriors ringing Strong Bow, Booth and Charlie led their horses down the narrow trail to the stream where White Eagle had been captured. Once on the other side, Booth hastily tied the boy to his saddle and the two men climbed into their own, leaving their former allies behind them.

From his position high on the ridge, Trace watched the Sioux camp prepare to ride. Riders were sent out to call in the scouts who had spent the night watching the soldiers to make sure they didn't attempt to escape under the cover of darkness. Trace remained where he was until the riders returned. In a matter of no more than an hour, the band of close to two hundred warriors deserted the valley, moving off toward the Powder River. When the last Sioux pony disappeared from view, he rose to his feet, the silence of the now-empty valley laying heavy on his ears. "Well, that's that," he muttered softly and turned to descend the ridge.

*   *   *

"Why the hell don't they come?" Turley demanded of no one in particular as he stalked up and down behind his line of troopers. It was half-past seven by his railroad watch, and no sign of hostiles anywhere. "Somethin' ain't right," he mumbled, then called out, "Keep a sharp eye on them flanks."

"Could be they're trying to draw us out in the open again," Luke Austen speculated as Turley crawled up beside him on the creekbank. He was about to say more when Turley suddenly grabbed his arm.

"Look there!" Turley interrupted in a loud whisper. "There's somebody coming across the rise." Turning toward the men to his side, he cautioned, "Get ready. Keep a sharp eye, but don't shoot till I say so—pass it on."

Luke had been studying the lone rider while Turley alerted the troops. "It's just one man," he said, "and he's waving his . . . Hell! That's McCall!" Turning quickly toward the men, he yelled, "Hold your fire! Hold your fire!"

When Trace was sure that he had been identified, he rode down the slope to meet Luke and Turley coming up from their holes in the bank.

"Well, you're a sight for sore eyes," Luke said as Trace dismounted.

"Where the hell are the damned Injuns?" Turley blurted. Behind him, the embattled troopers slowly began to crawl out of their emplacements, seeing that their lieutenant had abandoned his caution.

"They pulled out about an hour ago," Trace replied.

"You mean they're gone?" Luke asked incredulously. "For good?"

"'Pears that way," Trace answered with a shrug.

"Gone," Turley marveled. "We didn't even hear 'em move out."

"Hell," Trace said, "they're Injuns." He figured that was explanation enough.

Luke realized they had been damn lucky that day. But he knew there had to be some reason why the Sioux had decided not to press the attack on his men, and he questioned Trace while his troopers prepared to celebrate their survival with a hot breakfast. Trace modestly explained that the Sioux had lost their desire to fight when their chief was killed. "That was bad medicine, and Injuns don't like to fight if the medicine ain't right."

Luke thought about that for a moment. "But we could hear them all night . . . what sounded like a war dance to me. I know they were still sneaking around out there all during the night. We could hear them, even fired at them a couple of times. If they decided to quit because their chief was killed, why didn't they leave before this morning?"

Again Trace shrugged off the question, but Luke was insistent, so Trace finally told him. "They didn't know their chief had been killed until sunup this morning."

Luke was still somewhat puzzled. After all, the Sioux had them badly outnumbered. They could have kept his soldiers pinned down on that creek bank indefinitely. It didn't make sense to him that the hostiles wouldn't know their chief had been killed in the fighting the day before . . . unless . . . and then it dawned on him. "You mean you got into that Sioux camp last night and killed Iron Pony?"

He got no more than a nod in affirmation, then Trace quickly changed the subject. "Any of you boys got any coffee? I swear, I sure could use a cup."

Luke and Sergeant Turley looked at each other and shook their heads in amazement. Trace McCall was a piece of work all right. Luke had occasion to talk to many of the old mountain men—trappers and scouts—since he had been assigned west of the Missouri. Almost to a man, he had found them to be the biggest collection of boastful storytellers he had ever met. Jim Bridger and Buck Ransom came to mind—either man would have vocally painted a masterpiece of their daring assassination of the Sioux war chief, with every detail a brush stroke of vivid color. Trace, on the other hand, was modest to the point where Luke had to dig the details out, fact by fact, to get a clear picture of why his detachment had been spared another conflict with a superior force of hostiles. *Maybe, when he gets as old as Buck, he'll learn how to exaggerate like all the other old trappers.* Luke chuckled to himself at the thought.

While Trace helped himself to a cup of coffee, Turley turned to Luke. "Well, sir, it looks like we can get moving again. What have you got in mind to do? Are we still goin' on to the Powder like Captain Leach said?"

Luke, who had been watching the tall mountain man with amusement while Trace gingerly sipped boiling hot coffee from a tin cup, turned abruptly to face Turley. "Sergeant, do I look like a damn fool to you?" Not giving Turley time to respond, he went on. "We'll bury our dead, and return to Fort Laramie while there's still a few of us left." Turley touched his hat in a casual salute that signaled his silent approval and turned to get the men ready to move out. Luke turned back to the sandy-haired trapper squatting by the fire. "How about you, McCall? You riding back with us?"

"Reckon not, Lieutenant. I've still got some business out here to take care of." He had been thinking about White Eagle while he sipped his coffee, wondering about the boy's whereabouts and the possibility that he might be following the band of Sioux himself. Surely the boy could not have missed sighting a band as large as Iron Pony's. Trace regretted the fact that he had been detoured by the conflict between the soldiers and the Sioux. It would just make it that much more difficult to find the boy.

Sergeant Turley had a burial detail digging graves when Trace climbed on his horse and turned to ride up toward the ridge again. Luke pulled up beside him. "Thanks for sticking your neck out for us, Trace. When I get back to Laramie, I'll see if there's any way to get some scout's pay for the time you put in on the army's behalf." Trace shrugged indifferently. Luke gave voice to a thought he had come up with earlier that morning. "You know, with the fur trade gone to hell, you might consider signing on with the army as a regular scout. We sure as hell need men like you."

"I don't know, Lieutenant. I've been riding alone for some years now." Buck had frequently suggested the same thing, but Trace wasn't sure he could tolerate a constant crowd of soldiers around him.

Luke could see the hesitancy in the big trapper's face. "Give it some consideration. All right?"

"I'll consider it," Trace allowed and gave his pony his heels.

CHAPTER 11

It was no trick to follow the large band of Sioux warriors as they made their way back to their village, a village Trace guessed to be located somewhere on the Powder River. They wasted little time, evidently intent upon returning to their women and children. They were not overly cautious, either—not even employing rear scouts to alert the band of any enemies that might be following. As a result, Trace was able to tail the band a little closer than he expected.

Sioux scouts weren't the only riders he was watching for. He could not be sure that White Eagle wasn't trailing the war party, too. He wouldn't expect an eleven-year-old Snake boy to know the country—probably never having been as far east as the Bighorns. But then again, the kid appeared to be pretty smart, and he certainly had the spunk. He just might be determined enough to find the Sioux war party.

Trace would have made a more intense search for the boy if not for the fact that he had seen the white man in the Indians' camp. He could not permit Blue Water's killer to ride out of his sight, so he felt he had no choice but to follow the Sioux and hope he got to the white man before White Eagle attempted to.

Fearing no danger deep in their own territory, the Sioux, now led by Strong Bow, did not travel far the first day, making camp on the Belle Fourche with plenty of daylight left. There being little cover for concealment, Trace was forced to do most of his scouting of the camp on his belly, crawling through the grass. He managed to make a complete circle around the camp before darkness settled in, constantly searching for the white man in the black hat—but to no avail. There was no sign of the thin-faced white man anywhere. Trace began to experience a nagging fear that the man had parted with his Sioux friends somewhere back along the trail. But how could he have turned off the trail without being seen by Trace? Unless, Trace realized, he had left the camp before the Sioux even started for the Powder River country. The more he thought about it, the more worried he became. He had to be sure, though. He couldn't go riding all over the territory like a horse without a halter, hoping to stumble upon the white man. He had to know for sure that the man he searched for was no longer with the Sioux, so he decided to ride on ahead of the Indians and wait for them to start out in the morning. The trail they were taking to the Powder was fairly obvious, used quite often by many bands of Sioux, Cheyenne, and Arapaho. He would find a spot where he could watch the whole band as it filed by. If the white man was still with them, Trace would surely see him.

The place he picked was a narrow draw the trail passed through as it led up from the Belle Fourche. Perched high up on the side of the draw, Trace waited, lying close to the ground behind a screen of spindly scrubs. By the time the morning sun had begun to ingest the night chill, the advance scouts were already approaching the draw. Invisible to the unsuspecting warriors plodding below him, Trace looked hard at every man that passed. When the last few riders left the draw, rising to the plain beyond, Trace had the sinking feeling that he had wasted a whole day's tracking. There was no white man with the Indians.

Knowing that the man he hunted had evidently left the Sioux camp before it moved—and angry with himself for not discovering it when it happened—Trace lost no time in backtracking. As soon as it was safe, he left his hiding place and went back to the other side of the hill where his horse was hobbled. There was a strong sense of urgency about him as he urged the paint along. The possibility that he might never find the boy or the man who killed Blue Water weighed heavily on his mind. It was a big country—it could swallow up an eleven-year-old boy—and make a white man in a black hat damned hard to find.

With no clue to start with, there was nothing Trace could do but scout around the site of the Sioux camp back at the foot of the ridge. It didn't help to know that he was relying heavily on pure luck, since there were hundreds of tracks left by the comings and goings of the Sioux warriors. But having no choice, and unwilling to give up, he began a careful study of the many trails around the former campsite.

He spent an entire morning studying various tracks. They told him many things—here, a warrior tied his favorite pony near his bedroll, instead of with the pony herd; here, a dozen hunters rode out to get meat; here, they returned, their ponies loaded with meat; here, a large party galloped through the camp— the tracks told him many things—but they did not tell him where a white man in a black hat rode out of the camp.

Resigned to the fact that he was getting nowhere, he paused to spend some serious speculation on the white man's thinking.

Who could say where a man might decide to go? He thought back to where he had watched the camp from the ridge. If a lone rider had left the camp, heading for Fort Laramie, he would have passed close to the very ridge where Trace sat. Anyone riding off to the north or east would have also been seen easily from his position.

Perplexed for a moment, Trace rode halfway back up the ridge, almost to the exact spot he had watched from, and looked back over the abandoned campsite. The only part of the camp that could not be seen from high up on the ridge was the western edge, where the stream took a turn back to the north. The brush and trees were thick there, close to the water. It would have been possible for someone to slip down across the stream without being seen. It was a long shot, but he had run out of options. So he rode back down the ridge and began a careful search of the creekbank.

As before, he discovered many tracks leading back and forth to the camp, as well as several common paths worn through the brush. There were no clues that held any meaning, beyond the accounts of a typical campsite. He was about to determine his search a waste of time, when he crossed over the last little path to the stream and almost stepped in some evidence of some warrior's successful bowel movement. He stepped to the side just in time to avoid fouling his moccasin. "Damn!" he uttered in disgust, and started to return to the path. Something stopped him, and he turned to take another look.

It was obvious that the man who had squatted here had made his way carefully through the brush to perform his toilet. The thing that caught Trace's eye were the tracks leading away from the spot. There were broken branches and deep prints, like a man makes running. Why would a man squat, finish his business, then go charging straight through thick brush like a wild man? Had something scared him? Trace found no tracks that would support that thought. Deeply curious now, Trace made his way through the brush and small trees, following the tracks as they crossed the path and entered the bushes on the other side. *Either something was after him, or he was after something*, Trace thought. A few yards farther and he came to a spot where the brush was flattened, showing signs of a struggle, answering the question as to whether or not the man was chasing or being chased.

A thorough search of the area provided Trace with enough signs to construct a picture of what had happened there. The warrior performing his toilet had suddenly sighted an enemy of some kind and had immediately charged him, evidently overpowering his adversary. From the tracks nearby, it appeared that there had been a pony tied close to the path. Trace could imagine someone waiting in ambush, probably for a rider coming down the path. Whoever it was had been very careful about leaving any footprints. Trace could find none. The horses were a different matter, however, for he found various sets of hoofprints leading from the path. One of the horses was shod, no doubt a stolen army mount.

His scouting made him curious, but it offered no help to solve the puzzle. It told him nothing beyond the fact that someone had jumped someone else. He stood up and looked around him, exasperated, ready to admit that he had been whipped. Then he saw it. It was a plain, undecorated arrow lodged in a tree limb high up the trunk. It was the very plainness of the arrow that struck him—no designs, no tribal markings that he could see from the ground. He was aware of an increase in his pulse as he led his pony under the tree. By standing on his pony's back, he could just reach the arrow. It only took a glance when he had it in his hand to know that it was his own. He had made it himself, fashioned the razor-sharp stone point, inserted the three black feathers to make it spin true. *White Eagle had been the person lying in ambush!*

Once again, the dire sense of urgency returned, and Trace scouted the area in the brush again, this time concentrating more on the downstream side. After studying numerous footprints leading to and from the water, he finally found the confirmation he searched for—one small moccasin print leading up from the stream toward the spot behind the berry bushes. The boy had led his horse into the brush. Scouting the place where White Eagle had been attacked, Trace was relieved to find no sign of blood. Maybe White Eagle was captured, not killed. He would hope for that, and assume it to be so. Although he had a vague picture of what had taken place there, there were too many unanswered questions for him to be certain. For lack of better evidence, he had to guess that White Eagle had made an attempt on someone's life. Trace had to assume that it was the white man the boy had left to find. There were many tracks around the stream, but the only set that Trace could definitely follow were the prints from the shod horse.

There was still not much to go on, but Trace followed the shod horse from the stream, back to the camp. It took some time, but he was able to find the place where the horse was tethered while the owner slept nearby. From the small shallow holes in the ground, Trace determined that the owner of the horse had constructed one of the tentlike beds that Trace had seen from the top of the ridge. *More like something a white man would fix for himself,* Trace thought, and he became more and more convinced that he had found the trail of the man who had killed Blue Water—and now had captured his son. He was determined to follow the trail of the shod horse, wherever it led from that spot.

"Stop tormentin' that young'un for a minute and git me some firewood," Booth Dalton fumed. If Booth would let him, Charlie would pick at the Shoshoni boy until he killed him. Now the half-breed half-wit was entertaining himself by yanking on a rope tied around the boy's neck. "This meat'll be done in a minute or two, anyway." This last statement seemed to catch Charlie's attention and he dropped the rope, leaving it tied around White Eagle's neck. Trussed up like a hog heading to market, the boy offered no threat of escape. Charlie favored him with a leering smile before he turned to fetch some more dead limbs for the fire. White Eagle met his stare defiantly, causing Charlie to chuckle delightedly.

"When you gon' let me have him, Booth? Nobody's gonna trade you anything for that little rat." He looked back at White Eagle, and grinned, "Lemme skin him."

Booth cocked his head to the side, gazing at White Eagle, a smirk upon his face. "How 'bout that, boy? You want me to let ol' Charlie skin you? I will, by God, if you try to run away again." The smirk faded from his face, replaced by anger at the boy's blank expression. "Cain't you speak no American, dammit?" Booth barked. When that, too, was met with no reaction from the boy, he growled to Charlie, "Tell him what I said . . . 'bout runnin' away."

White Eagle listened to Charlie's translation of Booth's warning. Through Charlie's limited knowledge of Shoshoni and sign language, the boy got the meaning of Booth's threat, but it did nothing to dampen his desire to escape. The blocky half-breed was dangerous; White Eagle knew Charlie would like nothing better than to amuse himself by torturing him.

The white man wanted him alive for some other reason. White Eagle guessed that he wanted to make him a slave. Whatever the reason, the boy decided not to give Booth any trouble until he saw a real opportunity to strike. Then, he was as determined as ever to kill the man who had murdered his mother.

"Leave him be, Charlie. He'll be worth somethin' to the Gros Ventres," Booth finally said. "That young'un might have had a Snake mama, but he looks more white than Injun. I'm thinkin' we can pass him off as pure white, captured by the Snakes. Them Gros Ventres like white children."

Booth had expressed his intention to visit the Gros Ventres a couple of times already, and it appeared he was serious about it. Charlie had hoped Booth would change his mind. He didn't care for the idea of traveling into Gros Ventre country. Masquerading among the Sioux as a Sioux himself was bad enough. The Gros Ventres had an even stronger dislike for Flatheads. Besides, it was getting late in the year to be traveling that far north. It already felt like snow in the mountains—it was time to be holing up for winter.

"Gros Ventres already going to winter camps—maybe Missouri River, maybe Milk River. Too far north." He turned to point toward the mountains, hoping to influence Booth's thinking. "Too many mountains to cross."

Booth's thin lips slid back into a wry smile. "You ain't afraid of a little snow, are you, Charlie?" Then just as quickly, the smile faded and he stated, "We're goin'."

White Eagle rode his spotted gray pony behind Booth Dalton's large black horse with the U.S. brand burned in its rump. Sitting straight and defiant, his hands tied to a rawhide rope attached to Booth's saddle, he swayed back and forth with the pony's gentle walk. Behind him rode Charlie White Bull, leading two packhorses. They had traveled that way for two days, keeping the peaks of the Bighorns on their left, crossing the Powder River and going on until striking the Tongue.

The weather had suddenly turned colder, and already there was snow on the mountaintops. The boy would not complain, but he was secretly thankful when, after a cold day's ride, Booth pulled a buffalo robe from one of the packs and placed it around White Eagle's shoulders. "Gotta keep the merchandise from freezin'," he said and winked at Charlie White Bull. The robe would serve to keep him warm as well as provide him with a bed at night.

After reaching the Tongue River, Booth followed it toward its confluence with the Yellowstone. It seemed that every mile they rode toward the north, the weather got colder and colder. And with it, Charlie complained more and more.

"Quit your griping," Booth told him. "Look at that kid there—he ain't complainin.'"

Charlie snorted his displeasure. "He cain't complain. If he complains, I'll cut his tongue out." Never passing up an opportunity to harass the boy, he said, "Maybe I'd eat his tongue. I et a woman's tongue one time, smoked it over a hot fire till it was plumb black— tasted like buffalo tongue."

White Eagle gave no indication that he had heard Charlie's ramblings. He was determined to give the simpleminded half-breed no satisfaction. The boy was not afraid. He was disappointed that his attempt on Booth's life had been unsuccessful, but if they decided to kill him, he would die like a Shoshoni warrior, with no crying and no pleading for mercy. Even at his young age, life was not so precious to him that he would choose an existence as a slave over death. His one regret at this point was that he had not fought to the death with the other Shoshoni warriors when the Sioux attacked Broken Arm's camp.

As one day piled upon the next, and they made their way north, White Eagle spent the long day's ride thinking about the people he might never see again, and his Shoshoni family who were now all dead. Plodding along behind Booth Dalton's black army mount, he would allow a tiny bit of regret to creep into his thoughts, wondering if he should have gone with Trace. It was a decision he could not question, he reminded himself, as it was his duty to avenge the murders of his mother and grandfather.

Thoughts of escape never left his mind for very long, but Booth and Charlie kept such a close eye on him that there had been no opportunity. And at night, he was always tied securely. Near the end of his first day of captivity, he had tried to make a run for his life while crossing the Powder. Thinking the rope that bound his hands was looped loosely around Booth's saddlehorn, White Eagle kicked his pony hard when he was in the middle of the current, yanking at the rope at the same time. The pony responded as he was bade, jerking away downstream. But the rope was tied more securely than White Eagle suspected. As a result, the boy was wrenched from his pony's back and landed in the chilled waters of the river.

Instead of anger, Booth's reaction to the attempted escape was amusement—especially when he saw the predicament in which the boy's action had placed him. To teach White Eagle a lesson, Booth turned the big black stallion's head upstream and plunged along in the shallow water, dragging the flailing, sputtering boy behind him. Charlie had joined in the fun, splashing along behind Booth, packhorses in tow, yelling and laughing. Before the two had satisfied their impulsive entertainment, White Eagle had been dragged, half-drowned, for over a quarter of a mile in the cold water. The boy had decided after that experience that he would bide his time, waiting for a more promising opportunity. Without knowing it, Booth had purchased some valuable time for himself with his own cruel amusement at White Eagle's expense. The extended time spent in the shallow waters of the river effectively covered his trail.

A full day before reaching the mouth of the river, the morning clouds tumbled over the Bighorns, heavy and gray. Before noon, the first snowflakes began to fall. By evening, when the Yellowstone was first sighted, there was a half foot of snow on the ground and the storm had intensified, causing the travelers to seek shelter for the night.

A day and a half behind and to the east of the two renegades and their Shoshoni captive, Trace McCall looked up at the leaden skies, cursing the timing of the first real snow of the season. He had followed the trail left by five horses—one of which was shod—until it led to a crossing of the Powder River. There the trail ended. He scoured the banks of the river on both sides, looking for the point where they had left the water, but he could find no tracks for a hundred yards in either direction.

With no earthly notion as to the possible destination of the party he followed, he could not even hazard a guess on which way to search—upstream or down. For no particular reason, he decided to ride downstream, and after about two miles' ride, he came upon a crossing where many horses had forded the river. Intermingled with the hundreds of other hoofprints, he found several prints from shod horses. It was obviously a frequently used crossing, and it was possible that White Eagle's captors had crossed there, too. However, a few minutes' study told him that the tracks were too old to be the horses he was looking for.

Disappointed and discouraged, he had crossed over to the other side of the river and turned back upstream, searching the bank carefully. Ignoring the feeling of urgency to catch up with the white man on the heavy army mount, he forced himself to take his time so as not to overlook any sign. It had seemed apparent to him that the man he followed had taken great pains to hide his trail. For what reason, Trace had no clue. He was certain the man could not be aware of Trace's existence. The fact that he had slipped out of the Sioux camp unobserved might have indicated that he was possibly covering his trail so his Sioux friends couldn't follow him. A renegade like that, maybe he was just in the habit of covering his trail—Trace could only guess. The fact of the matter was that the man was increasing the distance between them with every hour Trace spent searching these riverbanks.

He had worked his way back to the point where he had first lost the trail when darkness caught him and he was forced to make camp. He didn't spend a great deal of time looking for a campsite, since he felt certain there was no one but him within miles. Settling for the first spot that offered plenty of grass for his horses, he made a fire beside a fallen tree, using the trunk to shelter him from a cold wind that had risen at sundown. After a supper of buffalo jerky and coffee—with plenty of wood to feed his fire—he settled in for the night.

The first sight that met his eyes when he awakened the next morning was his paint pony, gazing forlornly at him, a white frosting of snow covering the pony's ears and mane. *Dammit it to hell*, he thought, as he threw back the heavy buffalo robe and peered up at the sky. Looking around him, he was dismayed to find a blanket of snow already covering the riverbank. He got to his feet and shook the snow from his hair, scanning the silent cottonwoods along the bank, their leaves still and muffled by huge wet flakes as big as silver dollars floating down from the gray ceiling.

A feeling of despair swept through him as he stood there contemplating the impossible task now presented to him. How could he hope to find the trail under the snow? At that moment, he was stung by a reality that he was reluctant to admit—he had been beaten. His heart filled with remorse. He sat down by the fire thinking about the boy and what it must be like for him. Those thoughts served to rekindle his intense passion to avenge the murder of the boy's mother, causing a deep frustration such as he had never known.

With a morbid feeling that he was now reduced to stumbling around in a trackless world of white, hoping to chance upon the party he searched for, he nevertheless broke camp and started upstream. With no trail to follow, he had to rely on lucky guesses. And since any tracks that he might have found were now hidden under the snow, he found it difficult to feel lucky. With any direction as good as another at this point, he decided to follow the Powder north, hoping that the white man had done the same. Still determined, he urged his horses on. Looking back over the way he had come, he noticed that the falling snow was already beginning to cover his own trail.

"Damn, Booth, I told you snow was coming." Charlie White Bull pulled his robe over his head as he hunched over in the saddle. "We'll freeze our balls off if we don't git outta this cold."

"Well, where the hell are we gonna git outten it?" Booth shot back impatiently. He was as cold as Charlie and tired of hearing the half-breed complain about it. "We cain't just flop down in the snow and wait for spring, dammit. We got to keep movin' till we find someplace to hole up." What Booth hoped to find was a friendly tribe in winter camp, some group of Indians that wasn't acquainted with his reputation.

CHAPTER 12

After four more weeks of wandering between the Powder, Little Powder, and Tongue rivers, slowly making his way through drifts sometimes as tall as the paint's belly, Trace finally admitted his search was hopeless. After the first week the weather had cleared, still the storm had been so severe that the snow lay frozen on the ground. Crusted hard in the lower draws, sheltered from the sun, the snow scraped and tore at the horses' shanks and fetlocks, making travel difficult. He had hoped to stumble upon the boy's captors, but he was now resigned to the fact that it would take no less than a miracle to do so. With game scarce and supplies exhausted, he knew he would have to abandon his search for White Eagle and the white man who captured him. Reluctantly, he turned back to the south, headed for Fort Laramie. He had a few furs he could trade, and maybe Luke Austen had been able to authorize some scout's pay for him—possibly enough to supply him with the basics again.

The weather improved steadily as he rode south, and pretty soon he was able to make better time. When he reached the North Platte, the horses were moving easily through a six-inch covering of snow. Although the weather was brighter, his thoughts were troubled and heavy, for he felt he had failed White Eagle. His common sense told him that it was just bad luck—the early snowstorm—a man could not follow a trail hidden under a blanket of snow. That bit of wisdom did nothing to relieve his mind of its burden. He would find the boy, and he would avenge the death of Blue Water. These two things he solemnly promised himself—if he had to search forever. But for now, he had to wait out the weather.

Sergeant J. C. Turley stood passing the time of day with the sergeant of the guard near the post bakery. Turley was off duty, it being Saturday afternoon, and he had just come from visiting with Lamar Thomas. As the two sergeants stood there talking, Turley's gaze was captured by a lone rider approaching in the distance. Not many travelers passed through Laramie this time of year, so Turley continued to watch the visitor with an ample measure of curiosity. The rider was leading a packhorse, and when he got within a few hundred yards, Turley recognized the paint he was riding.

"Well, I'll be . . ." he interrupted the sergeant in midsentence, and abruptly turned and started walking across the parade ground, stopping in the middle to watch the rider approach.

Riding easily in the saddle, his rifle cradled across his forearms, Trace McCall passed the outer buildings and headed for the structure that housed the post commander's office. Recognizing the sergeant standing in the center of the parade ground, he nodded. "Turley."

"Trace McCall," Turley returned in greeting. "We wondered if you would ever show up again. Did you finish that business you had to take care of?"

"Nope—trail got covered with snow."

"I heard it snowed pretty heavy up in the mountains." Turley fell in step with Trace and walked with him as Trace led his horses to a hitching rail. "There ain't been much going on around here—the old man sends out a patrol once or twice a week, lookin' for God knows what. The Injuns ain't doin' nothin' but settin' by the fire." Trace offered no comment, so Turley went on. "Lieutenant Austen got you some pay for the part you had in that little shindig near the Belle Fourche. From the looks of them horses, I reckon you could use it."

"I reckon," was all Trace replied, but he was mighty pleased to hear it.

"You're just in time for the social event of the season," Turley continued, his face a broad smile. "We're gonna have a weddin' tomorrow. Lieutenant Austen and Annie Farrior is gittin' hitched."

"Do tell," Trace replied and raised an eyebrow. "I thought those two might tie the knot—make a fine coupling." It was good news. Trace had taken a liking to both of them. It helped take his mind off of White Eagle for a moment. "Where they gonna have the wedding?"

"In the post trader's store—only place big enough. We've got a chaplain now—come up from Fort Kearny a month ago. He'll tie the knot. Everybody's invited."

With Turley tagging along, Trace stepped up on the small wooden walkway and entered the sutler's store. Lamar was in the back storeroom, mending a hole in a sack of grain, so he didn't hear them come in until Turley called out, "Mr. Thomas, there's a feller out here lookin' to trade with you." Trace glanced briefly at Turley, wondering if the sergeant intended to do all his talking for him. Turley met Trace's glance with an open-faced grin. Trace couldn't help but be amused.

After a moment, Lamar came from the storeroom, still holding a large needle and a ball of twine. "Damn rats," he offered in explanation. "Mr. McCall," he acknowledged when he saw who his customer was.

"Trace," was the quick reply.

"Yessir, Trace," Lamar countered. "What brings you back to these parts?" Lamar had always held a certain curiosity for this tall sandy-haired friend of Buck Ransom's. To Lamar, Trace McCall was a strange one—a loner who just appeared, mostly in the summer, but at any other time of year as well. He always seemed dead serious, although Buck claimed McCall had a sense of humor about him—if you got to know him. As far as Lamar could tell, very few people got to know him that well. Buck said Trace was mostly raised by Crow Indians, lived four years with old Chief Red Blanket's band. Maybe that explained why Trace never wore whiskers, even in the dead of winter—and he looked more Indian than white if there was such a thing as a sandy-haired Indian.

The man had a way about him that Lamar found hard to define. Many so-called mountain men had passed through Lamar's store—including Jim Bridger, Buck Ransom, and Frank Brown—but none to match the likes of Trace McCall. Looking at the towering, broad-shouldered trapper, whose eyes seemed to penetrate a man's very thoughts, Lamar could understand why the Indians called him the Mountain Hawk.

In answer to Lamar's question, Trace said, "I'm needing some supplies. I've got a few skins and four buffalo hides. It ain't much, but I reckon I'll take whatever you can give for 'em."

"We can always use buffalo hides," Lamar said, "and I'll take a look at the other plews, maybe I can give you a little something for them. I reckon you know you've got a voucher for credit that Lieutenant Austen arranged for you."

Luke had been as good as his word, a fact that didn't surprise Trace. The young lieutenant had already established himself as a man of character in

Trace's book. "Good," Trace said. "Maybe I'll take a sack of that grain, then. My horses could use a good feed. They've been living off mostly cottonwood bark for the past couple of weeks."

After Trace had completed his dealings with Lamar Thomas, Sergeant Turley walked along with him to the bachelor officers' quarters. Trace wanted to express his thanks for the line of credit Luke had established for him, as well as offer his congratulations on Luke's marriage to be performed the next day.

Luke Austen seemed every bit as happy to see Trace as Sergeant Turley had been. He came striding across the snow-covered parade ground in front of the bachelor officers' quarters when he caught sight of his sergeant and the tall mountain man approaching. "Trace McCall," he exclaimed when within hailing distance. "I should have known you'd show up. You always do when you're needed. I damn sure need someone to stand up with me tomorrow when I surrender my freedom."

Trace smiled. He was happy to see the young officer again. "I heard you'd gone a little crazy in the head," he teased. "Turley here told me you'd decided to stick your head in the yoke." He dismounted and extended his hand.

Luke shook Trace's hand vigorously. "That's a fact," he said, beaming unabashed.

"Well, if I can put in my two cents' worth, you couldn't have got yourself a much better woman than Annie Farrior."

Luke's face remained awash in a grin that seemed permanently afixed, making no effort to hide his excitement. "I mean it, Trace, I want you to stand up with me when I get hitched. I'd appreciate it."

Trace hesitated. "I don't know . . . 'course I will I guess. . . . What do I have to do?"

Luke couldn't help but laugh. "Nothing, really, just stand up with me, and hold the ring, I guess. For a man who walked into the middle of a Sioux camp and killed the chief, you ought not be afraid to face a chaplain."

Trace laughed and shrugged his shoulders. "All right, then, we'll do her."

Sergeant Turley, an amused witness to the exchange, laughed with him. "I don't know, Trace, your job might be to make sure the groom don't cut and run."

When they had finished with the off-color jokes and asides that most males indulge in when teasing a prospective groom, Trace took a serious moment to thank Luke for the line of credit. Luke affirmed that Trace had certainly earned it, and Leach's replacement, Captain Theodore Benton, heartily approved.

"Have you thought any more about what I said when we left you near the Belle Fourche? About hiring on as a scout?"

"Well," Trace replied, "not really." In truth, he hadn't. His mind had been too heavily occupied with graver thoughts. But now the idea held more merit. There was no disputing the fact that he needed the income. And it was useless to try to find White Eagle until the snow had cleared the mountain passes. So why not? Although he was still uncertain what being a scout for the army involved, and how much it would infringe upon his freedom.

"We sure as hell need scouts who know the country as well as you do," Luke prodded. "Why don't we go talk to Captain Benton?"

Trace continued to hesitate, then said, "I ain't saying I'm not interested, Luke. I reckon I could try it till spring. But when spring gets here, I've got something I've got to take care of, and I'm gonna take care of it, come hell or high water. I can't tell you how long it'll take—it just depends on how lucky I get."

"Let's go talk to the captain," Luke said. He knew that spring was the time of year Trace would be needed most, when the wagon trains would start passing through, and the Indians would most likely be riled—treaty or no treaty. Still, there were patrols occasionally during the winter months where a competent scout was necessary. It was Luke's guess that the captain would be anxious to hire Trace, even with the conditions he set.

Luke was right. Captain Benton was more than agreeable to the idea. He was in desperate need of more white scouts experienced in the ways of the Indians. Like Luke, Benton pressed the tall mountain man to consider permanent employment, but Trace was steadfast in his conditions. He allowed that, if his few months' service were satisfactory to both parties, he would consider coming back after his spring leave of absence. He and the captain shook hands on it and Trace was now a scout for the army.

Sunday at noon, Trace rode over to Lamar Thomas's place of business, where a small gathering of friends awaited the arrival of the bride and her party. Although he was not completely comfortable being inside with that many people, he had promised Luke he would be there, so he went in the door. On the counter where he had traded his plews with Lamar Thomas the day before, a small altar had been placed. In lieu of flowers, a spray of willows had been arranged for a romantic touch, and a clean white cloth laid across the altar to represent the purity of the occasion, Trace supposed. Off to one side, at the end of the counter, next to a molasses barrel, Luke stood talking to the chaplain. When Luke spotted Trace, he immediately signaled him over. All eyes turned to watch an uncomfortable and self-conscious army scout as he made his way through the gathering. Trace became acutely aware of his animal-hide attire in a room mostly filled with soldiers in dress uniforms and a couple of ladies in the finest they had.

Luke greeted his best man with a wide smile. "I don't know who looks more scared, me or you." Trace answered only with an embarrassed grin. Luke turned to introduce the chaplain. "Trace McCall, Captain Gunter." The chaplain grabbed Trace's hand and shook it enthusiastically. Turning back to Trace, Luke took a thin silver ring from his pocket. "You take the ring. All you have to do is give it back when the chaplain asks for it."

Feeling his face slightly flushed, Trace said, "I reckon I can do that. Anything else?"

"Nope. When it's over, you get to escort Grace Turner out the door. That's all."

At that moment, Grace Turner entered the store, followed by Rose Thomas. "All right," Rose announced cheerfully, "the bride's here." Grace walked down to stand before the counter while the chaplain went around behind and prepared to receive the happy couple. Luke took Trace by the elbow and guided him over in front of the counter beside him. When Annie appeared in the doorway, the gathering parted to form an aisle and an enlisted man attempted to force the wedding march through a protesting squeezebox.

Trace glanced across at Ned Turner's widow. He had never met the lady. Meeting his gaze, she returned a pleasant smile, and he immediately looked away. Grace Turner looked to be about the same age as Annie, maybe a year or two older. She was comely enough—not really a pretty woman—but attractive in a homespun way. Trace decided that she probably had a good heart. When he stole a second glance, she was looking back at the bride. Trace turned his head to watch Annie as well.

Smiling graciously, Annie nodded to the few people on both sides as she walked slowly toward the counter where Luke waited.

Trace was almost startled. This was the first time he had seen the young lady in anything but an ill-fitting army uniform. Walking gracefully now on the arm of Lamar Thomas, she was a vision of innocence and beauty. When she made eye contact with Trace, her smile became wider and she beamed up at him. Trace was suddenly overcome with thoughts of regret. He glanced at Luke, the young bridegroom obviously joyfully enamored. Then he dropped his gaze to his crude buckskins, wishing he had not come. Feeling pitifully out of place, he realized that this kind of happiness that Luke possessed was never to be in his own life—a life of his own choosing, so there was no blame to be assigned. It might have been, he told himself. Maybe he was a damn fool for not finding Blue Water years ago. But he was so young at the time, and inexperienced. He believed that she had left because she did not want him to follow. *Well* he thought, *you passed up that chance for happiness with a woman.* And that was most likely the best chance he would ever have, because Blue Water's lifestyle was his lifestyle. His thoughts skipped for a moment to Jamie Thrash. At least she told him that there was no future for them. He knew it, anyway. He was never meant to be a farmer. *I wish to hell I hadn't agreed to do this*, he thought as the chaplain began the ceremony.

It was a brief ceremony, delayed only when Luke had to nudge Trace with his elbow in order to get the wedding ring. At last over, Luke and Annie kissed and turned to receive congratulations from the few friends gathered there. Grace smiled up at Trace and reached for his arm. Holding it out stiffly for her to hold onto, he walked her to the front door.

"Well, I reckon that's that," Trace sighed and tried to retrieve his arm from Grace Turner.

"You can't go yet, Mr. McCall. Rose and Annie, and I have been cooking all morning. Somebody's going to have to eat the food we prepared after we slaved over it."

"That's mighty nice of you, ma'am, but I don't think . . ."

"Oh no you don't," Grace interrupted. "You have to be there. What kind of best man doesn't even go to the wedding banquet?" He was about to tell her that nobody told him where to go, when she said, "Please," so sweetly that he couldn't bring himself to be abrupt with her.

"Mrs. Turner . . ."

"Grace," she interrupted.

"Grace," he began, "I like a big feed as well as the next man. It's just that I feel kinda out of place, what with all you folks dressed up in your fine clothes. These buckskins are all I've got. It was bad enough having to go to the wedding."

"Is that what's bothering you? My, my. And Lieutenant Austen said you were the most fearless man he had ever met. Surely you can face a few dinner guests," she teased. "I'll tell you what. I'll stay right beside you to protect you. We can even eat outside the house if it makes you feel more comfortable."

Feeling completely cowed and a little foolish, Trace gave in. The lady might as well have grabbed him by the ears and slipped a halter over his head. Trace frankly did not know what to make of it. After making him promise not to move from that spot, Grace left him for a few moments while she talked to Rose Thomas. When she returned, it was to say that she had told Rose to go on to the house without her, she planned to walk over with Trace.

"Where's the house?"

"About a mile away, by the creek," Grace answered.

"A mile?" Trace replied as Lamar Thomas's wagon pulled away from the store. He looked at the wagon, then back at Grace in her church dress, and scratched his head thoughtfully. "You can ride my horse and I'll lead him, if you don't mind straddling him. He's kinda particular who climbs on him, but he'll be all right as long as I'm leading him."

Grace laughed. "Oh, I could straddle him if I was of a mind, but I'd prefer to walk with you."

So they walked, their feet crunching along a dirty brown layer of snow where wagon tracks and horses' hooves had churned the white powder in with the mud. Grace stepped carefully along the wagon track, avoiding as much of the mud as possible, all the while rejecting Trace's repeated offers to put her on his horse.

About halfway to the cabin, the track dipped slightly where a branch crossed it and covered the trail with about three inches of water. It was no more than two feet wide and certainly no problem to step across, but Grace paused.

"I'm afraid that's too wide for me to step across in this dress. I know I'll ruin these shoes." She looked up at Trace expectantly, but the mountain man was too dense to be courtly, and her obvious hints were left lying at his feet. Rather than irritate her, his manner seemed to delight her. With a teasing lilt in her voice, she prompted him. "Mr. McCall, do you suppose you could assist me?" She held out her arms, indicating that she wanted to be carried across.

"Oh," he blurted, and before he knew it, she was pressing against him.

When he still made no move to respond, she chided, "You have to pick me up. I can't jump that high." Then she laughed, delighted by the sudden flush of red on his suntanned cheeks. She was not a frail girl, but he lifted her as easily as if picking up a child. As she was swept up from the muddy trace, she could feel the strength of his arms and the solid muscle of his chest. She instinctively locked her arms around his neck and laid her head in the crook of his shoulder.

Trace found himself in unfamiliar territory. At first, he was confused by suddenly finding this woman—a complete stranger short hours before—in his arms. Then he became acutely aware of the softness of her body, and the subtle hint of perfume in her hair—and he knew that he wanted to hold her longer. Lost in the warmth the sensation of her body generated inside him, he didn't realize until she spoke that the narrow branch of water was some twenty yards behind him.

"I think I'm safely across now," she said softly. There was a twinkle in her eye as she smiled up at him.

Flushing with embarrassment, Trace quickly set her feet back on the ground, and started to stammer an apology. She stopped him before he could get the first word out, and with a giggle, grabbed his elbow with both her hands, and strode merrily on to the cabin. Trace, still uncertain as to what was happening, let himself be led.

Grace released his arm and went inside the cabin while Trace tied his horse. As he looped the reins around a corner post of the porch, he paused to examine the moments just past. Had Grace Turner been flirting with him? A rough mountain man like himself? It wasn't likely, he decided. She was probably just teasing him, having a little fun at his expense. The only woman who had ever wanted him was Blue Water, and that was long ago. The thought of the Shoshoni maiden tore his mind from the joyous occasion of this day, and he felt a moment of melancholy when reminded of the mission he had set for himself.

Bowing his head to clear the door frame, Trace stepped inside the cabin. He was immediately hailed by Luke Austen, who along with Annie, motioned for him to join them. Before he could seat himself at the table, Annie stepped up and kissed him on the cheek, whispering, "Thank you for bringing Luke back safely to me." Trace was too flustered to reply, blushing for the second time in the last hour. He was ready to leave right then, feeling an overpowering desire to be back outside and away from the cabinful of people. But Rose Thomas set upon him with a plate of food and threatened to brain him with a skillet if he didn't finish it all.

While he ate, he was careful to mind his manners, feeling a dozen eyeballs watching his every mouthful. *I guess they expect me to eat with my hands*, he thought, as he chased some corn pudding around his plate with his fork. Occasionally, he glanced over toward the opposite corner of the room where Grace Turner was involved in a spirited conversation with Lamar Thomas and a young lieutenant. She had not given him so much as a casual glance since he came in the door—a fact that made him feel all the more foolish for some of the thoughts that had crossed his mind before.

As soon as he finished eating, he thanked Mrs. Thomas for the fine meal, wished Luke and Annie a long and happy marriage, then begged to be excused, saying he had some things to take care of before dark. Luke reminded him that he would be going out on a patrol the next morning, and Trace acknowledged with a nod of his head. As he made his way to the door, he glanced around, looking for Grace, but she was nowhere to be seen. Missing also, he noticed, was the young lieutenant.

Once outside, he breathed in a great lungful of air to clean out the close, smoky atmosphere of the crowded cabin. There had been too many folks in a confined space to suit him. Untying the paint, he stroked the pony affectionately on his face—snow white down to the muzzle—and prepared to step up in the saddle.

"Trying to sneak away from the party? Some best man you are."

Startled, he turned to find Grace Turner directly behind him, the same impish grin on her face that she had teased him with before. "I expect I'd better be going," he offered in defense.

Ignoring his remark, she said, "Come on. I'll show you where the groom proposed to Annie." With that, she promptly turned and started walking toward the creek. Dumbfounded, he stood there. After taking a few steps, she stopped, turned back to him and scolded, "Well, come on," turned again, and strode toward the cottonwood trees by the creek. He shrugged his shoulders and followed, leading his horse.

"This used to be Annie's secret place," Grace said as she stepped across a frozen rivulet and stood beside a large log near the edge of the creek. "Only it wasn't so secret," she added with a laugh. "Rose and I both knew she was meeting Luke down here."

Trace wondered why she was telling him all this. He really had no interest in Luke and Annie's courtship. When it appeared that Grace intended to walk no farther, he dropped the paint's reins to the ground, knowing the horse would not wander.

"It really is a lovely spot, don't you think?"

He glanced around as if judging for himself, but he didn't answer before she started brushing the snow from the log, clearing a space for them to sit. "You'll get your dress wet," he offered in his practical manner, not being a man of impetuous nature.

"It'll dry," she tossed back lightly. "Come sit by me."

"Wait," he said, and unrolled a buffalo robe that had been tied behind his saddle. He laid it across the log, and they sat down together.

"Now, I've heard nothing but tales about you," she said, "some wild and some downright hard to believe. So, Mr. Trace McCall, I want to know the real you. Are you really as wild as an Indian?"

The question was so ridiculous that he couldn't help but laugh. "No, ma'am, I'm not wild. I'm just the same as any other man. There isn't anything to tell."

She was insistent upon knowing all about his past, but all she found out was that he was an extremely private man who was reluctant to talk about himself. Encountering a stone wall with him, she instead began to talk about herself, her marriage to Ned Turner, their hopes and dreams—in short, more than he cared to know. Still she talked, and as the afternoon wore on, bringing a chill in the air, she moved closer to him in an effort to keep warm.

"We'd best get back now," he said. "You'll catch a chill with no more clothes than you got on."

"No, let's not go back yet," she said, moving even closer. Then, with that mischievous glint in her eye that he had seen earlier, she whispered, "I bet I could stay as warm as can be if I was wrapped up in this heavy robe—even with no clothes on."

He looked at her for a long moment, puzzled by her remark. "I suppose you could. I'll get up so you can wrap it around you."

Throwing up her hands in exasperation, she stood up and faced him. "I swear, Trace McCall, you are the thickheadedest man I believe I've ever met. Am I that unattractive? I meant wrap the robe around me and you." That said, she reached up and pulled his head down to her and kissed him hard on the lips.

Too startled to think straight at first, he almost jerked free of her embrace. Then realizing that she had planned on this encounter from the beginning, he dropped all the reservations he had harbored and let it happen, returning her kiss. After a long moment, they parted, but only long enough to pull the buffalo robe from the log and spread it on the ground.

It had been a long time for both of them, and the need was overwhelming, creating a mating that was feverish in its urgency. They came to each other with animal-like passion, frantic to know the release each needed so desperately. It had happened so fast that there had been no time for words of love or gentle caresses. And when it was over, there had been ecstasy—wild, violent release even—but no fulfillment or complete satisfaction. Grace lay in his arms then, thinking of the years she had been married to Ned, and how much she missed the intimacy they had shared. She wanted that back in her life. But even in this starburst of ecstasy, she knew there would be no future with Trace McCall for her. She had purposely selected him to fill a physical need that had been growing within her. He did not disappoint, and she had been left with the feeling that she had mated with a wild stallion.

They lay there until their heated bodies began to feel the chill of the winter air. Then Trace wrapped the robe around them, and she cuddled closer to him. In a little while, the flame of passion brightened again, and he began to explore the mysteries of her body. With his fingertips, he gently traced the contour of her breasts, marveling at the softness of her skin, watching in wonder as she responded to his touch. In a short time, his passion was reborn, and they came together once more. This time it was gentle and warm, of longer duration, bringing the complete satisfaction that Grace so longed for.

"We'd better go now," Grace whispered, gently kissing him on the cheek. "The wedding party may be winding down, and someone might wonder where I am."

Trace helped her up and rolled up the robe while she got back into her clothes. Still amazed by what had just happened, he found conversation difficult, even when Grace made joking remarks about the disheveled state of her dress. Confused before, when she had insisted that he follow her down to the creek, he was even more so afterward. He didn't know what to make of this sudden development, and he was struggling to put some meaning into it. Already, he felt a sense of responsibility for compromising the lady's virtue.

She studied the perplexed scout's face as she buttoned the last buttons on her dress, sensing the uncertainty in his thoughts. *The Mountain Hawk*, she thought. *You are a magnificent animal, but inside you are like a child.* "Trace," she said, placing her hand on his arm, "I owe you an apology. I used you shamefully. I hope you won't be angry with me." She gazed directly in his eyes, noting the uncertainty she saw there. "I think you needed me as badly as I needed you." She smiled and gave his arm a little squeeze.

Trace could not understand why she felt she should apologize until she explained as they walked back toward the cabin. "You are a good and decent man, Trace, but I've got sense enough to know that you belong to the mountains. There is really no room for a woman in your life, unless she could live like an Indian—and I can't do that. Lieutenant Masters has asked me to marry him, and I've accepted. We're going back to Fort Kearny in two months where he's permanently stationed. We'll be married there." Reading the astonishment in his eyes, she pleaded, "You can understand why I can't make love with him, can't you? I want him to think more highly of me than you probably do right now."

Masters, so that was the young lieutenant's name with whom Grace had been talking so intimately before. Trace wondered why he felt so dejected. He was certainly not in love with Grace Turner. Still, there was a definite feeling of despondency. He had an inclination to defend his character, to assert that he would make as good a husband as any man, even though deep down he knew he wouldn't. Instead, he said, "No, ma'am, I'm not mad at you. You did me a great honor, and I'll always appreciate it."

She smiled, relieved. "You're a good man, Trace McCall, and I thank you for this day."

Thinking it more discreet, they said good-bye before they reached the clearing before the cabin. Trace climbed aboard the paint and wheeled him around, riding back along the creek. He didn't look back to see her standing there watching him until he disappeared into the trees. He felt the need for a ride, and after a hundred yards or so along the creek, he crossed over and emerged on the open prairie.

Urging the paint into a faster pace, he rode across the snow-covered grass, feeling the chilly wind on his face, clearing his mind and sharpening his senses. He did not deny that he might have needed the tryst with Grace more than she. He had lost touch with those feelings. He thought about her plans to marry the young lieutenant and the urgency to find his son suddenly returned. He desperately wanted some sense of family. Even a hawk had family.

CHAPTER 13

During the next month, patrols were sent out when weather permitted, most of the time merely to keep the men in some form of readiness. Trace went on every one—even those he was not scheduled for—on the lookout for the rare party of Pawnees or Poncas, on the wild chance they may have heard word of a white man with a Shoshoni boy. A mystery that white men never could explain was the transmitting of information among various Indian tribes. Even though he had been a Crow for four years of his early life, Trace could not explain it, either. But it was a fact that he did not question. So he continued to hope for information that might at least give him a point to start searching come spring.

He saw very little of Grace Turner in the weeks that followed their meeting by the creek. It was his nature to keep to himself, so there was little opportunity for even a chance meeting. Luke and Annie had set up house in an army tent, waiting for better accomodations that would probably not be available before spring. Luke often extended invitations to join them for supper, but Trace never made it. He also avoided Lieutenant Ira Masters, never really having any desire to get to know the young man.

Trace was on his way back from visiting a band of Pawnees that had made their winter camp about thirty-five miles down the Platte, near the mouth of Horse Creek, when he was met by Sergeant Turley.

"Captain Benton's lookin' for you," Turley said before Trace had a chance to dismount. "Woodcutting party that went out yesterday morning still ain't back. Captain wants you to lead a party out to look for 'em—fifteen men, two wagons missing."

"Who took 'em out? Luke?"

"No. Lieutenant Masters took 'em out."

"Masters, huh?" Trace considered that for a moment before pulling on the left rein and nudging his pony toward Captain Benton's office.

"Where the hell you been?" Captain Benton wanted to know as soon as Trace dismounted. "I've had people looking all over for you."

"You told me to take the day off," Trace answered in a matter-of-fact tone.

Benton, all set to castigate his new scout, had to bite his lip to keep from sputtering. "Damn, that's right. I did at that. Well, I didn't think you would be running off where nobody could find you." Trace made no reply, but his eyes told the captain that he would go where he damn well pleased. Realizing this, Benton didn't push it. "Never mind," Benton quickly changed his attitude, "Lieutenant Austen is taking out a search party of thirty men. I want you to scout for him."

Trace found the detachment already assembled and waiting for him when he left the captain. He stopped briefly to tell Luke that he had to get a fresh horse—the paint had already done better than seventy miles in the past twenty-four hours. As he rode past the line of troopers waiting for the order to march, he could hear a lot of grumbling about starting out so late in the day. It would mean a cold night's sleep on the trail. Trace grunted to himself, *You boys have got too used to your warm beds*. They were right, though, they should have gone out long before it got so late in the day, instead of waiting for him to come back. It didn't take a scout to follow two wagons and thirteen mounted soldiers in the snow.

As Trace had figured, the detachment was not on the trail for more than three hours when Luke halted the column to make camp. The place selected was a shallow draw that afforded some protection from the wind that had constantly swirled the snow around the horses' hooves all afternoon. There had been no trouble in following the plainly marked trail up the Platte, so Trace spent his time out in front of the column to make sure Luke didn't ride into an ambush.

When Trace returned to the column, he found them already in the process of making camp, with the men busily clearing snow to set up their two-man tents. The grumbling started anew as the troopers spread their rubber mats and unrolled their blankets. Some of them already had on all the clothes they owned. As for Trace, when it was time to turn in, he wouldn't bother to clear a space in the snow. He would spread the big buffalo robe on the ground and roll up in front of a fire, sleeping peacefully with one ear alert for any sounds that didn't belong.

Trace scooped up a coffeepot full of clean snow and set it on the fire to boil while he gave his horse a measure of grain, supplied by the army. Hearing footsteps behind him, he turned to find Luke approaching.

"You know, I can get a tent issued to you if you want it," Luke said, eyeing the huge buffalo hide.

Trace smiled. "No thanks, Luke. I can make a tent outta this robe if I need to. Besides, this is a helluva lot warmer than a tent."

Luke stepped over closer to the fire. "I see you've got some coffee working."

Finished feeding his horse, Trace moved back to the

fire beside his young friend. "I haven't got anything but hot water right now, but I'll have coffee directly."

The small talk over, Luke knelt down beside Trace, who was now solemnly grinding a sack of green coffee beans between two rocks. "I've told Sergeant Turley to post pickets. I don't honestly know if there's any danger from Indians or not. What do you think?"

Trace reached into the coffee bean sack, took out a calculated handful and dumped them into the pot. Brushing the residue from his hands over the pot, he put the sack away and moved the pot closer to the fire again. "Well, Luke, I reckon it's always a good idea to keep a watch out for trouble. Most of the time, there ain't much chance of a war party in weather like this. An Injun ain't any more likely to wanna freeze his butt than you are. But I've known Injuns to raid in the wintertime. I reckon it just depends on the situation—and the Injuns."

"What do you suppose happened to that woodcutting detail? What kind of trouble could they have gotten into? We haven't seen any hostile activity, especially since the treaty."

Trace took the top from his coffeepot and peered into it, then replaced it. "It's hard to say. I've been wondering about that myself. 'Course, you know there's a heap of Injuns that didn't come in to sign that treaty, that don't know nothing about any treaties." He shrugged. "I reckon we'll just have to wait and see what happened."

It was obvious that his answers did little to satisfy Luke's curiosity, but Trace didn't have a clue as to the trouble Masters might have gotten himself into. They might have simply gotten themselves lost, although even a damn fool could turn around and follow his wagon tracks back home. Masters was newly arrived from the east and still a good bit green in dealing with Indians. *Hell, he might have gotten lost.*

The night passed without incident, and it was back on the march at first light, Trace having ridden out some thirty minutes before the column was in the saddle. They had not ridden two hours before rifle shots were heard in the distance. Luke immediately ordered his men to check their weapons and to remain alert. Turley rode back along the column, berating those who were slow in responding and waking those who were dozing in the saddle.

"Where the hell is Trace?" Luke wondered aloud.

In answer to his question, at just that moment, Trace appeared, riding along the bluffs on a line to intercept them. His horse was loping along at a good pace, but not running full out. Luke halted the column and waited for Trace to arrive.

"Lieutenant," Trace called out when he reached them, "maybe you'd better come take a look."

"What is it?" Luke wanted to know. "Is it Masters?"

"Oh, I found 'em, all right. I just ain't sure what they're doing. Why don't you and Turley come with me to look things over before you bring the troop up."

Puzzled and wanting answers, Luke nevertheless did as Trace suggested. Turning to Turley, he said, "Sergeant." While Turley gave the men orders to stand down, Luke turned back to Trace. "What the hell's going on? Who's shooting?"

"Soldiers," was Trace's simple reply.

Before Luke could ask who they were shooting at, Trace wheeled his horse around and moved off toward the bluffs again. Not waiting for Turley, Luke galloped after his scout. He caught up with him on a low ridge overlooking a bend in the river. Trace motioned for him to leave his horse and come up beside him. Following Trace's pointed finger, Luke saw the source of the occasional rifle shot. Bunched in a narrow gully, their backs to the river, were what appeared to be all of the fifteen-man wood detail plus Lieutenant Masters. Feeling a tap on his shoulder, Luke looked at Trace who was now pointing at the two wagons, lying on their sides halfway down the bluffs. Just above the wagons, Luke counted a sizable party of Indians scattered in a half circle. They seemed to be merely watching the trapped wood detail, for the shots fired at random intervals came from the soldiers huddled in the gully.

"We'd better get the troop up here fast," Luke gasped, and turned to pass the order to Turley, who had just then caught up.

"Hold on a minute, Luke," Trace said, catching his young friend by the elbow. "Let's don't go off half-cocked."

"Hold on?" Luke blurted. "Every second we delay might cost a soldier's life! That's probably the same bunch of Sioux that ambushed us in the Black Hills."

"They ain't Sioux," Trace explained calmly, "they're Crow."

Luke failed to see the significance. "Crow? They're a long way from home, aren't they? Are you sure they're Crow?"

"They're Crow," Trace answered flatly, not bothering to tell Luke that he had once lived with a band of Crows, so he could damn sure recognize them. "And you're right, they are a long way from home."

Luke was getting antsy. "Crow, Sioux—what's the difference? They've got Masters in a pocket."

"That's just it," Trace patiently pointed out. "Masters has got himself in a pocket. The Crows are just watching him." Taking Luke by the arm, he pulled the lieutenant along after him, moving to a closer point on the ridge. "Look. Those warriors aren't firing a shot at them. All the firing is coming from that gully. Hell, the Crows have been friendly to the army."

Gradually, Luke came to see that what Trace was telling him was true. The Crows seemed to be intent only upon watching the soldiers crammed into the small gully. Safely behind cover, and in no danger of the rifles below them, they appeared to be no more than interested spectators. Amazed, Luke shook his head and said, "What do you wanna do?"

"Let me go down and talk to 'em. Might be a good idea to keep your boys behind the ridge till I can find out what's going on. They might think we're trying to ambush 'em if they see a bunch of soldiers behind 'em—and then we might have a real fight." Luke agreed. He and Turley stayed back while Trace got on his horse and started down the bluffs toward the Crows.

"Where did he come from?" Big Turtle said, alarmed to discover a solitary rider making his way down the bluffs toward them.

Black Wing jerked his head around quickly, searching the ridge behind the rider. "Be alert!" he cautioned. "There may be more." The small band of Crow warriors moved to better situate themselves to counter an attack from above. Black Wing made his way farther up the bluff to a position where he could watch the rider more closely.

"Be careful," Big Turtle warned, "he may be as crazy as the soldiers in the gully."

Black Wing didn't answer right away. He was busy studying the lone figure approaching them. Something about the way the man sat his horse seemed familiar to him, yet he couldn't identify the man. He was not a soldier. He could even be an Indian, but Black Wing was unable to identify the tribe if he was. As the stranger approached, he held up his hands in a sign of peace. Black Wing made no sign of recognition and continued to scan the ridge behind the rider, watching for any sign of deception. Black Wing and his warriors were deep inside Sioux country. He could not afford to be careless. Still the man kept coming, and was now within fifty yards of the Crows.

"I come in peace," the man called out in the Crow dialect. "Let's talk."

Black Wing and Big Turtle exchanged puzzled glances, still uncertain. Finally Big Turtle shrugged and Black Wing nodded in silent agreement. He stood up and returned the peace sign, saying, "If you come in peace, you are in no danger from my warriors."

Dismounting some twenty yards away, he stepped down into the thin layer of snow and led his horse the rest of the way. Trace and Black Wing recognized each other at the same time. For a brief moment, both men were stunned, not believing what their eyes were telling them. Trace was the first to break the silence.

"Well, I'll be damned," he uttered in English, then in Crow, "Black Wing?"

Black Wing's stern face was transformed into a smile of delighted discovery. "Trace. It has been a long time."

The two boyhood friends stood there staring at each other, each one amazed to find the other still alive. Then, as if on signal, they suddenly broke into laughter and clasped hands, patting each other on the shoulder. Amazed, Big Turtle came forward to join the reunion.

"Do you know this white man?" Black Wing asked Big Turtle when his friend was obviously doing his best to recognize the tall stranger dressed in buckskins. When it dawned upon Big Turtle that this was the boy who had been taken in by his people years ago, the joyous reunion erupted again with more laughing and back slapping. The reunion continued as a few more warriors in the party came forward to greet Trace. Most of the others were too young to remember him.

The celebration was cut short by the crack of a rifle from down below in the gully, the ball imbedding itself high up in a cottonwood. Remembering the situation at hand then, Trace remarked, "They ain't exactly good shots, are they?" Turning serious then, "What's going on here, Black Wing?"

Black Wing then told Trace how they came to find themselves watching the soldiers in the river bottom. "We came to this country to avenge one of our people who was killed by a Sioux raiding party. We encountered a Sioux hunting party of six men and killed them." He indicated two fresh scalps on his lance. "We started back to our village when we saw the soldiers with the wagons. We thought, maybe the wagons are filled with coffee and beans, maybe flour, and we might trade some pelts for them. But the soldiers went crazy." He turned to Big Turtle for confirmation and Big Turtle nodded.

"I made the sign of peace when I rode up to them, and one of the soldiers shot at me. I wanted to tell them that we were peaceful, but they ran away, riding their horses hard toward the river. The wagons turned over and the soldiers cut the horses loose. Then they all jumped into that small hole on the riverbank. We tried to talk to them, but they shoot at us when we come near. We were going to leave when you came." He shrugged. "There was nothing in the wagons but wood, anyway."

Astonished, Trace could only shake his head, and he thought, *Grace, you're gonna be a widow again if that damn fool greenhorn doesn't get some sense about Indians.* To Black Wing, he said, "I'll see if I can talk to them."

He got on his horse and started down the bluffs, waving his arm back and forth and calling out, "Hold your fire!" Stopping halfway down, he called out again, "Hold your fire! You boys can come out now."

His answer was a volley of half a dozen rifles from the terrified soldiers in the gully. The shots were wild, and far from the mark—all except one—and that one struck his horse in the chest. The animal screamed and dropped immediately. If Trace had been a fraction of a second slower, he might have been pinned under the beast. Trace hit the ground rolling. Shocked at first, then angry as hell, he crawled back to the stricken animal to retrieve his rifle. "Damn fools!" he roared as he pulled his pistol out to put the unfortunate horse out of its misery. A shot behind the ear quieted the animal's thrashing legs. The frightened soldiers by the water's edge mistook the shot as one aimed at them, and another round of shots were sent his way. "Damn fools!" Trace repeated and scurried back up the bluff to safety.

When he jumped into the snowy trench that Black Wing was using as cover, his friend could not hide the smile on his face. "Are you a scout for those soldiers down there?"

"No," Trace replied frankly, "I just go out to round up the crazy ones." Knowing now that it was not worth the risk to stick his neck out again, he stood up on the edge of the trench and signaled to Luke and Turley, still watching from the ridge. Turning back to Black Wing, he explained. "There's about thirty soldiers on the other side of the ridge. I'm waving them on down." When he saw the look of concern in Black Wing's eye, he hastened to reassure him. "Don't worry, these ain't the crazy kind. They know you're friendly."

Several minutes passed, then a line of troopers appeared on the top of the ridge, making their way down toward them, Luke and Turley in the lead. The Indians came out of their defensive places and stood watching the arrival of the soldiers. Trace walked out to meet Luke.

"I guess you could see what happened when I tried to talk to that damn fool down there," Trace said as Luke rode up.

Seeing that Trace was not injured, Luke found the incident rather humorous and could not help but smile. He started to remark on it when he was interrupted by a cheer from the wood party in the gully. Seeing the arrival of Luke's detachment, they assumed they had been saved from an Indian massacre. "I think Masters is happy to see his rescuers," Luke said, his grin spreading.

Trace didn't say anything for a long moment while his bile lowered a bit. "You can send somebody down to tell him he can come out. Maybe he won't shoot at soldiers."

Luke laughed. Turning to his sergeant, he said, "Turley, go down there and rescue Lieutenant Masters and the wood party."

While Turley proceeded down the slope, Trace introduced Luke to Black Wing and Big Turtle. Black Wing suggested that it would be a good thing if they sat down and smoked together. While Luke's soldiers and the Crow warriors looked each other over, Trace, Luke, Black Wing, and Big Turtle sat down on a buffalo hide and passed a pipe that Big Turtle carried. The meeting went well, with Black Wing declaring his friendship for the Great White Father in Washington. After the polite talk and rituals were observed, the conversation was mostly between Black Wing and Trace. When Trace inquired about the welfare of Black Wing's father—and Trace's adoptive father—he was told that Buffalo Shield had become too old to ride with the war parties.

Soon, Lieutenant Ira Masters and his detachment of fifteen dragoons made their way up from the river and sheepishly stood off to one side while several of their number attempted to right the overturned wagons. Some of the Crow warriors helped round up the army horses that had run off during the soldiers' panic to reach the safety of the gully. Trace took one of the horses from the wagon team to replace his. While he was recovering his saddle and bridle, Lieutenant Masters approached.

"Sorry about the mistaken identity, McCall," Masters said, his tone condescending even in the face of his blunder. "I suggest you find an attire less like that of an Indian while you're working for the army."

Trace stopped what he was doing and turned to look the young officer over thoroughly. He could overlook greenhorn stupidity—and no harm done—but arrogance was another thing. He fixed Masters with a penetrating glare and in a low, even tone, said, "Let me tell you something, sonny. If you're lucky, you might keep your scalp long enough to learn how things are out here. You're lucky I wasn't riding my own horse, else I'd still be kicking your ass."

Masters recoiled. "Do you realize you're talking to an officer in the United States Army?" he demanded indignantly.

Trace didn't blink. "I'm talking to the ass I'm gonna be kicking if you ever shoot at me again. Now, get the hell away from me before I decide to start practicing right now."

Masters was completely unnerved. Insulted and

confused, he was uncertain what he should do about his dressing down from a civilian scout. His sense of manhood called for him to demand satisfaction from this half-wild lout. But Trace had risen to his full stature, a good head taller that Masters, and half again as wide across the shoulders. As a compromise to his honor, Masters glared back at the mountain man for a few moments before turning on his heel and departing. *I would not soil my hands*, he told himself.

Trace stood talking to his friend Black Wing until the troopers were ready to move out. They reminisced about the times they had when they were boys, living in Red Blanket's village. They were good times, both agreed. "Why do you live with these crazy soldiers?" Black Wing asked. "Come back to the mountains with us, live as a man should live. We could hunt the buffalo together again, follow the elk and the deer, take horses from the Blackfoot."

"It would be good," Trace admitted—and it did have a great deal of attraction for him—"but I have something I must do now. There is a white man that I must find and kill."

Black Wing nodded his head slowly. "This white man, what has he done to earn your vengeance?"

Trace told him of the union with Blue Water that had produced a son, of the murder of the Shoshoni girl, and the abduction of the boy. "I lost his trail in the snow, but I will search for him again when the snow melts."

"There is a white man who lives with the Gros Ventres," Black Wing said.

This captured Trace's attention at once. He was interested in any rumor about a white man living with Indians. "How do you know this?" Trace asked, knowing that the Gros Ventres were allies of the Blackfeet and no friends of the Crows.

Black Wing explained. "A Hidatsu man came to our village. He had been a prisoner of the Gros Ventres for two years where they made him a slave. One day when he was gathering wood with the women, he saw a chance to escape. He happened upon our village after the first snow. He told of a white man who came to the Gros Ventre camp with a boy tied with a rope around his neck."

Trace's blood went cold inside his veins. Without realizing it, his hand tightened around the handle of his knife until his knuckles were white. *It had to be him!* After a moment, he regained control of his emotions. "Where was this village?"

"He said it was on the Big River, beyond the land of the Assiniboine, near the mouth of the Yellowstone."

"I'll find it," Trace said, his words slow and hard as granite. Heating now, blood rushed through his veins, and he was burning with an urgency to ride. Fighting to keep his emotions from taking control of his senses, he told himself that he would have to wait. There were too many miles of frozen country between here and there. Two more months and the passes would be free of snow. That was time enough. The Gros Ventres would not likely leave their winter camp before then. Even if they did, he would find them, for now he had a trail to follow. Taking control of his emotions again, he took a deep breath and promised himself that he would not be denied.

They camped side by side that night, the soldiers and the Crows. The troopers shared their hardtack, salt pork, and coffee with the Indians, since Black Wing's warriors had found little game in the area. The next morning, when the wagons were righted and minor repairs were completed, Luke gave the order to mount and the troopers prepared to return to Fort Laramie. At Trace's suggestion, Luke had his men donate half of their coffee ration as a gift to the departing Crows. It seemed an appropriate gesture of goodwill. And since the men had drawn rations for ten days, there was coffee to spare. Once again, Trace bid his boyhood friend farewell and turned his horse toward Laramie.

Guiding his horse in beside Luke's, Trace looked toward the east where the rising sun had lit the cloudy sky in shades of fiery red, waves of brilliant color that spread across the prairie until they faded to a pink glow in the dark clouds over his head. Trace knew the radiant display was no more than a tease, and it would soon disappear. As he suspected, within an hour there was no evidence that there was ever a sun, the clouds grew dark, and it would probably snow before they reached the fort. But with Laramie only one day's ride, the soldiers were in a lighthearted disposition as the column retraced their march of the day before. Trace sat easy in the saddle, trying to adjust to the uneven gait of the horse he now rode. It was a hardheaded beast with a broken rhythm in its walk, and there was little wonder that it had been relegated to pulling a wagon. Behind him, he could hear the almost constant banter of the soldiers, as the men from Luke's patrol chided the members of the wood detail on their panic-stricken flight to the riverbank upon sighting "hostiles." Trace supposed that Lieutenant Masters, who was even closer to the banter, was getting his ears singed a little. That thought led him to thoughts of Grace Turner, and for a moment, he recalled the chilly afternoon on the creekbank. It caused him to glance back at the boyish face of the young lieutenant. He unconsciously shook his head as he decided that Grace was too much woman for Masters to handle. As quickly as thoughts of Grace had come, they were pushed aside by the news Black Wing had given him. Suddenly the banter of the soldiers got on his nerves and he needed quiet time to think.

"I'm gonna ride on ahead," he said to Luke, and without waiting for Luke's reply, gave the balky horse his heels. When he had spaced about a quarter of a mile between himself and the column, he let his horse settle back to a slower pace. From long habit, his eyes scanned the trail before him, darting back and forth, never fixing on one spot for any length of time. While that part of his brain stayed alert, working on instinct, another part worked furiously to sort out the recent events that served to trouble his mind.

While thoughts of finding the boy had never been far away, the fact that he had resigned himself to wait until the spring thaws had diminished the urgency somewhat. Now that urgency was renewed and he ached to set out for the Missouri right away. *The Big River*, as Black Wing called it—where the Yellowstone began—that's where White Eagle was. It would not be easy. The Gros Ventres were strong friends of the Blackfeet, and not especially cordial to white men. To be tolerated by this hostile tribe, the renegade who had taken White Eagle must have been useful to them in some way—probably supplying guns and powder. This man he sought, this thin-faced white man in the flat-crowned black hat, showed a talent for allying himself with various bands. The one common thread seemed to be that each band was hostile and savage in its intent. Trace had the distinct feeling that the entire world would be a far better place without Mr. Black Hat.

The sky became darker and darker as the clouds continued to hover close to the earth, and Trace's mind wandered to the Crow war party making its dangerous journey back to their village. It had been a daring raid Black Wing had undertaken, especially at this time of year. A thought struck him that Black Wing's raid might well have been inspired by the Great Spirit for the primary purpose of telling Trace where he might find the boy. He had been reluctant to admit it, but without help from some source, it might have taken him years to track down the white renegade. He realized that he was thinking like an Indian, but the teachings of old Buffalo Shield seemed to make more sense to him than the white man's beliefs. Then he thought of Black Wing's invitation to come back to the people. It was tempting—a way of life that Trace had found most fulfilling—he would think about it. But first he must find the boy—and settle a score with Black Hat.

A light snow was falling by the time the column approached Laramie. Plodding silently now through a veil of white, the wind stirring eddies around the horses' hooves, the column appeared ghostly, as if floating through a cloud. Cold and stiff from hours in the saddle, the men began to rouse themselves from their cold-induced stupor as they closed on the encampment. The wood party was back, although a couple of days late.

CHAPTER 14

By his own evaluation, Trace was not fit to live with for the next couple of months. So he kept to himself and his own thoughts as much as possible. There were a few patrols, but they were organized more for training purposes than actual missions. Some of the free time was spent in the company of Sergeant Turley and occasionally Luke, but most of the time Trace sought his own company. Thoughts of White Eagle with a rope around his neck kept recurring no matter how hard he tried to put them aside. Several times he determined to pack up his horses and start out, snow or no snow. Each time he would have to remind himself of the distance he must ride, most of it through hostile country. His best chance of accomplishing all he needed to do was if he was successful in traveling through that territory unseen. He wouldn't be doing himself or the boy any favors if he was wandering all over the territory, leaving tracks in the snow. Even though he would keep to the mountains as much as possible, the slopes were too treacherous for his horses when covered with snow and ice. And many of the passes would be blocked. He had no choice but to wait.

A week before Lieutenant Masters was scheduled to transfer back to Fort Kearny, Trace did have occasion to see Grace Turner. She made it a point to bump into him in the post trader's store one Saturday morning.

"Well, hello, stranger," Grace said, smiling. "Where have you been keeping yourself?"

"I've been around," Trace allowed.

"We were talking about you the other night at supper. My fiance seems to think you're a little too rough-cut for his liking." There was a definite twinkle in her eye when she said it. "He says you lack the proper respect for an officer. What did you say to him, anyway?"

"Nothing that I recall," Trace replied and quickly changed the subject. "I reckon you're making big plans for your wedding. I surely wish you and the lieutenant all the happiness in the world." Trace wanted to let Grace know that he harbored no resentment toward Masters, just in case she had the notion that he felt jilted by her. *Hell*, he thought, *no woman in her right mind would tie up with a drifter like me.*

Grace was outwardly pleased by his sentiment. "Why, thank you, Trace. You know I'll always have a special place in my heart for you."

Trace began to become uncomfortable. "Well, I guess I'd best get on about my business," he said. "Hope you have a safe trip downriver."

She caught his sleeve as he started to go. "Trace, I was thinking about taking a walk down by the creek to that spot Annie used to call her secret place—around four this afternoon, I expect." Her eyes searched his, her smile warm and inviting. Then she turned to leave, but in case her message was a bit too demure, she paused and whispered, "If you're out riding, you might want to take your buffalo robe with you. It's still pretty chilly out." Not waiting to witness his reaction, she promptly turned on her heel and was off.

Trace stood there a moment, watching her as she

made her way toward the door. Finding it difficult to believe at first, he marveled at the woman's blatant invitation, practically on the eve of her wedding. He thought back to the last time they had met by that creek. He had certainly been surprised at what came to pass at that meeting. He was more surprised now. *Damn!* he thought, *I must have done something right.* Wrestling with his emotions, he changed his mind several times during the balance of the morning.

But at a little before four that afternoon, he saddled the paint and rode off toward the cottonwoods that lined the creek behind Lamar Thomas's house.

He saw her once more after that day, passing her on his way to the stables. They came no closer than twenty yards of each other. Neither spoke—Trace nodded a solemn greeting, Grace smiled warmly. There was an unspoken understanding between them, a bond created by a mutual fulfillment of a deep need. There was no need for words. Two days later, a mail wagon with an army escort made it through from Fort Kearny. Assured that the trail was passable, Grace and her husband-to-be left Fort Laramie the following day. From a low rise along the riverbank of the Laramie River near the site of the old fort, Trace watched them depart—none of the parties involved knowing that he had presented Ira Masters with a son for a wedding present.

"Come'ere, boy." Booth Dalton jerked on the rawhide rope, causing the boy to stumble, almost falling on the floor of the tipi. On the other side of the lodge, sitting close by the fire, Charlie White Bull chuckled, always delighted by pain administered to others. "We need some more wood," Booth said.

White Eagle silently began the routine that was now all too familiar to him. He reached up and started working at the knot that tied the rope to the noose around his neck. Once the rope was untied, he removed his moccasins and leggings. Next he pulled his shirt over his head. Down to his breechclout, he then left the tipi to gather wood for the fire.

Booth laid back by the fire, smug in the knowledge that he needn't fear that the boy might run away. He felt certain that the desire to escape had been sufficiently dampened when earlier attempts had been dealt with severely. He smiled to himself when he thought of his latest method of clipping the little eagle's wings. Jumping around barefoot and almost naked in the snow, while gathering wood, effectively discouraged any thoughts of running away. It also sped up the wood-gathering process.

"When you gonna let me have that boy?" Charlie asked. "These Gros Ventres ain't gonna give you what you want for him."

"Shut up!" Booth snapped, tired of hearing Charlie's constant nagging. "It don't give no profit to me, you skinnin' that boy." A thin smile cracked his stern countenance. "What you complainin' about, anyway? Maybe you'd rather go git the wood." He stretched his legs out to make himself more comfortable. "It suits my fancy to have me a slave, even if I can't trade him."

Near the center of the camp, Wounded Horse stood talking to Fire That Burns. Both men paused to watch the nearly naked boy searching along the riverbank for deadwood. After a moment, Wounded Horse spoke. "I do not think we should permit those two to remain in the village. There is a stench about them that offends my nostrils."

Fire That Burns nodded, understanding the war chief's feelings. Most in the village shunned the white man and his half-breed friend. They were only tolerated because the white man promised to supply them with guns—and the fact that the half-breed was said to be the son of a Blackfoot woman. "Maybe you are right," Fire That Burns replied. "Maybe we should drive them out. I would have driven them from our camp before if we didn't need the guns they promised."

Wounded Horse frowned, his eyes still on the boy, who was now making his way back to the lodge through the snow. "They say they will leave in the spring to go get guns for us. I think they're lying. I think they just want a warm place to spend the winter." He looked back at Fire That Burns. "I don't like the way they treat the boy. I think maybe we should kill them instead of letting them go free when the snow melts."

"Maybe you are right, but we need the guns. Already, the Shoshoni and the Sioux have many guns. If this white man's word is true, it would help us against our enemies. It might be best to let them stay until spring, and see what happens."

"What about the boy?" Wounded Horse asked. "They claim he is white. He looks white, but he looks Indian, too. Maybe we should take him away from them. They ask too much to trade him—ten buffalo hides and four ponies—I say we should just take him."

"Maybe. Let's wait a while."

Back inside the tipi, White Eagle dropped his load of firewood, and shivering with the cold, hastened to climb back into his clothes, ignoring the lascivious grin on Charlie White Bull's face. Booth might be secure in his belief that White Eagle's will to run away had been broken, but it did not escape the boy's notice that the ice was beginning to melt along the riverbanks. It would not be long before the first signs of spring would appear. Then he would try again—clothes or no clothes. His spirit was far from broken.

*   *   *

Wounded Horse came out of his lodge to find Booth approaching his tipi, Charlie at his side, and the boy once again led by the rope around his neck. "Good morning, Chief," Booth said, combining his scanty knowledge of the tongue with sign language. "I come to trade this white boy."

Wounded Horse glared at the two men he had come to detest while some of the other people of the village came up to listen. Without warning, the boy spoke. His words came slowly as he was not totally confident in the few words of broken English he had picked up from Booth. "Not white—Shoshoni."

"Shut your mouth!" Booth hissed and jerked hard on the rope. "He don't know what he's sayin'. He's white, he was just raised by the Snakes."

Wounded Horse was taken aback by the sudden announcement by the boy. The boy had never spoken before. Now, Wounded Horse could see that it had possibly been out of fear of punishment from Booth. "Go and find Three Toes," Wounded Horse said to a warrior standing near him. Three Toes knew the Shoshoni tongue. Within minutes, he joined the gathering around the war chief's tipi. "Ask this boy where he comes from, and who his people are," Wounded Horse said, and all eyes turned to look at White Eagle.

"I am White Eagle, Shoshoni," the boy replied boldly. "I am from Chief Washakie's village in the Wind River country." Pointing toward Booth, he said, "This man killed my mother and my grandfather."

A low murmuring began to build within the growing crowd of spectators as Three Toes translated the boy's words. The people of the village had little use for the white man and his half-breed partner, so White Eagle's accusations were not surprising to them. When the boy spoke again, Three Toes jerked his head back abruptly, his eyes shifted briefly to fix on Booth Dalton, a look of shock on his face. Then he looked back at Wounded Horse and translated.

"The boy says that this white man and his friend were riding with a Sioux war party when the boy's mother was killed."

There was an immediate swell in the crowd, lifting the low grumbling of the previous moments to sharp protests of individual voices. In the next moment, all eyes were turned toward the two renegades. The Sioux were traditional enemies of the Gros Ventres. Instinctively, Charlie White Bull began to inch away from Booth's side in a feeble attempt to disassociate himself from the white man.

"Now wait a minute, Chief, me and Charlie wasn't riding with them Sioux, no sir." His face a shade whiter than before, Booth blurted the denial so quickly that he forgot Wounded Horse couldn't understand English. Seeing the stern face of the chief, he quickly groped for the proper Gros Ventre term, finally spitting out, "Captive! Captive! We were captives . . . The boy's wrong."

The situation had rapidly turned ugly for them, and Booth knew he had some fast talking to do. The little Shoshoni rat had thrown their fat in the fire for sure if Booth couldn't convince these Gros Ventres that he and Charlie had taken no part in any raids with the Sioux. *I told the little bastard to keep his mouth shut. I should have let Charlie skin him.* Feeling the angry crowd of warriors closing in closer and closer, their faces reflecting the contempt they held for anyone who rode with the Sioux, Booth held up his arms, asking to be heard.

"Chief Wounded Horse and the great Gros Ventre warriors, know that I have always been a friend to your people. I have brought you guns and other gifts in the past, and I will bring you more in the future. This boy does not see the truth as it was. Things don't look the same from the other side." He gestured toward Charlie. "My friend, the son of a Blackfoot woman, and I were trying to steal guns from the Sioux to give to the Gros Ventres. But they caught us and made us captives. We got away the first chance we got, and came straight to our friends, the Gros Ventres." He paused to examine the chief's expression, hoping to see some sign that Wounded Horse believed him, but the chief's expression remained stony. "We brought this boy with us—saved him from the evil Sioux—they would have killed him."

"But you keep him tied like a camp dog," Fire That Burns interjected.

Booth nodded in agreement, racking his brain for creative thoughts. "That's for his protection," he replied, "so he won't run off and get caught by the Sioux again."

"So you are protecting him," Wounded Horse stated with more than a hint of sarcasm in his tone.

"Yes," Booth eagerly replied. "Me and Charlie are protecting the boy."

"And yet you want to trade him for buffalo hides and horses," Fire That Burns said.

"Well, yeah," Booth admitted, looking nervously from the chief to the medicine man, and feeling like he was not going to come out ahead on this discussion. "But only because I think the boy would be safer with you."

Wounded Horse looked long and hard at the thin-faced white man before he spoke again. Glancing at the boy who was lost amid a sea of strange languages, the chief made his decision. "You are right, the boy will be safer with us. We will keep him."

Booth forced a wide smile. "That would be a good

thing—keep the boy." Then he quickly added, "But I need the skins and horses—a fair trade."

Wounded Horse gazed at Booth as if his eyes were tired of looking at the offensive white man. "We will trade," he said, "but not for skins and horses. I will give you your life for the boy."

Booth didn't understand. "You wouldn't kill me and Charlie, would you? We're gonna git many rifles for your warriors."

A wry smile parted Wounded Horse's lips. "That's why I am giving you your life. You and the other will leave my village now. When you come back with guns, you will get many skins and horses then. I think this is a good trade for you."

"Well now, I don't know, Chief," Booth started, but Charlie grabbed his sleeve and pulled him aside.

"It's a good trade," he whispered in Booth's ear. The half-breed had been gauging the temperament of the crowd gathered around them, and he didn't like the surly looks he received. It was obvious that the chief's decision to spare their lives was not a popular one with the warriors. He looked at the chief and nodded excitedly, "It's a good trade. We'll go to get the guns right now."

Booth had always been the self-appointed brains of the partnership with Charlie White Bull, but it was the dimwitted half-breed who realized there might not be another opportunity to leave the village with their scalps. Many of the assembled warriors were already grumbling among themselves as they cast a hostile eye in Booth's direction. "Come on, we go to get the guns now," Charlie said, speaking for the benefit of the sullen warriors. Booth resisted, still intent upon turning a profit for the sale of the Shoshoni boy. But Charlie took him by the arm and forcefully moved him away from the chief's lodge.

Angry at first, Booth then saw the look in Charlie's eyes, and it suddenly occurred to him that his defiance of Wounded Horse's will would most likely lead to a scalping party—with him and Charlie as the guests of honor. Realizing then what Charlie had already surmised—that their lives weren't worth a plugged nickel—Booth nodded nervously, and stammered, "All right, all right . . . let's git outta here."

Three Toes removed the rawhide collar from White Eagle's neck and held him by the shoulders while he examined the boy from head to toe. "They did not give you much to eat," he commented.

The boy remained silent, looking around the tipi apprehensively. As far as he knew, his people, the Shoshonis, had never been very friendly with the Gros Ventres. The Gros Ventres were one of the few tribes who were close to the Blackfeet—and the Blackfeet were hated by most. White Eagle was not sure what his future would be with these people, but he was glad he had spoken up when Booth tried to trade him again. He was still a captive, but anything was better than staying with Booth and Charlie. This man, Three Toes, did not appear to mean him any harm. There was no hatred in the curious eyes that looked him over.

"You spoke of your mother and your grandfather," Three Toes said. "Where is your father? Was he killed by the Sioux as well?"

"No," White Eagle shook his head. "My father will come for me." Although the boy had no way of knowing if Trace McCall would search for him, he truly believed that he would. Even though spending just a short time with his father, he felt a strong kinship for the tall man whose eyes had looked into his. White Eagle had seen no deceit there.

"Your skin is light," Three Toes said. "Is your father a white man?"

"Yes."

"How is he called?"

"Men call him the Mountain Hawk," White Eagle answered proudly.

White Eagle was puzzled by Three Toes's look of astonishment. The old warrior drew back as if he had seen a snake, or a rabbit had suddenly bolted across his path. He seemed to examine the boy anew, as if for the first time. Three Toes asked no more questions, but continued to watch White Eagle while the boy ate from a bowl of boiled meat Three Toes's wife had brought for him.

White Eagle ate hungrily, causing Three Toes and his wife to exchange amazed glances. It was apparent that he was not accustomed to eating his fill. In truth, White Eagle had been surviving on the scraps left over after Booth and Charlie had eaten. For the first time since his ill-fated attempt upon Booth's life, White Eagle forgot thoughts of escape. Content for the present to concern himself with filling his belly, he wasn't even aware that his former captors had packed their possibles and were already hightailing it down the Yellowstone. Thoughts of vengeance would return, but for now the boy was content to be in the lodge of an Indian family, even if that family was Gros Ventre.

Wounded Horse looked up to see Three Toes hurrying across the open space between the tipis. From the serious expression on the old warrior's face, Wounded Horse's first thought was that something had happened to the boy. Before Three Toes could speak, Wounded Horse asked, "Is something wrong?"

Three Toes shook his head excitedly. "No," he answered, "the boy is resting." Seating himself beside the fire across from Wounded Horse, he could barely contain his news. "The Shoshoni boy is the son of the Mountain Hawk," he said, then waited for the chief's reaction.

Wounded Horse's eyes opened wide, his usual placid features registering the depth of his surprise. "The Mountain Hawk!" he echoed. Could this be true? It had been rumored that this Mountain Hawk might be a white man—or spirit. "How do you know this?"

"The boy told me," Three Toes replied. "There was no deceit in his eyes." He waited while Wounded Horse digested this, then said, "He has said that his father will come for him."

"I see," Wounded Horse said, his mind now churning with questions regarding the possibility that the storied Mountain Hawk might descend upon their village. Their allies, the Blackfeet, had originated the name for the man, or spirit, that dwelled in the high mountain meadows. They claimed that three of their bravest warriors had been slain by his hand. Only a few others had seen him, and that was only a fleeting glimpse before he disappeared into the rocks.

There was one question that confronted Wounded Horse now, if the boy really was the son of the Mountain Hawk. Was the Mountain Hawk not a spirit, but simply a man? Or was the boy in part spiritual as well? He would have to discuss it with the medicine man— old Fire That Burns had a strong sense about things of this nature. The two of them got up from the fire and went to seek him out.

Fire That Burns was as amazed as Wounded Horse had been to hear the news his chief brought. "If what you say is true, then this is a very serious matter, and we must think on it a while."

"How do we know that the boy speaks the truth? He may have only heard of the Mountain Hawk,"

Wounded Horse suggested. "I do not doubt that the boy's father is white, but he might not have the slightest idea who his father is."

"That is possible," Fire That Burns allowed, nodding his head slowly as he considered that possibility. After a moment's thought, he said, "Bring the boy to me. I'll know if he speaks the truth."

Three Toes was off immediately to do the medicine man's bidding, leaving Wounded Horse and Fire That Burns to speculate upon this fateful turn of events. "This could be a very important thing for our village," Wounded Horse said, his mind already jumping ahead to thoughts of glory. "Our friends, the Blackfeet, have been trying to kill this spirit of the mountains for many moons but have failed. Our medicine would be very big in their eyes if we are able to lure him into a trap and kill him."

"This is true," Fire That Burns agreed, "but we must be careful. The Blackfeet are fierce warriors, and they lost three of their best trying to kill this spirit," he reminded the chief.

Further discussion was delayed by the arrival of Three Toes with the son of the Mountain Hawk. With Three Toes acting as interpreter, Fire That Burns talked to White Eagle. Being cautious not to make the boy think he was anything other than welcome in the Gros Ventre camp, he first asked White Eagle if he had been offered food. When the boy replied that he had been treated like a friend in Three Toes's lodge, Fire That Burns nodded solemnly, smiling. He then questioned the boy about his tribe and his mother, then finally, his father. White Eagle answered the medicine man's questions, telling him all that his mother had told him of his father. When Fire That Burns asked why White Eagle thought his father would come for him, the boy told of his recent meeting with Trace.

"He is as tall as the pines on the mountainside, hi
shoulders wide, his arms powerful," White Eagl
boasted, eager to impress the Gros Ventre medicin
man.

Fire That Burns believed the boy might be telling
the truth, but he searched for more proof. He remem
bered the description of the mysterious Mountai
Hawk told to him by one who had seen the legend. Lit
tle Bull, a Blackfoot war chief had seen the Mountai
Hawk once. Although it was from a distance of per
haps that equal to one tall lodgepole pine, still h
could see him fairly well. Little Bull had said that th
Mountain Hawk stood on a rocky ledge above him
and when he and his war party climbed up to th
ledge to capture him, the man was gone, but a hawl
circled away above them.

"Your father," Fire That Burns began, "I am tol
that he has hair as black as night, and black bushy hai
on his face like many white men."

White Eagle immediately shook his head, as the pic
ture of Trace McCall returned to his mind. "My fathe
is not a hair-face. His face is smooth, like a Shoshon
warrior. And his hair is the color of the mountai
lion."

"Ahh," Fire That Burns responded. This matche
the description given him by Little Bull. He turned t
Wounded Horse. "The boy speaks the truth—he is th
son of the Mountain Hawk."

"Then you think he will come for the boy?"
Wounded Horse asked. When Fire That Burns nodded
the chief's eyes gleamed with excitement over the op
portunity to capture or kill this mountain spirit. "We
must call the elders to the council fire to talk of this."

There was a great deal of excited discussion among
the elders when they gathered to discuss Wounde

Horse's startling news. Not all believed the rumors that the Mountain Hawk was in fact a spirit of the mountains. One among them, Lame Elk, was particularly skeptical of the tales told by the Blackfeet, and spoke his contempt passionately. "I don't think this Mountain Hawk is a spirit. I think he is a white man, like all the others who came to our lands to trap our beaver and kill our buffalo. He is just more clever than the others, staying high upon the slopes where the Blackfeet would not go to look for him. I say let him come and we will see if he is spirit or man when I shoot some arrows in his body."

When Lame Elk sat down again, a few of those around the council fire nodded agreement with his words. But the majority of the warriors were not ready to refute the stories the Blackfeet had told of this hawk. If he was not a spirit, then he must surely be a man with special medicine. And it was the general opinion that Lame Elk might be taking the hawk too lightly.

"Maybe if we greet this hawk in peace, and give him his son, he may come as a friend," Many Horses suggested.

The council rose against this idea almost to a man. Wounded Horse spoke then. "The Mountain Hawk is an enemy to the Blackfeet as well as the Gros Ventres. There are Blackfoot dead to tell us this truth. If he took a Shoshoni woman as a wife, how can we expect him to be a friend to the Gros Ventres?"

"Maybe we should send a runner to the Blackfoot camp to tell them this hawk is coming," Fire That Burns said. "He has been their enemy longer than he has been ours."

"No!" Lame Elk sprang to his feet. "This man is coming to our village to take the boy from the Gros Ventres. I say we watch for him and kill him. Then we

will send his head to the Blackfeet to show them we
did something they could not."

"I think Lame Elk is right," Wounded Horse said
and when the council was over, it was agreed that the
village would prepare for the arrival of this special
enemy. There was much discussion on when the hawk
might be expected. Lame Elk maintained that if he
waited until the snow had gone, it would be an indication that the Mountain Hawk was no more than any
other man. If he were indeed a spirit, as the Blackfeet
said, he would not have to wait for good weather. This
seemed reasonable to the gray heads of the village, so
they deemed it wise to prepare themselves now. The
boy would continue to be kept under the care of Three
Toes, since Three Toes spoke his language, but he must
not suspect that he was a captive. This was in case the
boy possessed special medicine himself and might be
able to send a message to his father and warn him of
the ambush. There followed a great amount of excitement in the Gros Ventre village as each warrior
checked his weapons, eager to be the one who killed
the Mountain Hawk.

While the Gros Ventres prepared a reception for
him, Trace McCall was two hundred miles away, as the
hawk flies, and making his way up the Powder River
valley. Unable to wait until spring officially arrived, he
decided to leave at the first break in the weather. He
had tried to be patient throughout the long winter
months, but each day that painfully dragged by only
increased his anxiety over the welfare of the boy, and
the unfinished business with Blue Water's killers. So
spring had not yet arrived when Trace informed Captain Benton that he was leaving.

Though his patience had worn through, he had not
grown careless. Without having to concentrate on it, he

naturally kept to the low side of the ridges, watching his back trail, and carefully looking over the trail in front of him before leaving cover. Luck seemed to be with him because winter had apparently lost its grip on the rolling hills with signs of runoff already spilling into the icy streams. In many places, the snow was little more than a light dusting. He was satisfied that it had been a good decision to leave when he did.

Although he could not make as many miles in a day as he would have liked, still he should be able to reach the head of the Yellowstone in a week's time. Then he would have to find the Gros Ventre village.

CHAPTER 15

"**D**amn that young'un," Booth spat, as he sat by the fire and chewed on a tough strip of buffalo jerky. "I wish to hell I had let you skin that brat to begin with."

"I told you them Gros Ventres wouldn't trade you nuthin' for him," Charlie said, patiently working on his own strip of the tough buffalo meat.

"Shut up, dammit," Booth fired back at his dimwitted partner. He swallowed hard, forcing a partially masticated wad of dried meat down his throat. "You're some damn Injun," he complained to Charlie, "can't find so much as a rabbit to cook."

It wasn't Charlie's fault that game was scarce, but Booth felt like assigning the blame somewhere so he could complain about it. He was still angry at having been ushered out of Wounded Horse's camp. Sitting on a snowy riverbank, his hands and feet numb with the cold, he thought about the warm tipi he had enjoyed for most of the winter and cursed his luck again. At least they were able to leave the Gros Ventre camp with an extra horse—the pony that belonged to the Shoshoni boy.

Travel had not been as difficult as Booth had expected. There was only light snow down the Yellowstone valley. Still, that was not enough to improve his outlook. Looking at his foolish companion sitting

across from him, chewing contentedly on his jerky—
slobber running down his chin—didn't help Booth's
disposition, either. An unattached thought ran
through his brain that this would be a good opportunity to rid himself of the half-breed. *One bullet between
those stupid eyes would be all it took and I wouldn't have to
listen to his damn bellyaching no more.* It was tempting,
but Booth was too lazy to do without the many chores
that Charlie performed for him—hunting, cooking,
gathering wood, slitting throats—all the things Booth
preferred having someone else do.

"Where the hell we goin'?" Charlie suddenly asked,
breaking into Booth's thoughts.

"I ain't decided yet." That was all the answer he felt
like giving Charlie at the moment. His plans to this
point had advanced no further than following the Yellowstone to the point where the Powder forked off,
following the Powder south, and cutting across to
South Pass. From there, he could go east or west, and
he was kind of favoring west—over toward Mormon
country. Thousands of Mormons had been emigrating
into the Wasatch country, thousands of folks who had
never heard of Booth Dalton. The thought brought a
smile to Booth's face, causing his disposition toward
Charlie to brighten a bit. Maybe he'd tolerate his dull-
brained partner for a spell longer. "Maybe we'll head
for the Bear River Mountains and the Wasatch," he
said to Charlie.

Charlie stopped chewing for a second to consider
this, then asked, "What kinda Injun I gotta be there?"

Booth laughed. "Snake, I reckon." He thought to
himself, *Dead Injun most likely.* Charlie's usefulness
was probably nearing an end. Booth didn't think it
likely that Charlie could pass for Shoshoni, and he
damn sure didn't look like a Mormon.

* * *

From the cover of a line of trees running the length of the low ridge that paralleled the river, Trace McCall lay on his belly in the snow watching the progress of the two riders. Sticking close to the river, the two appeared to be Indians, leading three horses, two of them heavily packed. He might have crossed their trail had he not been careful to look the broad valley over before descending from the ridge. Having no desire to encounter Indians from any tribe, Trace was content to remain where he was until the two had passed, then he would continue on his way up the Powder.

Keeping low, he made his way back over the top of the ridge to check on his horses. Satisfied that all was in order there, he returned to his vantage point in the trees to watch the progress of the two Indians. They had reached a point abreast of his position and would soon be far enough beyond for him to safely continue on his way.

While he waited, he pulled a skin pouch from his coat pocket and unwrapped the remaining portion of a young rabbit that had been his breakfast. Tearing off a leg, he contented himself while watching the two Indians as they slowly rode past. Suddenly he stopped chewing, forgetting his hunger, as something triggered his mind. The last horse in line behind the two packhorses looked familiar—a lot like the little spotted gray pony that White Eagle rode. Dropping the rabbit leg in the snow, he quickly scrambled to a better position where he could get a closer look at the horse. *It was the same pony!* He was sure of it.

Scores of hurried thoughts stampeded through his brain as he made his way along the tree line, working his way down as close to the edge of the trees as possible. Had he been too late to save his son? This didn't mean that White Eagle was dead, he quickly reassured himself. Maybe these Indians stole the horse. He real-

.zed that he was jumping to conclusions that made no sense. Why would the Gros Ventres kill White Eagle if he had been a captive all winter. He needed to get a closer look at the two, now approaching the edge of the trees where he waited. Maybe they could tell him of the boy's whereabouts.

Lying flat behind the trunk of a pine, and hidden by its low-hanging branches, Trace waited and watched as the riders came closer and closer. In the next instant, he felt a rush of blood to his brain and his heart pounded in his chest. For now he could see that instead of two Indians, it was *an Indian and a white man*!

Fighting an almost overpowering urge to spring upon the two, he forced himself to remain still. He could not be certain this was black hat, the white man he had seen in the Sioux camp. The two riders were almost opposite him now, and the white man turned to say something to his partner. Still, Trace could not get a good look at the man's face since it was partially masked by the heavy fur robe pulled up around him. Almost certain that he had stumbled upon the very man he searched for, Trace was frustrated now when a thread of doubt entered his mind. He had only seen the man before from a distance, wearing a flat-crowned black hat. This man now riding away from him wore a fur cap—which would be only natural in weather this cold. His gut feeling told him this was the man White Eagle described to him. And yet, there was a small margin of doubt, and Trace had no desire to murder an innocent man. His finger lightly stroked the trigger on his Hawken rifle, wanting to squeeze it, but unable to until he confirmed his target.

Damn! he swore to himself. There was no choice but to follow the two and find out for sure. And there was no way to find out unless he confronted them. He stood up and watched the two riders until they rode

out of sight. Then he made his way back up the ridge
to fetch his horses while deciding his best course of action. By the time he reached the paint and his packhorse, the decision was made. He would follow the
men until they made camp. Then he would ride in
peacefully. If they were the murdering renegades he
hunted, he should soon find out.

Charlie White Bull looked up when the horses
whinnied, startled to see the rider approaching their
camp. His first thought was to reach for his rifle, only
then realizing that it was propped against a tree some
twenty feet away. One look at the Hawken rifle resting
across the stranger's thighs told him it would be futile
to make a try to get his. Charlie glanced at Booth,
stretched out by the fire, his rifle still in its saddle
sling, the saddle serving as Booth's pillow.

"We got company," Charlie said, keeping his voice
low. Booth, unaware of their visitor until that moment,
bolted upright. "Who the hell . . ?" he started, trailing
off when he saw the solitary figure in buckskins.

Trace reined up some twenty-five yards away, and
called out, "Hello the camp."

Booth started to pull his rifle from the sling, thought
better of it, then answered. "Hello yourself. Who be
you?"

"Trace McCall," Trace answered. "I saw your fire,
thought you might have some coffee."

Charlie began inching toward his rifle, but Booth
stopped him. "Stand still," he whispered, "there ain't
but one of 'em. No sense in gittin' shot at." To Trace, he
called back, "Come on in, if you're peaceful. Friends is
always welcome at my fire." He was already evaluating the possible spoils to be gained with the stranger's
demise—two horses, a fine-looking rifle, and who
could say what might be packed on that horse?

"He's a big'un," Charlie noted under his breath, his hand resting on his knife hilt.

"Ain't he?" Booth confirmed, grinning widely.

Trace touched the paint lightly with his heels and the horse walked slowly into the camp. As he approached the fire, the two men watching him, Trace noticed the rifle leaning against the tree, the other rifle in the saddle sling on the ground, one pistol laying beside the saddle, another pistol and a knife stuck in the Indian's belt. He made it his business to know where all the weapons were before he stepped down, and he thought he had them all accounted for. But just as he was about to dismount, the weapon that caught his eye and held it for a long moment was lying by the Indian's blanket—an otterskin bow case and quiver, decorated with colored beads and porcupine quills. The expression on Trace's face never changed as the anger boiled up inside him. The gray spotted pony and the bow case were all the confirmation he needed to know that he had found the right pair. But he decided to continue to play out the hand he had already dealt just to be doubly sure.

"Well now, Mr. McCall," Booth piped up when the stranger dismounted, "where are you headed, all by yourself in this territory?"

"I'm looking for somebody," Trace answered, his rifle still in his hand as he positioned himself so he could keep an eye on both men. "Maybe you've seen him."

Booth shrugged. "Maybe. We ain't hardly seen nobody though." He sat back down by the fire. "Set yourself down by the fire and git warm." His show of hospitality failed to induce the stranger to put his rifle down. "Who is it you're lookin' for?"

"A boy, eleven or twelve, Shoshoni," Trace answered, watching Booth's reaction intently. Booth

never twitched, his expression remained as innocent
as a Sunday-school teacher. The half-breed was not so
adept at restraining his emotions. Trace did not miss
the sharp eye-jerk toward Booth and the hand tighten
on the handle of the knife he wore opposite his pistol.

Unfazed, Booth stroked his chin whiskers as if trying to recall. "Nope," he finally said, "we ain't seen nobody like that. What do you want him for, anyway?"

"He's my son. He was abducted by a couple of low-
down bushwhacking murderers." Out of the corner of
his eye, he noticed the half-breed slowly inching over
toward the rifle leaning against the tree. He turned his
head and looked straight at Charlie, stopping the half-
breed in his tracks. "You sure you ain't seen him?"
Trace pressed.

"No, friend, we ain't. Why don't you set yourself
down and rest a while. Help yourself to some of that
coffee there." Booth made a show of settling back
against his saddle, hoping to relax the stranger a bit.
"Why, I'll tell you what, why don't you camp here
with us tonight? And me and ol' Charlie will help you
look for your boy in the morning."

"Well now, that's mighty neighborly of you," Trace
replied, barely hiding the sarcasm. Charlie shuffled a
couple of steps closer to the rifle while Trace pretended
not to notice.

"No trouble at all," Booth said. "I swear, it's about
time to turn in, anyway." He took a pocketwatch from
his coat and held it up to the fire so he could see it.
"Yep, it's past my bedtime." He closed the cover on the
watch and wound it.

Remembering a comment that Annie had once
made, Trace said, "You know, if I was a betting man,
I'd bet a hundred dollars that watch you got there says
To Tom Farrior from Annie on the inside cover.

There followed a frozen moment when both Booth

and Charlie stared speechless at the imposing stranger who had invaded their camp. Charlie made his move first. Still too far from his rifle, he snatched the pistol from his belt. The barrel had barely cleared his belt when the rifle ball from Trace's Hawken tore into his belly, causing him to double up in pain, his pistol discharging into the ground.

Without waiting to see the results of his shot, Trace dropped the empty rifle, and in the wink of an eye, lunged toward Booth. Stunned for a second by the sudden explosion of Trace's rifle, Booth dived for his own pistol, only to be knocked sideways by Trace's hurtling body. Scrambling up from all fours, Booth stumbled and staggered, trying to regain his feet. Though much bigger than the thin-faced renegade, Trace was lightning-quick, and was upon the hapless man like a fox on a prairie dog, tumbling and mauling him viciously.

In one last desperate attempt to save himself, Booth managed to pull his knife from his belt. Fueled by the fury that had festered inside him over the long winter, Trace caught Booth's wrist, clamping down so forcefully that Booth was powerless to hold the weapon. Holding the terrified renegade helpless, Trace stuck his face inches from Booth's, and growled, "Is that the knife you used to scalp the Shoshoni woman you killed?" Booth's eyes were wide with panic, bulging from the powerful hand that crushed his throat. "She was my wife," Trace forced through clenched teeth.

Seeing that Booth was just about to lose consciousness, Trace eased his grip on the scoundrel's throat slightly. "Where is the boy?" he demanded. "Is he alive?"

His windpipe already partially crushed, Booth could barely whisper. "If I tell you, will you let me go?" he rasped.

Too enraged to lie, Trace replied, "I'll let you go to hell where you belong."

Clearly seeing the end of his evil life only moments away, Booth resigned himself to his death, and in one last act of spite, said, "He's dead, and you can go to hell."

The pronouncement hit Trace like a rifle shot, and he clamped down on Booth's neck, slowly crushing the life from his lungs. He held the hated renegade in his death grip long after Booth's body went limp—his face now a terrified mask with bulging eyeballs that seemed to have stared Satan in the eye. Finally, Trace flung the lifeless body from him and stood up. Looking back toward the fire, he discovered Charlie White Bull painfully straining to drag himself to his rifle.

Trace walked over to the tree, picked up the rifle and tossed it out of reach. Seeing that Trace was coming to finish him off, Charlie pulled his knife from his belt, and falling back on his side, waited for Trace to attack. Trace paused for a moment to stand over the mortally wounded half-breed, his eyes blazing with hatred. Then suddenly he struck, kicking the knife from Charlie's hand and pinning him to the ground before the half-breed could react.

Charlie tried to resist, but already he was too weak from the loss of blood to put up much of a fight. Seeing death reflected in the tall mountain man's eyes, Charlie gave up his struggles and started to chant his death song.

"Is the boy dead?" Trace asked.

"No," Charlie answered weakly, "he's with the Gros Ventres on the Yellowstone." The half-breed saw no reason to lie at his hour of death.

Trace released his hold on the dying man, and got to his feet. He stood over him once more and watched the man's agonized struggling. Then he pulled out his pistol and put a ball into Charlie's brain, ending the half-breed's torment, a payment for his honesty. With the sudden report of the pistol, everything seemed to go silent. Even the wind stopped its whispered song through the pine needles, and Trace felt a heavy cloak of melancholy fall about his shoulders. Instead of the sweet release of vengeance he had long anticipated when the score had been settled with Blue Water's killers, he found that he was only saddened more by her loss. The loss was even more devastating because he had really never had the opportunity to know her as his wife. Looking now at the two bodies sprawled before him, he wanted to cry out to the spirits that this was not enough. Then he thought of the boy—their son, his and Blue Water's, and he gathered his emotions again and tucked them away deep inside where he always kept private thoughts—away from the rest of the world—and turned his mind toward rescuing his son.

Without bothering to drag the two corpses away from the campsite, Trace lay down by the fire and slept the sleep of the weary. Sometime during the night, he awakened and, realizing his carelessness, unsaddled his horse and took the packs from his packhorse. Then he lay down again and slept until dawn.

Rested now, he was eager to complete his quest. Before bidding the late Booth Dalton and Charlie White Bull farewell, he gathered their weapons and ammunition. With his own bow and quiver once again on his back, he took the silver watch from Booth's pocket, opened it, and read the inscription. THOMAS L. FARRIOR, LOVE FROM ANNIE. It would mean a great deal to Annie to have this returned. He tied the gray spotted pony behind his packhorse and cut the other horses loose. With the job he had ahead of him, he couldn't bother with extra horses. Everything finished there, he turned the paint's head toward the Yellowstone.

For the past week, Wounded Horse had kept his village in a state of readiness. Every day scouts went out to scour the surrounding prairie and hills, watching for signs of the Mountain Hawk. Fire That Burns had told of dreams he'd had that foretold of the coming of this white man-spirit. For three nights in a row, he had dreamed of hawks—there could be no other interpretation. There had been many dances celebrating the honor and prestige that would come to the village when the golden scalp of the Mountain Hawk was displayed on the council lodge.

While White Eagle was treated with kindness, he soon found that he was still regarded as a captive. He was never allowed to leave the village alone. When he asked old Three Toes why the men of the village appeared to be preparing for war, he was told that it was nothing but springtime ceremonies. The boy suspected there was more to it than that, but he could not get any more information out of the old man, and Three Toes's wife never spoke to White Eagle at all.

Several miles away, Trace knelt down to examine the tracks of two horses in a patch of snow. They were recent enough to tell him that he must be getting close to a village. He must exercise even more caution now to avoid encountering any Gros Ventre hunting parties. After another mile or so up the valley, the hunting trails grew more numerous, and he decided it was time to find a place to hide his horses. Most of his scouting would be on foot from that point and under the cover of darkness.

On the eastern side of a low line of hills, he finally found what he was looking for, a sheltered defile that was ringed by thick pines—close enough to the village that he could hear occasional voices on the wind. Here he made his camp and waited for nightfall.

When the last few shafts of light finally faded away, he laid his rifle aside. Taking up his bow and knife, he left his hideaway and started for the Gros Ventre camp. There was still too much snow on the ground to avoid leaving tracks altogether, so he would just have to trust to luck, and try to mix his tracks with others that he encountered.

Long before he had made his way up a low hill some two hundred yards from the village, he could see the glow of a huge fire reflected on the dark clouds overhead, and hear the chanting of a war dance. *Sounds like they're getting ready for something big*, he thought. Upon reaching the top of the hill, he saw the Gros Ventre village before him, spread along the riverbank. He estimated over a hundred tipis, and a large pony herd below the camp. It would not be an easy task to find the boy, especially at night, but the risk of getting close to the camp in daylight was too great.

Twice, while making his way down the hill and across the narrow valley floor, he was forced to stop and take cover to prevent encounters with a Gros Ventre rider patrolling the perimeter of the camp. It caused him to wonder. It was not the usual routine for a camp this size, especially in winter. Possibly the village was expecting an attack from some enemy.

When at last he worked his way up behind the outermost lodges, he began to edge his way around the camp, sometimes on his hands and knees, trying to find some clue that might indicate where White Eagle was being held. There was not much he could see. Still he continued to work his way around the camp, watching the people of the village as they either joined in or watched the dancers. There were many children in the camp, but none that could be distinguished as White Eagle. Finally he had to admit that his efforts were meeting only with frustration, and he backed away a bit to contemplate his situation.

After giving it much thought, he decided that it would be impossible to find White Eagle at night. He could be in any one of over one hundred tipis. It was going to be risky as hell, but he was going to have to find a place to hide himself in the daylight, close enough to see the goings and comings of the village.

He spent the rest of the night trying to find a proper location to hide himself. An ideal spot would be on a rise on the west side of the camp in a stand of trees, but he rejected it because the sun would be directly in his eyes for much of the early morning. Stopping once again to lay flat on his stomach as another Gros Ventre warrior rode by, he then made his way along the riverbank until he found a place that might be suitable. In fact, it may have been made to order. A large log lay close to the river, held on the bank by two smaller trees. By scooping out the snow between the two trees, Trace found that he could fashion a sizable hole beneath the log. Once he had dug out enough to accommodate his body, he crawled inside. Using his bow as a rake, he pulled the snow back up to the log and smoothed it out as best he could. He could only hope he did an adequate job of disguising his handiwork—daylight would be the ultimate judge. There was nothing to do now but wait for morning, so he made himself as comfortable as he could under the circumstances, knowing that if he were discovered, this snowbank would be his coffin.

When the sun rose the following morning, Trace was surprised to find that he had dozed off during the wee hours before dawn. For now he could already hear sounds of the village waking up. Anxious to see if his snow cave gave him the vantage point he had thought it would during the dark of night, he raked a small observation hole under the log. He was disappointed to find that he could only see about half of the camp—but that half he could at least see clearly. It might be necessary to find a better spot, but for now, he had no choice but to stay where he was, maybe even until that night.

Hours passed and Trace watched as the daily life of the Gros Ventre village unfolded. A few of the women cooked the morning meal outside, even though there was still snow on the ground. Smoke from the smoke-flaps of the tipis was evidence that the majority preferred the comfort inside the warm lodges. Cramped and hungry, Trace envied those warriors still in their fur robes as he rubbed his arms and legs to stimulate some circulation.

Gradually the village came to life. Some of the men went to tend their horses, only a few prepared to go hunting, a fact that puzzled Trace. He saw many young boys running between the lodges, but none that looked like White Eagle. After a while, he began to wonder if the half-breed had lied to him about the boy. As he grew more and more uncomfortable, he started to question the wisdom in burying himself in this frigid hole.

Later in the morning he spotted the chief of this band of Gros Ventres. His lodge was in the center of the village, close to what appeared to be a council lodge. From the manner in which other men of the camp approached this man, Trace could tell that he was either a chief or at least a respected member of the tribe. As Trace watched, an old warrior came from one of the lodges close to the chief's and went to talk to him. Then the older man returned to his tipi and said something to someone inside. A few moment later, White Eagle emerged and went around behind the tipi to relieve himself in a patch of bushes.

He was no more than fifty yards away. Trace could feel the muscles in his arms tense, and he had to remind himself to remain calm. Had there not been twenty or thirty warriors milling about, he might have made a move to grab the boy right then. But he knew that would be suicide, and it would get both of them killed. He turned his attention back to the old warrior who positioned himself a few yards away from White Eagle, obviously guarding the boy. Even though he would have to wait for a better opportunity, Trace now knew which lodge White Eagle was being held in.

Suddenly he heard a voice behind him, and he was sure he had been discovered. Quickly turning over to defend himself, he expected to find someone pulling the snow away from the log. Instead, he saw two Gros Ventre women walking to the water's edge. During the early hours, the snow had evidently fallen away from the log, creating a long narrow gap through which he could clearly see the two women. Every nerve in his body seemed to be twitching at once. If they chanced to turn in his direction, they could not help but discover him, stretched out under the log. At that moment, he wondered how far he could get before a Gros Ventre war pony ran him to ground after the women screamed in alarm.

A stupid way to die, he thought. But the women turned away from him and began to fill their water skins. Lying as still as he possibly could, he listened to their conversation.

"My husband refuses to go out to hunt, and I have cooked the last of that puny deer. I'll see how he likes eating nothing but pemmican."

Her companion laughed. "Mine, too. None of the

men want to be away from the village when the Mountain Hawk comes for his son."

Hearing her words, Trace was astonished. *They know I am coming?* White Eagle must have said he would come. How else could they know?

Listening again, he heard the first woman say, "My husband says that Lame Elk thinks this hawk is a mortal man, but Wounded Horse is certain he is a spirit."

"My husband agrees with Wounded Horse," the second woman replied. "He knows the Blackfoot chief who saw the white man turn into a hawk and fly away."

Trace didn't listen closely to the rest of their conversation, his mind was too busy working on the startling information just heard. This news changed his plans dramatically. Thinking before that his task would be simply to steal into the camp at night and take the boy, hopefully while everyone was asleep, he now had to consider other factors. Now he understood the roving sentinels that constantly scouted around the perimeter of the camp. The whole village was waiting for him to show up. With his original plan, he felt it would have been highly likely that the Indians would think White Eagle had run away on his own. They might not have even cared enough to go after him. But now Trace could see the stakes were higher—the Gros Ventres were intent upon killing what they thought to be a spirit. When he took the boy, they would most definitely come after them. He would have to think on it, come up with some way to ensure a good head start after he got the boy.

During the morning, several more women followed the same path to the river to fill waterskins while Trace lay hidden in his cave. Stiff and fidgety, he longed to extricate himself from his snowy grave but was resolved that he must wait until darkness. Later on in the afternoon, he came to change his mind, for more than an hour had passed with no one venturing close to his hiding place, not even the mounted perimeter guards. His discomfort had advanced to the point where he was approaching a reckless state of mind, causing him to conclude that there was little risk that he would be seen.

Slowly at first, he raked the snow away, his hands red and stiff from the cold. Then, once he thrust his head and shoulders through the opening, his efforts became more rapid, as he wriggled his body out into the open, searching constantly from side to side, expecting to be discovered at any minute. His joints frozen from the long confinement, he staggered to his feet, taking care to remain behind the cover of the trees. *So far, so good*, he thought. There was no one around. Watching the people moving back and forth through the camp, he was satisfied to see that no one looked in his direction. Taking a few moments to smooth the snow around the log again, he then hurried down the riverbank, leaving the village behind.

It was necessary to make a wide circle around the Gros Ventre camp to avoid being seen. Even so, he was obliged to dive for cover once to avoid two warriors on horseback. When all was clear again, he crossed the river valley and entered the pines that ringed the line of low hills where he had made his camp. As he made his way back to check on his horses, he tried to formulate a plan to rescue White Eagle that would allow them enough time to gain a sizable lead on their pursuers. The only way that could happen, he concluded, was if there was some distraction to occupy the warriors when he made a try for the boy. At that moment, he didn't know what that could be.

As he neared the tree-lined defile where he had made his camp, he stopped to listen. Hearing nothing but the afternoon breeze stirring the pine needles, he continued on. A little closer—now he could hear the horses stamping nervously, sensing his presence, he presumed. *The paint's showing his displeasure for leaving him all night without any feed*, Trace thought as he entered the head of the defile. *Well, you ain't the only one that didn't get any supper*.

The thought had barely left his mind when he was suddenly knocked sprawling to the ground with such force that he was sure he had been attacked by a mountain lion. Instinctively rolling with the blow, he was on his feet in an instant, to find himself confronted by a painted Gros Ventre warrior. Knife in hand, the warrior attacked, slashing out at Trace as he charged, causing Trace to back away while he tried to pull his own knife. The warrior was quick and powerful. Trace had to lunge sideways, diving in the snow once again to avoid the slashing knife. Seeing his adversary on the ground, the warrior sprang upon him, his face a mask of triumph, only to register mortal shock a moment later when Trace's long Green River knife measured the depth of his belly. Still the Indian struggled, trying to find Trace's throat with his own blade. With his hand still on the handle buried deep in the warrior's belly, and his other clamping the wrist of the Indian's knife hand, Trace got to his feet, lifting the warrior with him. Once on his feet, Trace slammed the warrior down in the snow, withdrawing his knife as he did so. The warrior, gasping with pain that seared his innards, struggled to get up, knowing he was finished. Trace stood over him for a few moments, trying to catch his breath. When he saw there was still some fight left in the warrior, he reached down, grabbed his topknot and pulled his head up. One quick slash with his knife opened the Indian's throat before Trace let him drop to the ground.

When it was over, he sat down in the snow, still a little stunned by the sudden attack on his life. His assailant lay dying at his feet, his only motion a series of violent spasms as a scarlet stain spread under him in the snow. *That was damn close*, Trace thought, scolding himself for being ambushed so easily. He had been lucky, however. If the warrior had not launched his body so violently, he might not have knocked Trace out of reach of his knife hand. It was close, but Trace didn't dwell on it, having accepted the fact long ago that it took a generous portion of luck to survive as a lone white man in Indian territory. He got on his feet and checked on his horses.

"You tried to warn me. I just didn't listen," he said as he stroked the paint's muzzle.

He found the Gros Ventre's pony halfway down the back of the slope, tied to a small pine. Not willing to risk having a riderless horse wander into the Gros Ventre village, Trace moved the horse down the hill a few dozen yards to a thicket and tied the animal in the center of it. "At least you won't starve to death before somebody finds you."

The next question to be resolved was what to do with the dead Indian—if anything. If one Indian could stumble upon Trace's camp, then it was not out of the question for another to do the same. *Maybe I should at least cover him with snow*, he thought. And then a better idea occurred to him—one that might serve two purposes. To make good his attempt to rescue his son, he needed a diversion of some kind. Now he had one.

When it was just about dark, Trace began his preparations. Earlier that afternoon, he had selected his spot, a clearing on the highest point of the hill, a spot that could be easily seen from the Indian village. Now with twilight approaching, he gathered a great amount of

lead limbs and branches and stacked them just out of
sight below the ridge of the hill. When darkness finally
came, he went back for his horses. Lifting the warrior's
corpse onto the back of White Eagle's pony, he returned to the hilltop. Selecting a stout limb, he dug a
hole in the ground and drove the limb in it, pounding
it down with a large rock. When he thought it steady
enough, he carried the corpse over and propped it upright against the limb. The weight of the body proved
to be too much for the shallow footing of the limb, and
it promptly toppled over.

Not discouraged, Trace replaced the limb, then
piled rocks around the base of it. Again, the limb toppled. Refusing to be defeated by a dead Indian, Trace
dragged the body back a few yards to a tree at the edge
of the clearing. Taking a coil of rope from his pack, he
tied it under the Indian's arms and threw the other end
over a limb. Letting his horse do the lifting, he raised
the corpse off the ground and tied it off around the tree
trunk. *Hell, that's better, anyway*, he thought. *Makes him
look about ten feet tall.*

Satisfied with his Mountain Hawk, he brought the
dead wood up from below the brow of the hill and
formed a large stack behind the Indian hanging from
the limb. When he figured the time was right to start
the show, he spread some of his Du Pont black powder
along the base of the firewood, and then lit a dry
branch.

When the branch was burning with a healthy flame,
Trace began to yell at the top of his lungs. "Awaken,
Gros Ventre dogs! I am the Mountain Hawk. Come
and fight me, if you are not afraid!" He kept yelling it
over and over until he saw signs of activity outside the
tipis below. *I hope to hell this doesn't fizzle*, he thought as
he threw the flaming branch into the stack of wood.

It was better than he had hoped for. A huge, bright

fireball bellowed out from the stack when the fire ig-
nited the gunpowder, and the dead wood was soon
blazing, casting an eerie backlight behind the hanging
body. "I am the Mountain Hawk," he shouted once
more before jumping on his horse and hightailing it
down the other side of the hill, trailing his other two
horses behind him.

Time was important now. It was critical to the success of his plan that he should circle around behind the
Gros Ventre camp so as to be in position to act at the
peak of confusion. He raced through the night, dodg-
ing the gullies and breaks, praying that the paint could
find its footing. Out of the cover of the trees and across
the open valley he galloped, trusting to luck that he
did not meet one of the scouts who had been patrolling the village. He could already hear the sounds
coming from the Indian camp over the pounding of his
horses' hooves.

In the Gros Ventre village, there was an explosion of
frenzied activity. Chief Wounded Horse, confused at
first, quickly shouted to all who could hear his voice to
arm themselves and ride. Like a disturbed anthill,
angry warriors, long awaiting the fateful coming of the
Mountain Hawk, now scurried frantically to grab their
weapons and run for their ponies. Terrified women
screamed as they witnessed the fiery spectacle on the
hill where a spirit in the form of a man hovered over
the ground like a hawk.

In the midst of the stampede to charge toward the
hill, Wounded Horse looked around and discovered
Three Toes and his wife, standing and staring at the
fearful sight. "Go and guard the boy! Don't let him out
of your sight!" the chief commanded.

Three Toes nodded excitedly and hurried back to
his lodge, leaving his wife to gape horrified at the
ghostly scene. He reached the lodge just in time to stop

White Eagle from joining in the chaos. He had not learned many words of their tongue, but he was sure he had heard "Mountain Hawk."

"Back inside," Three Toes ordered. "It is not for you to see."

White Eagle resisted but was forcefully taken back in the tipi. "I heard them shouting about the Mountain Hawk," he insisted. "Is my father here?" Three Toes did not answer, pushing the boy back. "If my father is here, let me go to him!"

Three Toes sat the boy down, and tried to calm him. "Your father is not here," he said. "It is nothing—a fire on the hill, that is all. It's best that you stay here."

White Eagle made up his mind to dash around the old man, and go out to see for himself what had caused such an uproar in the village. He was on his feet when he heard the ripping of the tipi wall behind him. Turning at the sound, he was startled to see the long blade of a skinning knife as it parted the inner lining of the tipi. He jumped back in fright when Trace suddenly burst through the opening. Then recognizing the tall mountain man, his heart leaped for joy.

There was no time for a joyous reunion. Stepping past the stunned boy, Trace sprang immediately upon Three Toes, quickly pinning the old man to the ground. Three Toes struggled briefly in an effort to defend himself, but he realized at once that he was no match for the powerful mountain man.

"Don't kill him!" White Eagle cried out. "He has been kind to me."

Trace hesitated, looking at the boy, then back at the old man, caught helplessly in his grip. "Hand me that rope," he said, nodding toward a coil of rawhide line hanging from a lodgepole. When Three Toes was securely bound and gagged, Trace dragged the old man over to the side of the lodge. While Trace was taking

care of Three Toes, White Eagle stood at the entrance
to the tipi, keeping watch for Raven, Three Toes's wife.
She was apparently in the middle of the crowd of children and women who were anxiously watching the
fiery apparition on the hill.

"Come," Trace said, and pushed through the slit in
the back of the tipi. Outside in the cold night air, he
paused only long enough to see that White Eagle was
right behind him, then made for the riverbank at a trot.
Behind them, the sounds of the frightened women
drifted over the camp like the moaning of the wind, as
Trace and his son ran along the bank to the willows
where the horses were tied.

"Gray Thunder!" White Eagle cried when they
reached the willows.

"What!" Trace responded, reacting at once, ready to
fend off an attack.

"Gray Thunder," White Eagle repeated, rushing up
to the spotted gray horse and hugging its neck affectionately. "You brought my pony."

"Oh," Trace responded, relieved to find they had
not been discovered by the Gros Ventres. "Well, jump
on him, and let's get the hell outta here." They were
wasted words, for White Eagle was on his pony's back
before Trace finished saying them.

They rode hard, pushing their horses constantly to
keep up the pace. Trace led them down the river, always riding on the common trails so that their tracks
were intermingled with hundreds of others. After an
hour of hard riding, Trace eased off to let the horses
rest. There was no sign of anyone pursuing them, so
they let the horses walk for a while before picking up
a faster pace. Daybreak found them some thirty miles
down the river, and far enough from the Gros Ventre
camp to stop and rest.

Trace told White Eagle to gather some wood to

make a small fire, while he cut some cottonwood limbs to strip for horse feed. In short order, the boy had a cheerful fire going, and he knelt before it warming his hands, never taking his eyes off the tall man in buckskins who was now feeding handfuls of cottonwood bark to the three horses. After the horses were taken care of, Trace got some coffee and salt pork from his pack and proceeded to make them a little breakfast.

Fascinated by the man who had come to rescue him, and still watching his every move, White Eagle finally asked the question that needed definite confirmation. "Are you *really* my father?"

Trace paused for a moment to glance at the boy. "I reckon I am." Then he turned his attention back to the pork he was heating over the fire.

"You are the Mountain Hawk," the boy stated in tones of undisguised wonder.

While still focusing upon the strips of salty meat that had now begun to sizzle slightly, Trace said, "I think I already told you I ain't no mountain hawk. I'm an ordinary man, like everybody else." He was concerned that the boy was going to set standards for him that he couldn't live up to.

White Eagle smiled. *You are the Mountain Hawk*, he said to himself. Then he asked, "Then what do I call you? Father?"

"Hell no!" Trace reacted immediately, looking up at the awestruck face of the eleven-year-old. "Call me Trace," he said, then meeting the probing brown eyes of his natural son, reconsidered. "Whatever you want—you can call me father if you want to."

Pleased, White Eagle sat back and accepted the cup of steaming black coffee from his father's hand. "I am glad you came for me, Father. We will live in the mountains together."

Trace raised his eyebrows as he turned to face the

boy. "I kinda thought you might be anxious to get back to your mother's people with Chief Washakie."

"I want to stay with you."

This option was not really one that Trace had considered. There followed a lengthy pause while he thought about the possibility. Finally, he said, "We'll see. We'll have to think about it."

White Eagle smiled inwardly while he chewed the tough strip of meat. *I will stay with you.* There was a natural streak of determination in the boy—his mother would have said stubbornness—that he had apparently inherited from his father.

CHAPTER 16

Old Man Winter had come on with a vengeance that year, with the north winds blowing wave after wave of his icy breath through the tiny valley that a handful of settlers had christened "Promise." On this bitter morning, Buck Ransom stood outside the door of his simple one-room log cabin, his eyes squinting against the sun's glare of the frozen valley. It was the first time he had seen the sun in over a week. It had been a hell of a storm, the kind of trick Old Man Winter enjoyed playing on mortals—waiting until he had everybody fooled with signs of spring, then slappin' 'em down with one last blizzard.

He took a deep breath of air so frigid that it made his lungs ache deep down inside him. Holed up in his cabin for weeks at a time, Buck had all he could do to keep from becoming terminally melancholy. To combat it, he told himself stories from the past, reliving the days when he and his old companion, Frank Brown, trapped beaver for the Rocky Mountain Fur Company. When it reached the point where he was talking directly to Frank about things that happened at the rendezvous on the Green River or the Wind River, or Popo Agie, he suddenly realized that he had better get out of his cabin and see some real people.

Now on this frozen morning, his thoughts turned to his friend, Trace McCall, and the day they had parted company near the Bighorns. "I wonder if Trace has found that boy yet," he said aloud—a habit he had acquired during the long winter weeks. It had been months since Trace had ridden off after White Eagle. It was not the first time Trace had stayed away all winter, but Buck had a nagging fear this time because Trace was heading deep into hostile territory. If he caught up with the boy as soon as he had expected, they would have been back in a month. "Maybe he found the boy and took him up in Wind River country to find his mother's people," Buck speculated, hoping that accounted for his friend's long absence. *That young'un's likely dead*, Buck thought, as he made his way around the cabin to the lean-to where his horses were.

"You're damn lucky I took in some hay from Jordan Thrash," he said to the buckskin mare. "You'd be scratching around in the snow for your supper."

The mare whinnied and jerked her head up. Buck thought she was answering his comment until the other two horses in the shed snorted and whinnied also, announcing the presence of other horses. Buck turned to look out across the valley. Two riders leading a packhorse made their way slowly down the western slope to the valley floor. Buck could see that one of them was probably a boy. The other, even at that distance, could be none other than Trace McCall. No other man sat a horse like that, straight and tall, riding easy like man and horse came out of the womb together.

Buck felt his pulse quicken with strength as a flood of joy and relief overwhelmed him after the long solitary winter. His family had returned. The sight of Trace and the boy brought a tear to the eye of the grizzled old trapper. *Maybe I ain't gonna die alone in this damn cabin after all.*